DYING BREATH

Book 6

KORY M. SHRUM

This book is dedicated to my new family:
Francis, Eileen, and Steven.
Patricia and Neil.
Tita Alex and Uncle Craig.
Joey, Tophet, and Aunt Helen.

One of the best parts about marrying Kim
was inheriting you.
Thank you for all the love and kindness
you've shown me.

CHAPTER ONE

MAISIE

The truck slides to the right, hooking around a huge boulder. Desert sand sprays in a swooping arc through my open window and into my face.

"Slow down!" I cough and fumble for anything to grab ahold of. After groping air, I snatch the seatbelt dangling over my right shoulder. I miss the snap twice before I hear the reassuring *click*. The belt hugs me against the scalding seat.

Mom doesn't slow down. The truck bounces over another medium-sized rock, axles creaking, and the wheels pop up and skid. I don't think anyone is supposed to drive through the desert like this. There should be roads, right?

"You're going to kill us!" I scream.

"We have to lose her." Mom's blue eyes cut to the rearview mirror. Blood is smeared across her right cheek and I can't help but stare at it, fixated on the way it fills the creases around her mouth as she speaks. If she flicks out her tongue, she'd taste it.

Maybe she already does.

I look at my own hands. Blood everywhere. It's crusted under my fingernails and a bright crimson half-moon lines each of my cuticles.

My father's dead body slouches between us, oozing blood. It pools on the seat, soaking the side of my jeans. Most of him rests against Mom. But his head is barely attached and it flops, threatening to snap free and tumble into my lap at any moment. It's freaky and gross. Looking down at my blood-soaked jeans and grubby hands isn't helping my nausea.

I'm going to puke.

"Shit." Mom's focused on the rearview mirror, watching the road behind us more than the empty desert ahead.

I turn toward the open window between our seats. Beyond the bare truck bed, the black Mustang gains on us.

Jesse's coming.

But not for me.

She wants Dad's head, to blow him up and make sure the crazy bastard never wakes up again. Mom wants the exact opposite—Dad alive and Jesse mutilated beyond recognition. And here's me stuck in the middle.

You thought *your* family was dysfunctional.

Dad's oozing blood reaches my skin. It's sticky against the back of my knees. My stomach clenches for the billionth time, and I squeeze my eyes shut. Mom's jerky driving is probably to blame. I open my eyes and find a fixed point on the horizon. A white building in the distance squats between a beautiful blue sky and orange sand.

I focus on that building and draw in deep breaths.

Dad's body is starting to smell.

It's the heat. It's collecting in the black dashboard and seats. The hot air blowing through the truck's open windows is no help either. All of it makes Dad's body putrefy faster.

Mom calls up her power. Through our mental connection

or whatever you want to call it, I feel her power before I see it. It's like a blast of arctic air. Like the air conditioner kicked on and is pumping its guts through the dusty vents in the dashboard.

Phantom snakes, twin coils of black smoke, unfurl from Mom's abdomen. If she even grazes Jesse with this smoke, Jesse's dead meat.

I glare at Mom.

She sees me glaring. "I have to stop her."

No. An impulse to protect my sister overwhelms me, blocking out my conflicting urge to puke in the overbearing heat.

I've got to do something. Say something.

I'm not brave like Jesse. Jesse would leap across Dad's dead body and attack Mom. Maybe pull her hair or shove her out of the car.

I could never do that. Of the fight or flight impulse, I've got more flight in my veins. When danger shows up, everything inside me says, *run away! Run away!*

"You don't have a good shot. You'll probably kill me, and if you do, we'll all be dead." It's all I can think to say. "She'll use her shield to block you anyway."

With a frustrated hiss, Mom retracts her power.

I should've known self-preservation would do the trick. Mom wants to kill Jesse—and probably me too—so she can absorb our powers, but the moment she does she'll die. Her body will have to reboot in order to absorb our abilities. If Mom offs me, she'll be a sitting duck for Jesse. All Jesse would have to do is walk up and finish her.

That's probably the only reason I'm alive right now.

If Dad were alive, I might already be dead. The second he decides he wants my power, my ability, I *will* be dead.

It's only a matter of time.

"You have to wake him up," Mom barks. She yanks the

steering wheel, and the nose of the truck cuts a sharp right. The vehicle slides as it corrects itself. The white building disappears and now there's only blue sky. Nothing to focus on.

"No." Vomit burns in the back of my throat. I swallow it down.

"Damn it, Maisie." Mom grits her teeth. "We need his help to fight her. Wake him up!"

"We don't have to fight." I place one hand on my stomach and the other on the door to brace myself. "We can share the power. We were *supposed* to share it!"

I think of Monroe and his deep, infectious laugh and his sweet eyes. He had puppy dog eyes, like Winston, Jesse's pug. More importantly than being the kindest man I've ever met, Monroe told us the truth about our powers and abilities. Back at his house in Louisiana, back before my parents caught up to us, he told us we were never meant to use our powers against each other.

We were supposed to work together. The original twelve powers were to be shared by the people chosen to wield them. By the partis—some weird, ancient name for what we are and what we can do.

But Dad made a mistake early in the game. He killed another partis, and it broke the connection. It severed the link between all the abilities and the only way to unify the power and save the world is for one person to collect all the powers inside themselves.

We've been killing each other ever since.

Monroe tried to change that before Dad killed him. He reestablished the link between me and Jesse and me and Mom. We can share the twelve powers between us if only I can get her to listen.

Mom doesn't understand. She's been fighting forever,

since before I was born. I don't know what to say that will make her stop seeing Jesse as the enemy.

"She's a liar." Mom's face softens with pity. "Whatever Jesse told you was a lie."

"It's not a lie, and Jesse wasn't the one who told me."

Jesse's Mustang hits the back of the truck, and we lurch forward. *Bad timing, Jess. How am I going to convince Mom you're one of the good guys with you running us over?*

"Do you think she's going to let him live?" Mom's burning eyes cut to Dad's body. "She's going to kill him. For good."

"If he ever wakes up, do you think he's going to let *you* live? Or me? He's a monster."

"Maisie!" Mom reaches across Dad's body and slaps me. She's never hit me before. Not once. Not ever.

I cup my burning cheek and look at her like she's grown two heads.

She looks as shocked as I am. "What did she do to you?"

"What's he done to *you?*" I snap back. I uncover my cheek. I want her to see the mark she's left. She flinches like I knew she would. "Since when are you the crazy abusive one?"

Her hands wring the steering wheel.

"Leave him," I beg her.

"He's your father."

And a monster.

"We need him."

I snort. "How feminist, Mom."

"You know better." Mom scowls at me. "You know she'll kill me. It's why you woke me up."

Why you woke me up—

My anger dissipates. The battle we just escaped replays in my head. Less than an hour ago, my mother was killed. She collapsed dead on the hallway floor inside the abandoned military base where Jesse wanted to have our last stand. When

Mom was killed, I bent over her and blew into her nose, waking her up in that special way I do, because—because she's right. Because I knew Gideon, Gloria and Jesse would overpower me. They would kill my mom and make me watch.

I couldn't let that happen.

Mom isn't perfect. She's a borderline horrible person. She's selfish and cruel. She has this self-destructive streak I'll never understand.

But she's my mom.

She's always loved me. She's always told me how much she loved me. How special I was. How much she wished and prayed for me. And she's always protected me—until now.

The silence makes Mom think she's won.

"Whose side are you on?" Her expression is haughty again. "It's either her or me."

My fist tightens around the seatbelt pressing against my chest.

Whose side *am* I on?

The longer I don't answer, the more Mom's face pinches in betrayal. "This isn't you. Jesse did this to you. She turned you against your own mother."

"No—"

"We have to kill her. It's the only way to protect your father until—"

My temper explodes. "What about us? What about protecting *us*?"

"He won't hurt us," Mom says, but I know that voice. It's her *he will never hurt you while I'm alive* voice. But my mom won't always be alive. She was dead an hour ago. She'll probably be dead again before the day is over.

Jesse's Mustang whips around the side of the truck. The driver's side window rolls down, and there's my sister, all wide-eyed and freaked out.

She casts her shield. The shimmering purple light covers

me and part of the truck. She looks as surprised as I am she can do it. That's Jesse for you. She never seems to realize how awesome she is.

"Jump!" she screams. Her brown hair falls across her face, and she frantically wipes it away.

Jump? Out of a moving truck?

"Jump! I'll catch you!" She has to scream over the sound of sand, wind, and roaring engines.

Jump. But not *jump and bring Dad's corpse with you.* Dad's corpse isn't even in the shield.

She wants me.

She wants me more than she wants Dad's dead body.

Because she loves you, a voice whispers through my mind. A voice I haven't heard in a long, *long* time. I thought it was because I was with Jesse and Rachel. Their power dwarfed my own.

I'm stronger now because you are.

A weight lifts from my chest. *I thought you'd given up on me.*

Never.

With an angel on my side, it seems less insane: jumping from a moving car. I throw my door open and reach for the release on my seatbelt.

"No!" Mom cuts the wheel hard to the right, slamming the side of the truck into Jesse's Mustang. An invisible, angry hand rips away my door. Sparks spray into the cab as metal scrapes metal. Stray shards sting my cheeks. I cover my face, hoping my arms and legs stay inside the cab and won't be ripped off too. That would suck.

I open my eyes, and Jesse's there, keeping up with us. The side of her Mustang looks like it was stepped on by a huge boot. Through the open window, she's shouting.

"I've got you! Jump!"

"Fuck off!" Mom screams. With one flick of her hand, the

Mustang's two front wheels are lifted off the ground and thrown back into the air.

It's so unexpected I gulp air, gagging on the stray sand. It feels like scraps of sandpaper go down my throat. Mom didn't have the telekinetic power until she killed Rachel for it and already she's using it to kill my sister.

"No!" My screaming doesn't do anything to stop the Mustang from flying backward, and then dropping back to Earth like a bomb.

The black car rolls head over tail before slamming into the side of a boulder.

No! No!

Jesse's car explodes on impact, the black muscle car disappearing in a plume of fire and smoke.

"Oh god, no. Jesse, *no*."

I blink back tears, hanging out the open side of the truck. My mother's unforgiving fingers bite into the flesh of my upper arm, trying to drag me back inside. But I can't look away from the burning wreckage.

I'm desperate for a sign, *any* sign Jesse survived.

I don't get one. It's only fire and the mushroom cloud darkening the blue sky as Mom speeds away.

My sister's funeral pyre.

All that's left of her is a swirling, black blaze.

CHAPTER TWO

JESSE

I'm reaching out for Maisie, begging her to jump into my arms and away from her crazy mother. Then the horizon disappears. Impossibly, the car goes up which is a super weird direction for a car to go. The front wheels lift until it's a clear blue sky in all directions.

I start to rise out of my seat as if the gravity is turned off and I'm floating.

It makes me think of when I was a little girl and dreamed about flying. I'd hold my arms out and run through the yard making airplane sounds with my lips.

But gravity kicks back on and the car plummets.

Be careful what you wish for, right?

Jesse! Gabriel's scream cuts through my shock at being airborne. *Shield!*

Purple light spreads over my body, cocooning me the moment before the car slams to a stop. The sound of crushing metal is swallowed by *boom*!

An orange supernova engulfs my cocoon. Flames dance over the surface, along with swirling smoke—like ink in water. The leather seats and dashboard. The blinking clock. All of it's swallowed in the plume. I can't feel the heat, and that's probably a good thing since I'd totally be a melty marshmallow a second from falling off the stick.

A second explosion makes metal scream and my shield ripples again. Man, what if it fails? Are my eyeballs going to liquefy and ooze out of their sockets like they do in the *Tales of the Crypt* movie? Gross. And I don't think I'd look so great with a bald head. No thanks.

"Gabriel?"

Wait it out.

Ha! Like I have a choice. Even if I wanted to crawl out of the burning car, I wouldn't know which direction to crawl. I can't see anything but black smoke and fire.

I fall back against the shield with a sigh. I remember Maisie's terrified face, her desperate wiggling fingers as she reached out for me.

So much for my plan. I was going to get Maisie, hurt Georgia enough that she couldn't follow us, take Maze back to the base where she'd be safe with our friends, and then come back and finish off the current contenders for Worst Parents of the Year. But *nope*. Instead, I had to watch Georgia whisk Maisie away. Again. Dammit.

If anything happens to her—

There's time, Gabriel whispers.

There's time.

I repeat this over and over until the smoke thins, and certain shapes come into focus. I recognize the warped plane of the dashboard first, though it's about as solid as a chocolate bar left in the sun. The crispy seats appear next, the interior padding exposed and burnt. A pool of metal glistens in the seat. The buckle, I realize. The seatbelt buckle *melted*.

I'm sitting in a car that's hot enough to melt the seatbelt buckle.

As soon as the driver's side window appears, I start to shimmy out of it, drawing my shield in close to my body so I can squeeze through.

I hit the sand. Even with the shield, it's jarring, and I cough on impact.

Nothing feels broken. In a few places on my arms and face, there's the itchy burn of healing. Scratches, probably, sealing themselves shut with the healing power I inherited when I killed a psychopathic jerk named Jason.

I army crawl away from the wrecked car until I'm far enough away that a second explosion won't blow my butt off. I like my butt. It's always got my back. I can't go leaving it behind at the first sign of trouble.

When I drop the shield, the heat knocks me back. It's more than desert hot. Heat wafts off the burning car. I stand, brush the sand off my pants, and start marching away.

In every direction, there's only distance. A couple of white buildings sit spread apart. A few miles back I can see the military base where I left Ally, Gloria, and Gideon.

Alive, Gabriel assures me.

"So you keep saying," I tell him. But everyone I cared about *was* dead. I saw it. And frankly, I'm getting super tired of watching the woman I love die. I've done it twice now.

Thanks to Maisie's gift, they'll be up and moving soon. I hope.

I search every direction until I spot the plume of sand thrown up by Georgia's truck. They have miles on me.

"Well, fuck." I scowl at Gabriel where he stands in the middle of the desert. In an expensive suit and tie. Weirdo. "This is lovely."

"You need a vehicle."

I glare at him. "Thank you, Captain Obvious."

His brow scrunches. He never gets my pop culture references, and I'm not in the mood to educate him.

"Do you *see* a car?"

"Yes," he says. He turns and points.

"That's a cactus. Uh, humans don't drive those. Given the pointy parts. They're also rooted to the earth, and generally, lack propulsion of any kind."

"No," he says and extends one slender finger. "There."

I squint at the horizon. At first, nothing but heat shimmering on the sand and the half-buried road stretches out before me. Then I notice the squat white building he's pointing at. "The house?"

"A station. A mile away."

"You want me to walk a *mile* across the desert?" I practically flop down on the spot. I hate exertion of any kind. Adding the desert heat makes this ridiculous. "Why couldn't you give *me* the teleportation power? It's much cooler than walking, and we both know Caldwell doesn't deserve it."

I have no idea if the angels *give* us the superpowers. Gabriel said he chose me. But choosing me to be his end-of-the-world gladiator is not the same as giving someone a superpower, is it? Gabriel doesn't seem interested in clarifying this point. I have a theory the powers reflect the kind of people we are. I'm fiery and guarded for example, and Caldwell is a sneaky, evasive fuck. It makes sense. To me anyway.

"This would be an awesome time to reveal you can fly me places. How does that sound? Do you want to fly me to the station? Because I'm super open to the idea."

I turn back and gaze longingly at the military base where I left my friends. It's even farther than the station. No point in hiking back to take one of the other cars. I turn back toward the station. Ugh. Lesser of two evils, I suppose.

Maisie.

I hope she can feel me. I hope our empathetic connection

is letting her know how worried and afraid I am for her. Okay, maybe not afraid. I don't want to freak her out. Concerned? No one should have to go through what she's going through alone. I had to deal with some heavy shit when I was her age, and I killed myself over it.

Please god, don't let history repeat itself.

I start walking toward the building in the distance, squinting against the sun in my eyes.

I'm coming, Maisie. I pour all the mind juice I've got into this message. *Hang on. I'm coming for you.*

CHAPTER THREE

MAISIE

I wipe tears off my cheeks, and Mom doesn't even care. She just murdered my sister, orphaned Winnie Pug, and now she's driving across the desert like we're on our way to somewhere totally normal. Like the grocery store.

It's messed up.

At times like this, I'm sure I can finally give up on her. She'll never win Mother of Year. But one look, one reassurance—*Maisie, I'm doing this for us. For you. I'll keep you safe*—and the confusion creeps in. I don't see a lunatic. I see my mom.

Every Chicago winter, all bundled up in our mittens and caps, we'd go ice skating in Millennium Park. In the summer, we walked Navy Pier with drippy ice cream cones running over our hands. Or we'd take the water taxi across Lake Michigan to the museum campus and eat loaded hot dogs and drink lemonade until our bellies burst.

We laid in the grass and watched the clouds go by, and my

mom would tell me about her childhood in Nebraska on a horse ranch with her grandparents. It was a happy childhood with a pack of dogs and a horse named Storm. Storm for his gray fur and lightening white mane.

I love that mom best. The funny mom. The slightly crude mom. The one who laughs and sweeps my hair off my shoulder before kissing my temple. The mom who rubs my back with lavender oil when I can't sleep and begins sentences with *did I tell you about the time—*

—I jumped off a bridge naked into the river—

—I got a boy to undress down to his socks. Then when his eyes were closed for a kiss, I took his clothes and ran away as fast as I could—

—the first time I saw your father—the moment I saw those gorgeous green eyes—

I tumble out of my thoughts as soon as the truck's dashboard chirps a warning. Mom scowls, bending down to read through the dust. "We're low on gas."

"There's nothing out here." I crane my neck in all directions. This is an excuse to gawk at the black smoke growing smaller in the distance. I squint at the horizon, hoping I'll see Jesse there. Alive and unscathed, even if she's stranded. She's got her shield. She could have survived the blast.

If anyone could survive a car explosion, it would be Jesse. Not because of her healing powers and her impenetrable shield, but because she's the toughest person I know. She's been killed hundreds of times, and every time she gets up, brushes herself off and says, *bring it.*

She's amazing.

I squint into the glaring sun until my head hurts. I don't see her. I don't see anything but the black smoke.

But I didn't feel her die either, so there's that.

When someone dies, icy cold stabs me in the chest. It's like someone runs me through with an icicle. Or sometimes it's more like they poured a bucket of ice water over my head. My point is, the feeling is totally recognizable. I could never miss it or mistake it for something else.

But the car's going too fast. It's possible she was out of my range by the time she died. I don't feel everyone in the whole world, you know. Only people who are kind of close to me. Half a mile maybe? I'm not sure the exact distance because I've never measured it.

"Do you see anything?" Mom asks, fighting for my attention.

I'm forced to look away from the burning wreckage and scan the horizon for a gas station.

Unless she figures out how to run a nozzle from a cactus, we're out of luck. "We're going to run out."

I try not to sound too excited. God, I hope we run out. If Jesse survived, she might catch up to us then, especially if I drag my feet and pretend to die of heatstroke. And how will we carry Dad's body? Mom will never let us leave him. A dead body will slow us down. She might even have to walk to town alone, get help and come back for us.

My excitement falters. What if Jesse catches up to us? What happens then? She and mom try to murder each other. Again.

It's hard for me to understand why they can't stop fighting. Even with my partis power and an angel in my ear, I've never had this overwhelming desire to fight. Every time things get crazy I want to stuff my head in the sand. That's me. Maisie the Ostrich. Where's my circus sideshow?

It can't be genetic. Mom and Dad love to fight.

Jesse's reluctant most of the time, until the guns come out, and we're in danger—especially if Ally's in danger— because then Jesse jumps into the fray with the rest of them.

There's another way.

My stomach flutters at the memory of Monroe and his

last words. I can see him perfectly in my head, rolling a cigarette between tobacco-stained fingers. His slow southern drawl added to his sweetness.

Maisie, baby. You got a big heart in you. Hang on to it in the hurricane. Let it anchor you.

Monroe was like me. He wasn't a fighter. He never asked for his power or to be caught up in this struggle over the whole world.

Knowin' the fightin' be wrong and getting' people to stop—that's two different things. They've stopped listenin' to their hearts. Not you. And don't you stop now.

The last time I saw Monroe alive, he tried to warn me. He tried to explain it's going to be hard for everyone to stop fighting, but I've got to resist. Easy, considering I'd rather step into Millennium Mile traffic than attack anyone. Getting flattened by a Chicago taxi driver would be a blessing when I consider the alternative—having my head sawed off by someone I love.

I chose you for your strength, Azrael whispers.

My *strength!* I hiss in my head. *What about* your *strength? Why do I have to do anything?*

When I think about the angels, it makes me mad. If they are so mighty, why don't they fix everything? Why use us like pawns to start wars?

We are not meant to interfere. Together, you have no need of us, she instructs.

Before I ever saw Azrael, I imagined her as an uppity professor. Black-rimmed glasses, a sweater vest, and with a pen behind her ear.

Nope.

I couldn't have been more wrong.

Imagine my surprise when she appeared looking like Joan of Arc—full body armor, sword, shield, and long wild hair. I glance at my bloody nails again.

Azrael won't be able to materialize now. Mom's too close. That's probably for the best. It's super weird when an angel shows up in a shiny breastplate with a sword. Intimidating doesn't even begin to cover it. Acting like she's not in the room? Impossible.

"We'll get at least twenty miles, maybe thirty before the car dies. We'll ride it out." Mom's acting like we're having a normal conversation. It's hard to feel normal with a dead body beside you.

A shape pops up on the horizon. One, then three. An oasis forms in the watery heat, like a mirage materializing from the paper-thin air.

"A town," Mom breathes, relieved. Her hunched shoulders slide away from her ears.

I lean forward, trying to get a better look. Dust clouds swirl across the landscape making it hard to see. As it settles, stark white buildings shine in the distance. It must be Cochise. I saw a sign for this town when we were heading to the military base.

We don't say anything else. After a few miles, the wheels bump up onto pavement. This new road leads us into a cluster of buildings. They are all one-story, squat boxes in an off-white color. People *live* here. There are proper fences and stop signs, and painted parking spaces with yellow or white lines sprayed onto the sandy concrete. One house even has a pink bicycle sitting outside, the seat growing hot in the sun.

"We need somewhere to hide until your father wakes up."

I blink at her, trying to get my eyes to adjust again after staring at the blinding white buildings in the desert light. Spots dance in my vision until it clears.

"We need to sew him up. He'll never heal like this. Look at him."

She's right about that. Dad's head rolls dangerously on his

neck. The place where the skin stretches and pulls away from the nape makes me want to puke. I pinch my eyes shut.

Encourage delay. Give your sister time to find you, Azrael whispers.

Dad's body falls against my shoulder. I nudge him away and pivot toward the window—well, where a window would be if the whole door hadn't been ripped off. God, what if someone sees us? It'll be hard to explain away a missing door, let alone the dead body inside, slumping between two women covered in blood.

Real subtle.

We pass an elementary school. People's houses. A post office. I pretend to be interested in anything but the stinking corpse lying against me. It's hard to do. Dead people are so heavy.

"We'll commandeer a house," Mom says.

Commandeer. I suppress a snort. *You mean murder innocent people and take their stuff.*

To your left, Azrael offers.

I crane my neck and see it. The building is an old-timey saloon, complete with rickety porch and poles propping up a covered porch. Above the door in black paint, Cochise Hotel.

"There!" I point my finger. "Let's get a room. You can clean Dad up there."

Mom pulls the wheel and the nose of the truck points toward the hotel. *You can clean Dad up there*—why did I say that? I don't want to clean him up. If Dad heals and comes back to life—

One problem at a time, kid. I scold myself in Jesse's voice.

She's got to be alive. She's got to be. Azrael practically said as much. She wouldn't tell me to buy Jesse time if Jesse had exploded into a million pieces, would she?

Problem number one: Get Mom to stop driving and give

Jesse time to catch up. Because she did survive, please god, she *did* survive. I don't think Azrael would lie about that.

So how will I do it? How do I make sure Dad doesn't wake up?

It sounds horrible. No one should wish their Dad would stay dead, but I do.

It's more stupid that I love him. I want him dead, *and* I love him.

I'll be the first to tell you I need therapy.

God, I can see Jesse's face if I ever admitted these feelings to her. She'd totally freak. She'd say something like, *how can you love a homicidal maniac? Do you know how many people he's killed? Do you know how many times he's killed me?*

It's not clear to me, though. This is probably because shitty people aren't always shitty. Sometimes they can be kind too, and that's enough to blur the line between good and evil.

Dad's no exception.

I remember meeting him. It's hard to remember much from being five or six, but I remember my big pink room with candy-striped walls. I can remember my toy box, white and wooden, and a rocking horse I never used because it creeped me out with its uneven eyes. I used to stare at it before I'd fall asleep, convinced if I looked away for even a second, it would transform into a beast, crawl into my crib, and eat my toes one by one.

It never did, but a different monster came, long after my crib was exchanged for what my adoptive mother called a *big girl bed.*

One night I woke up and there he was. He introduced himself as The Tooth Fairy. He asked me if I had any teeth. The first few visits I didn't, so we talked instead. He told me silly stories and jokes. I remember thinking he was very handsome, and I liked it when he smiled at me. It was funny, not weird when he asked to put a Q-tip in my mouth.

He was checking my DNA, trying to make sure I was the same baby he'd shuffled into the adoption system years before.

One night, I did have a tooth to give him, and he gave me a dollar for it. It was cool. None of my friends had seen the tooth fairy come into *their* rooms and give *them* money.

In exchange for my second tooth, he gave me Freddy. Freddy the Teddy. Every time I lost Freddy, he'd find it. Dad would turn up when I was drowning in my tears and say with a big grin, *look what I found.*

For the third tooth, he said he was taking me to see my real mom.

My real mom.

The idea that the woman who cut the crusts off my bologna and cheese sandwiches wasn't my real mom blew my mind. As kind as I remember that woman to be, hearing that I had a real mom was a dream come true. I'd always felt different. Set apart. The Michaelsons were open with me about my adoption. They tried to make me feel loved. But it left me with a thousand questions about my parents and where I came from.

What little girl didn't want to find out she was special? A princess? From some magical kingdom? Destined for a Hogwarts letter or something?

When he told me he wanted to take me to where I *really* belonged, I went without a fight.

Maybe Jesse doesn't remember the times he was kind to her, but I do. Death replacement agents lose some long-term memory with each death. It's possible Jesse forgot how nice Dad can be. I'm sure he was a good dad before he got some superpowers and became a maniac hell-bent on world domination.

And my parents were good to me until very recently. So, it's hard to condemn bad behavior when it's served with a big side of *do you know how much I love you? Do you know what you mean to me? You're my world.*

Mom parks the car on the street outside the hotel and gets out.

"Wait here." She lifts a hand to shield her eyes as she gazes at the hotel. "I'll see if I can get us a room."

She slams the door to the truck. I watch her march up the small slope toward the hotel's dark doorway. She pauses at the threshold and then slips through the open door. A faint bell chimes.

I look at Dad's dead body. A large black fly licks at his salty skin inches from where Jesse tried to saw through his neck.

I bet if I grabbed his head and pulled hard, I could pop it right off. I could finish him for good and save millions of lives. I grab a handful of his hair and find it cold. It should be wet with sweat. But he's dead. My heart pounds as I tighten my fingers on his soft hair. It's the same color as Jesse's. I got Mom's Nordic blond hair and her blue eyes. Even with the plastic surgeries meant to hide his past, Dad looks like Jesse. To me anyway.

I can't do it.

I can't finish him, and Mom knows it. That's why she left him alone with me, not afraid for a second I'd hurt him while she was gone.

I let go of Dad's hair, my hands shaking.

Hurry, Jesse. I beg, hoping she can hear me. *I can't do this alone.*

CHAPTER FOUR

JESSE

"**O**h my god," I whine. "Why is it so *hot?*"

Sweat droplets form on the back of my bare neck, beneath my ponytail. When the droplets get too big, they slide down my skin into the collar of my shirt. It's gross, and I can't do shit about it since the sun is directly overhead.

"This is an arid landscape—" Gabriel starts.

"No science, please. I understand this is a desert, and how the sun works. I wish my shield could work more like a portable umbrella."

It protected me from the car explosion, so using it to cool myself isn't out of the question. But using my superpower for something as silly as a walk through the desert makes me feel wimpy.

And let's be honest, my pride's all I have now.

"You will reach the station soon." Gabriel consoles me as if he isn't wearing a three-piece suit and looking like he just stumbled out of a starlet's bed and into a Gucci ad. Despite the suit, he isn't sweating one bit. His skin is free of perspiration. Bitch.

"I do not think you will die before you reach it," he adds, turning his big green eyes on me. Cat-eyes with an upward tilt at the outside corners.

"You do not think," I mock him. "Well, that's comforting. Nice to know my body won't become the next carrion buffet."

Every step is hotter than the last.

I groan. "Seriously, why didn't I get the fancy teleportation power? I could think shade and *poof*!"

"You each have access to the same power source. It is not different," Gabriel says. His tie shifts to green. I never did figure out what the mood ring tie meant.

"It's entirely different," I argue. My foot slides on the sand, and for a moment, I lose my footing. I catch myself with my hand, and the ground is blistering hot. My anger flares. Stupid desert! With its stupid sand! And stupid sun! And stupid hotness! "I can't zap people dead with Georgia's death ribbons. Or bring people back to life with the breath stuff like Maisie. I can't move things with my thoughts alone like Rachel does. All of those things are different."

My mind snags on something I said, and my heartstrings vibrate.

Like Rachel *did*.

I stop walking. I lift the bottom of my T-shirt up to wipe my dripping face and then my wet palms. Like Rachel *did*.

Past tense.

Because she's dead, and I was the one who killed her.

My heart compresses, becoming a heavy stone in my chest. A throbbing pain radiates from its center down each of my limbs. Somehow I keep standing.

"I am sorry." Gabriel opens his wings wide, monstrous and

black. They block out the sun. It's ten degrees cooler instantly.

"What? You should be sorry! Why didn't you shade me before?"

He isn't apologizing for holding out. We both know he's apologizing for Rachel and what I had to do to protect Maisie and the others.

But *I'm sorry* doesn't undo the whole best-friend-went-dark-side thing.

I replay her last attack again and again. Her body slamming against the shield as she tried to wring the life out of Maisie. The horrible way my purple light wavered, shimmering under her assault. I thought it was going to give. I thought she was going to break through and tear Maisie apart right in front of me.

I would have never forgiven myself.

The moment Ally's face pinched, and her breath went shallow, Rachel sealed her fate. Before Ally's eyes bulged, and she choked, there was hope of reconciliation between us.

"You could not have done anything differently."

"Man, I'm stupid." I try to will my legs to start moving again. "Everyone tried to warn me about Rachel and I wouldn't listen. A fucking moron."

"You loved her."

"That doesn't make me smarter."

The smell of rain washes over me. Gabriel's smell. "Love is above reproach."

"Stop. You're making this awkward."

He frowns at me while I replay those last moments in my head again. Rachel's betrayal and Ally's death. The images loop over and over. I'm not sure I'll ever forgive myself for getting Ally killed. Again.

"She will survive."

"Thanks to Maisie." It was Maisie who saved Ally, blowing

her magic *wake up* breath into her nose. I hadn't done a damn thing.

And I'm not doing much now either except hoping Maisie doesn't wake Caldwell before I can catch up to them.

Gabriel keeps his wing arched over my head as we walk. He doesn't watch the approaching horizon as I do. His eyes are trained on his feet.

My throat tightens the more I think about Ally, Rachel, and Maisie. The more I think about them, the more stupid and useless I feel.

Man, I'm going to cry like a loser out here? Is there anything more pathetic than walking through the desert with your imaginary friend and *crying*?

"Tell me a story," I beg. I will not rub my runny nose. I sniffle "Anything."

Gabriel turns his face up to the blazing sun for a moment and seems to consider my request. "She was once a partis."

"Who?"

"You call her the sun. At times your kind uses the word *star*. This particular star was once a partis."

I stop walking. The toes of my sneakers slip beneath the hot sand in my sudden stop. "Excuse me?"

"You must make the same choice. You can be the fourth star, or you can be this planet's shield."

A mule has kicked me in the chest. "The sun was a human?"

He tilts his head. "No. I believe you reserve the term human only for Homo sapiens."

My voice wheezes as I continue to struggle to draw in enough air. "Some conscious being evolved on a planet like Earth. I mean, she had to have brains and verbal skills if you gave her superpowers and made her choose the future of her whole freaking race. She couldn't make a choice without a brain, right? I mean, she *could*, but it's a pretty bad idea."

I wasn't sure this conversation was much of an improvement over *hey your best friend turned out to be a psycho who killed your girlfriend*. I don't exactly want to be reminded of the universal bullshit that's going to tear apart my world soon. But maybe this is a good chance to get some answers.

I exhale. "A civilization evolves, becomes conscious and then they get a choice as to whether to preserve what they've built or blow it up and start over. Three people have chosen to blow it up?"

"Yes," he says. His wing twitches, raining black feathers down on my head.

"And how many have chosen to shield everyone instead of blowing everyone up?"

"None."

I groan. "Damn. Do we fuck it up *every* time?"

Imagine, after billions and billions of years, chance after chance, and we're total asshats. Bummer.

"Did they have French fries before? Chocolate? Pugs?"

Gabriel's big green eyes fall on me again.

"Well, clearly we're already doing better," I tell him. "How can I possibly destroy a world with pugs?"

He blinks. "When the time comes, I will show you the world. Your world as it truly is, and you must choose."

"Don't you think that's a lot to put on one person?"

"There were twelve," he reminds me with a stern look of admonition.

Right. Twelve original partis. This time anyway, since Gabriel keeps insisting this is *Take Four: A Perfect World*.

Too bad we killed each other off. I'd love it if someone else could handle this whole save the world crap. Now there are only four of us, counting Caldwell.

I sigh. "I knew trying to get you to have a normal convo was stupid. Listen, I don't know if anyone ever explained this to you, but sometimes people like to talk to be distracted from the horrible bullshit they are dealing with. You talk about food, or sexy butts, your favorite television show. Sometimes it's about the food you love to eat while you're staring at the sexy butts in your favorite television show."

His frown deepens.

"My point is every time I try to talk to you, it's not an invitation to drown me in somber discussions about death and responsibility and horrible impending choices, okay?"

"You do not want to talk about your decision," Gabriel repeats, only he says it with an air of astonishment and disgust.

I sigh. "*Exactly*."

"I do not watch television or eat food."

I shrug. "That leaves butts."

"I do not often consider glutei maximi—"

"How about we play the quiet game then? Hmm? It's hard enough walking in the heat without trying to walk in the heat and use my air for talking."

"We are here." He folds his wings in, and the sun hits me hot and heavy. I could fall dead on the spot.

But he's right. Here's the station.

Only he's wrong about it being a station. A metal over-hang canopies the pumps, but they're outdated. They don't even have credit card readers. The numbers used to calculate gallons and cost aren't digital. They're black and white tiles which would rotate toward a total sum.

To the left of the pumps, across a slab of concrete, is a garage. Three stalls with dusty glass windows sit closed. A doorway stands empty, revealing dark shapes within.

"There's someone inside," Gabriel says.

"Friend or foe?" The hair on my neck rises. Or it would rise if it wasn't plastered to my skin with sweat.

Gabriel doesn't answer, so I erect my shield.

"Is there a car in there?" I ask. I'm also wondering about a phone, but that won't be much help. I need a car if I hope to catch up to Maisie and Georgia.

A man appears in the doorway, wiping his hands on a blue grease rag. I'd know that gesture anywhere. The action conjures a sharp memory of Eric Sullivan in navy coveralls, rubbing his hands before opening his arms to catch me. The smell of orange soap and grease-caked fingernails blooms in my mind.

"Hey there," the guy calls. He steps out into the light and grins at me. Once the light hits his sandy hair and scruffy face, I'm able to refocus on the present and push thoughts of my father, the man who would become Caldwell, out of my mind.

This mechanic is middle-aged. Forty, maybe forty-five. One of his bottom teeth is gone, revealing a black socket as his lips move. "What're you doing way out here?"

No weapon. No guns or noticeable threat. I drop the shield and step forward, hoping he'll think the purple shimmer was a trick of the light.

He looks over my shoulder as if searching for a car.

"I'm Donnie."

"Hi, Donnie. My car, uh—" *freaking exploded* "—broke down. I was hoping I could use your phone? Or you could give me a lift to the nearest town?"

He turns his left ear toward me. "Speak up, sweetheart. I can't hear worth a damn."

I repeat myself, projecting my voice in a way I haven't since the junior high Princess and the Pea production. I was the pea and my part largely consisted of lying sandwiched between two mattresses while wearing a pea suit. Oh, and the wailing. Whenever Annabelle Jerkins—thankfully the tiniest girl in our class—flopped down on top of me, I was supposed to howl in pretend pain.

Thankfully, Donnie hears me on the second go-round and

nods. "Jimmy's got the tow. I can call him, and he'll be here in twenty. Come on in out of the heat. I've got some Orange Crush."

They still make orange soda? The prospect is both exciting and promising. I can't recall being this thirsty. *Ever.* Something about trudging through the desert makes even plain old water seem like a godsend.

I drink half the orange soda in three swallows.

It hits me Jimmy won't have a car to tow because there's nothing left of the Mustang I took from the military base. What is Jimmy going to do? Drag back the blackened pieces?

"What're you doing out here?" Donnie asks after he hangs up on Jimmy.

I fumble for a lie. "I'm lost. I was heading for Tempe." I name the only city in Arizona I can think of.

"You've got about three hours to go," he says, wiping at his face with the cloth.

Inside the garage, it's twenty degrees cooler. Part of it is the three large industrial fans blowing overhead. They are loud as hell, and now I understand why Donnie is deaf. I would have to yell over their thunderous roar for anyone to hear me. But getting out of the sun, if only for a minute, is fantastic. The iced soda bottle cooling my hands is icing on the cake.

"After I get Lauraine's engine going, I'll be happy to look at your car."

I gulp down another mouthful of orange soda. It burns my nose, and I love it. "Uh, thanks. That'd be great."

What the hell, Gabriel? What do I say?

Take his car. Gabriel flutters his wings in the direction of a beat up white truck. It's got huge tires and a utility box in the bed. I've seen those before. Big silver boxes full of tools and gadgets, whatever a person might need. Eric Sullivan had a box on the back of his truck like that.

It will be easier to take the vehicle now with only one man to wrestle rather than when the second arrives. I've learned in my short time as a badass, the more people involved, the more quickly shit gets messy.

But this guy gave me an orange soda and sat me in front of the fan. It seems awful to beat him up and take his car.

About twelve of the twenty minutes have passed. The radio overhead blasts classical rock, *Highway to Hell* this time. I can barely hear it over the fan. With Donnie's electric socket wrench whirling and his head buried under the hood of the beige Taurus, I don't think he can hear the song at all.

I suck down the last of the orange soda and stare at the empty glass bottle in my hand.

I sigh. "Damn it."

I cross the garage to the Taurus and tap Donnie's shoulder. He comes up for air, pulling himself out of the car's mouth.

He gives me another one of those wide, trusting smiles. "What is it, honey?"

I regret this already. "I'm sorry."

"Speak up, I can't hear you."

"You've been so nice. I'm sorry about this," I shout.

His face screws up in confusion and stays that way as I bring the orange soda bottle down on the side of his head. The moment the glass connects with his cranium it breaks. Shards fly, scaring me into thinking I hit him too hard.

It doesn't help his eyes roll up in his head, and his knees give. Donnie goes down hard, hitting his head for a second time on the concrete.

"Ouch, damn." I groan. "Gee-*zus*, Gabriel. Why did you stand there? You should have caught him!"

I bend down and touch his throat under the jaw, searching for a pulse. His heart hammers away under my fingertips. I roll him over and inspect the big gash on his head. The skin is split wide open.

"Is he going to be okay?" I ask, frowning at the glass glittering on the concrete.

"He will live," Gabriel assures me. "Now we must go. His friend is close."

I bend over and search Donnie's coveralls for keys. I find them in the right front pocket, resting beside a pack of Spirit cigarettes. I fish them out and run out to the white truck. I hop in, turn the engine and speed away without looking back.

When I finally do look back, only the shrinking garage and wide open desert are there.

"Whew! That was close." I thrust out my lower lip at Gabriel. "Poor Donnie!"

That's the problem with having firebombing power. It doesn't leave much room for subtlety. If I *don't* want to melt someone's flesh off their bone, I must resort to other means.

A small black box on Donnie's dash buzzes.

"All Cochise County officers, we have a double 187 at the old Cochise saloon. All available units, Code 2. Proceed with caution."

It's a scanner. A *police* scanner. I don't know what 187 or 2 or any of that means.

"Georgia?" I ask Gabriel.

He levels his green eyes on mine, turning only his head to gaze at me. His body's lounging in the passenger seat as if we're two buddies on a pleasant afternoon drive.

"She murdered them."

Of course, she did. Georgia's death toll surpassed mine ages ago, and mine's far from low.

Gabriel faces forward, his eyes on what lies ahead. "She means to survive by any means necessary."

I sigh. "Don't we all."

CHAPTER FIVE

MAISIE

It's getting too hot in the car. For an instant, I start to worry about Winnie Pug. An article I read about leaving dogs in hot cars flashes in my head. Minutes. That's all it takes, and they're dead. We're not even talking a hundred degrees. My gut knots.

Winnie Pug isn't here.

He's back at the military base with Gloria and Gideon.

I'd give up a whole pack of peanut butter cups in exchange for a pug kiss right now. I love kissing his smooshed face. I don't even mind the dog breath.

My heart kicks a second time.

I'm never going to see Winnie Pug again. Or Gloria. Or even Gideon.

Gideon. His dark eyes behind glasses and his one-sided smirk. Okay, yes, he's six or seven years older than me. But he's got thick lashes as long as my little finger.

And horrible taste in women. I don't know what he saw in Rachel.

It got him killed.

Dad's body slumps against me again. I elbow him away.

Don't think about it, I tell myself. *Think about something nice.*

Gideon's dark eyes and warm scent come to mind. When I bent over him, ready to blow air into his nose and bring him back to life, I almost kissed him.

Okay, I've got some stupid school girl crush on him. It'll go away once my hormones sort themselves out. Then I'll find someone who goes to Whole Foods and buys me Lemon Cookie ice cream at ten o'clock at night because I'm sad. Like a hot accountant or nurturing veterinarian, not a wealthy international super spy likely to drop me for the first Bond girl he sees.

I want someone normal. Someone who dreams of a calm, boring life like I do.

Maybe I'll meet this awesome guy in college—though who the hell is going to admit me without proper transcripts, I don't know. I could do a couple years in a high school first. Make friends whose worst drama is some cheating boyfriend. If my grades are good enough for two years, I can probably get in somewhere. I'll work if I have to. Maybe somewhere cool like a coffee shop. Even better if they host goth bands on weekends. And my friends and I will get dressed up and go out for drinks and somehow pass all our tests on Monday morning. When I graduate, I'll get an apartment in a big city. New York. Or maybe even go back to Chicago.

I snort, choking on a laugh.

Who am I kidding?

I'm never going to college or getting over Gideon. I'm going to die a horrible flaming death like every other partis. No amount of wishing and dreaming is going to change my fate.

I shove the dead body off me and slip out the truck's cab. My ankle hurts the second I put pressure on it. I'd forgotten all about my twisted ankle. It was Rachel's fault. I hurt it trying not to get murdered.

I lift my pants leg and examine it. It's totally swollen. This heat is probably making it worse, but I can't do anything about it right now. It'll have to wait. For now, I'll keep the weight off it.

I push Dad over so he's lying flat on the seat, hidden from view.

I take a big gasp of fresh air.

I can smell him. He must've gotten his dead body stink all over me. I gag.

I step farther away from the truck and the smell dissolves. Now all I smell is dry, hot desert.

Good. Maybe it's the truck that reeks to high heaven. I look down at my clothes. My shirt's wet with sweat and blood has soaked my right leg.

I look like I fell out of a horror movie.

First stop: the bathroom. If I run into anybody before I have the chance to shower, I better have a good story.

I shade my eyes and peer at the hotel. It looks dead. No maids are coming out of rooms or pushing towel carts. No music from the door marked *office*. I turn in all directions and don't see a single soul on the street either. If tumbleweeds rolled across the street right now, it'd look natural.

Creepy ghost town, that's what this is.

"Hey."

I whirl with a scream bubbling from my lips.

"Sorry! Sorry," he holds his hand out. "I didn't mean to freak you out."

I put one hand over my heart. Not a man. A boy. My age, give or take, and balanced on the seat of a bicycle. He's wearing a Sun Devils cap on his head and a yellow jersey that shows off his considerable biceps.

"Are you okay?" he asks. "Do you need help?"

"Oh hi," I manage to choke out. "You scared me."

"Were you in an accident?" he asks, his eyes big.

I look down at my bloody clothes and gimpy leg.

"Yeah. But we're okay. My mom went inside to use the phone."

"Can I get you something?" he asks. He's already off the bike and moving closer. I take a step back, and he stops. "I'm not going to hurt you."

"I bet you say that to all the girls," I say. What a weird, dumb thing to say.

He frowns and lifts his cap. He scratches his head before yanking the cap back down. It gives me a chance to see his big ears. They stick out on either side of his head, but surprisingly, it's not goofy. It adds to his charm. "We don't have a hospital here. It's about fifteen miles up I-10. If you've got car trouble..."

"No, no." I force a smile when I realize how weird that came out. He's looking back at the truck. I don't want him to look at the truck, think about the truck, or go *near* the truck. Not with a dead body baking in the cab. "We're fine. The truck's fine. I'm waiting for my mom. That's all."

"Are you sure? We've got Stanley. He was a medic in the army." He leans over the shiny silver handlebars and grins up. "And I could at least get some ice for your ankle."

Okay, athletes aren't usually my type. I prefer pasty goth boys who like to talk about relationships in terms of centuries, but here I am, grinning at this big-eared boy.

Maybe those big ears and goofy grin got half the girls in Cochise pregnant.

One never can tell.

"I'm okay." I'm grinning because if one random boy from

Cochise can make me feel all aflutter, chances are I'll get over Gideon in no time, which is *awesome* because I don't want to spend the rest of my short life pining over a playboy.

"What's your name?"

He looks pleased by the question. He pushes the bill of his cap up enough to look at me with both eyes. "Sam."

"Like Sam Winchester?" A hunka hunk of burning love on my favorite television series. "Great name."

"No, I'm Sam Mercy. Never heard of Winchester. He play ball?"

Okay, the cutie isn't a geek. -10 points. Maybe he has many other redeemable qualities. "No. He's a character on a TV show."

"Oh," he says. "You going to be in town for long?"

"Nope. Passing through. We're heading to—" *to my immediate demise.* Can't say that. I blurt the first city that comes to mind. "Uh, San Francisco. To visit family."

"Cool."

"What about you? You live here?"

"Oh yeah. All my life. But I ain't going to die here. Next year I'll start up at ASU. I'm gonna be a Sun Devil. I can't wait." He pulls on the handlebars of his bike, yanking it up into a wheelie. On his feet, I realize how tall he is.

"What do you want to study?" Honestly, I don't care. I'm hot. I'm sweaty, but I can't go back to the truck. Sam might come over and try to talk to me. That'd be horrible, given Dad's dead body. But I can't walk away either. What if he gets curious about a truck with a door missing? I shift my weight and wipe at my soaked neck, already considering what I might ask him after he runs out of things to say about college.

"They've got a great sports med program."

"So you want to be a sports doctor?"

"I want to play ball if I can, but you've got to have something to fall back on."

"So practical," I say. "Still, it's got to be hard packing up and leaving your home like that."

I think about Chicago and the beautiful lake stretching as far as the eye can see. My chest aches.

He shrugs, grin bright. "Got to see the world while you're young. That's what my daddy says. I can't wait. It's gonna be the best four years of my life."

"Your dad sounds like a smart guy."

He lifts his cap and scratches his head again. "He is. I got real lucky there. You could meet him if you want. He's right inside." He points toward the saloon-like hotel. "My dad owns the place."

And you could meet mine. He's dead. Over there in that truck.

"Maybe later. If I leave this spot, Mom will freak out." Another half lie. Mom's freaking out all on her own.

"Do I know you?" he asks, his brows coming together. "You sure do look familiar."

"I have one of those faces." I force a laugh. I hope it doesn't sound as tight and crazy to him as it does to me. If he does recognize me, it's because my face was plastered all over the news for the last couple of days. I'm the victim of a supposed kidnapping...total B.S., or at least it was total B.S. when the bulletin went out. I *am* kidnapped now.

Sam tilts his face up to the sky. "I wish you'd let me get some ice for your ankle. And maybe a coke. You look thirsty."

Is that another way of saying I look like a red-faced pig?

I frown. "I don't have any money on me."

His enthusiasm doesn't falter. "I've got ya. I'll be right back."

He pops another wheelie and angles his bike in the direction of a store two doors down from the hotel. My chest relaxes as he peddles away. He doesn't even glance at the truck as he heads toward the storefront with cases of Pepsi filling the glass windows.

I try to picture Sam at Arizona State, in his Sun Devil jersey, carrying all his books from class to class. Going out with friends on the weekend.

I sigh. The kid doesn't know how good he's got it. Not because he's got an awesome dad, but with the long, bright future ahead of him.

Ice stabs me in the chest, melts and pours into my guts. A sucking sensation tugs at my insides, and I reach out and grab the side of the truck to steady myself. I barely register the scorching metal as I'm pulled underwater by a strong hand.

Someone's dying.

Someone's life is draining away, and they are taking me with them. Then as quickly as the feeling came, it shuts off. Kaput.

I look around, but I don't see anything. No bodies in the street. No running or shouting or screaming. No cause for alarm.

But I know death when I feel it.

Mom bursts out of the office and into the sun.

I know something's wrong as soon as I see her.

She hurries down the stairs, practically running toward the truck. Her face is tense, all the muscles screwed up with emotion.

"What—" I begin, but I don't get the whole sentence out of my mouth.

"Get in the truck."

I look at the storefront where Sam disappeared through clear bright doors. No sign of him.

"Get in the truck!" My mother screams. "Now!"

I hop up into the cab, and the truck is thrown into reverse before I manage to buckle myself in. Seatbelts are always important, but more so when you don't even have a door.

The truck lurches forward.

"What happened?" I ask.

"There's no gas station in this town. Can you believe it? What a shithole!"

I want to defend Sam's town. How bad can it be if it's got someone like him?

"We need to ditch this anyway. We'll trade it." She's not even looking at the road as she drives. She's looking at a small piece of plastic and then up at the street signs.

"What are you doing?" I shove Dad off me for the hundredth time. I'm reaching my limit of corpse contact for the day. I don't complain because all Mom will say is *he wouldn't be a corpse if you'd wake him up.*

"There!" She points at the sign and whips the truck onto Main Street. She slams on her brakes in front of a house at the corner of Main and Smith. She looks at the plastic square in her hand again, and I realize it's a driver's license.

My stomach drops. "Whose license is that?"

"This is the house. Help me get your dad inside."

"Mom, whose house is this?" I ask again, but she's already thrown her door open and is dragging Dad out the driver's side, her arms laced under his.

I hop out and go around to the other side of the truck. Dad sags in her arms. His neck is stretched to the left, and I can see the gristle of his esophagus. I swallow vomit.

"Pick up his feet. We need to get inside."

I lift Dad's dusty shoes up by taking a heel in each hand. My lower back cramps like I'm a hundred instead of sixteen years old.

We carry him through a white gate and across more sand and clumps of dead grass. Mom makes me take most of his weight while she fishes some keys out of her pocket.

"Seriously, whose place is this? Why do you have their keys?"

"The hotel's out of order," Mom says. "But the owner was

nice enough to give me the keys to his house and his license for his address."

I frown harder. I wouldn't give some stranger my house keys. And didn't Sam say his dad was the owner of the saloon? Is Sam's dad really that nice? Is that where Sam gets his kindness from?

"He said we can make ourselves at home. By the time he gets off work, your dad will be awake, and we'll be long gone."

The door to the one-story ranch house pops open, and we fall inside, pulled by the gravity of Dad's body. Mom helps me drag him into the kitchen before marching out again.

"Where are you going?" I call after her.

"I want to hide the car in the garage," Mom says. "So no one will see it on the street."

Then she's gone, leaving me alone in a stranger's house with a corpse at my feet.

I'm a fool if I think it can't get any worse.

CHAPTER SIX

JESSE

The police scanner is surprisingly helpful. Who knew cops worked so hard to fully inform each other when they conversed via radio?

As I try to put as much distance between Donnie's garage and moi, I learn a few miles away, two people working in a hotel were killed.

No signs of trauma. Just dead.

Georgia's calling card.

Her black death ribbons render a person lifeless. No visible signs of violence like split skin or bruises. Rachel's telekinesis could do that too. Georgia has both powers now.

I remember Cochise, the tiny desert town we passed on our drive to the military base. I'm certain I can find it again.

The only problem is by the time I get there the town will be swarming with cops. It's likely someone will recognize Donnie's truck if he's the only mechanic around here, and they'll wonder what the hell I'm doing driving it. Or maybe my face will give me away.

I am a wanted fugitive after all. Anyone who watches the news is going to recognize me on sight.

It's only fifteen minutes before Cochise appears on the horizon.

I don't see any other way to drive into the town except head on. It's not like there's a forest to hide in or a big mountain to creep around. Barren desert stretches in all directions.

If Georgia and Maisie are there—that's where I'm heading.

How will I know if they're there? They could have hit and run. That would have been the smart thing to do.

"Find her," Gabriel says.

I frown. "I didn't put a tracker in her butt."

Black tufts of his hair fall across his cheeks and cover his bright eyes briefly before it's sucked back toward the open window. "You can find her."

"Again, no way I can call her up and ask for directions," I say, and I point at the scanner. "And cops are the only people I can find with that thing. So...*nope*."

"Monroe reestablished a connection between you. Sense her location using this connection."

I remember the bizarre chicken blood ritual Monroe did to reestablish said connection between Maisie and me. It was a connection that was always supposed to exist between the partis, but apparently, it was severed the moment Caldwell murdered Chaplain, a psychopath with a penchant for snuff films.

God, it seems like a million years ago since I sat on Monroe's floor and let him smear blood on my face. But it was days. *Days*.

"I can feel her?" I ask.

Gabriel surveys the horizon with a thoughtful expression.

He looks like he should spout some poetry right now. "Her angel does not oppose me. She will not be hidden."

"You have a friend?" I can't hide my surprise. "I thought I was your only friend."

I pout and he only grins.

"You've been *cheating* on me?" I finally comprehend what he said. "Wait, Maisie has an angel?"

"Yes," he says. He turns away now, gazing at the horizon. "She is not like the others. She is more—" He searches for the words.

"Maisie has a *lady* angel? You're cheating on me with a lady angel?"

Gabriel's face blanks, becoming unreadable.

He stiffens as if he isn't entirely comfortable with my assessment.

"Gabe, how could you?" I quiver my lower lip for show.

His eyes go all squinty. "I believe the word designated for this affiliation is 'ally.' One whose objective is the same as your own."

"If two people want sex, then they have the same objective," I say, grinning. "But I wouldn't call them allies."

"She is my *ally*. She will not resist your connection."

It's funny watching him insist it's only platonic between him and this so-called lady angel. I want to tease him more, explore this opportunity to learn more about Gabriel and his people and their purpose, but I'm distracted by the city manifesting on the horizon.

Heat shimmers along the desert floor, glimmering in the air like gasoline. Through the haze, I can see buildings. They're bleached by the sun, amplifying the sunlight assailing them. Some shadow flits over the hood of the car, and for a minute I'm sure it's Gabriel. When I turn and look out the driver's side window, it's a bird of prey. The sleek outline of its body and fan of its tail unmistakable. But from this distance, I can't tell if it's a hawk or owl or something else.

"Contact her," Gabriel says again.

"Using this connection?"

"Call to her."

"That's super vague. If I opened an owner's manual that only said *use me*, it would be the shittiest manual ever."

"Here," Gabriel says and taps the side of his head with an index finger.

Like I do with you, I say, mouth closed, mind open.

Yes.

I don't close my eyes. *Hello*, I'm driving. But I do think about Maisie. I conjure a picture of the kid in my head. She rolls Winston over onto his back and exposes his little pug belly. She scratches him ruthlessly as his feet kick the air. A large pink tongue hangs out the side of his mouth.

Maisie? I pretend I'm talking to her. To the kid scratching the pug belly in my mind. *Maisie, can you hear me?*

Nothing.

I try again, concentrating. *Maisie!*

This time, I get a reaction. No words. No mental picture comes zinging back across the desert. But something like a *ping* goes off inside me. The deep, resonant echo of a homing beacon. My mental signal bounced off something and has come sailing back

"They're still there," I say, smiling at Gabriel.

He doesn't look surprised.

"You knew!" I accuse, gripping the steering wheel.

He says nothing.

"Well, do you also know how I'm going to sneak into town without running into the police? I bet they already see me coming, dust clouds and all." I turn in my seat and look out the back window. Dust billows up behind me into the sky. "So much for subtlety."

"There." Gabriel points toward a road right of town. It's far right of the central cluster. And probably about the closest thing to a back road I can hope for. "Take it."

I don't argue. Either he's a supernatural being who can see the situation better than I can, or he's a figment of my imagination. If the latter, then wouldn't his choice be my choice anyway? Brings a whole new meaning to *his guess is as good as mine,* right?

The tires gain traction as the sand turns into a paved road. After so long blasting across the wild desert it's weird to drive on something solid.

I slow my speed but not enough to look like a creeper. Off-white buildings line the roads, but they are spaced kind of far apart. The houses huddle closer together once I turn down a side street, and I pass an elementary school and a laundromat.

There's the saloon with the words Cochise Hotel painted in drippy black paint over the door. Out front, I count them, one, two, three, *four* cop cars are parked, lights and sirens off. Near the entrance stands a cluster of cops in brown uniforms, buzzing like flies around a corpse.

Speaking of a corpse, two men in white uniforms wheel out a gurney with a lump of a body on it. I assume it's a body. I can't see what lies beneath the sheet, but it seems like a lot of pomp and circumstance for a couple of pillows.

I pull the car to a stop two full blocks away, parking Donnie's ride behind a big ice truck.

"So Georgia went whacko and knocked off a couple of people?" I whisper to Gabriel. I don't know why I'm whispering. I mean, I know *why*. I'm worried the cops will hear me. But I'm not sure they can hear me from way over there.

I'm not going to take my chances and find out.

"She was recognized," Gabriel says. "As you will be. Do not linger here."

"Hey, it's not my fault you didn't give me invisibility. Invisibility would be super useful right now." I'm arguing, but he's right. I'm already backing the truck out from behind the ice truck, on the lookout for a nice quiet side street to hide in.

I'm going to stash this truck—get rid of it before Donnie reports it—and use the *ping* call and response to find Maisie. She's got to be around here. Of course, she's probably also with Georgia, and I'm sure that will go over well when I demand she gives Maisie up without a fight.

I slide the car from reverse to drive and slam on the brakes lest I run over the guy blocking my path.

"Freeze!" a man shouts. Not one voice, but at least three blat at me. Two cops in front have their guns raised, pointed through the windshield at my head. Another cop steps into my periphery, ready to yank open the driver's side door and drag me into the dirt.

I only have a second to suck in a sharp breath before I hear the door click open and the hot desert air rushes in.

CHAPTER SEVEN

MAISIE

*J*esse?

Maisie, where are you?

Jesse's voice blows through my head like a creepy poltergeist.

"Jesse?" I say her name. "Jesse, is that you?" I'm talking to an empty living room. Dad's stretched out, dead at my feet. His feet beneath a coffee table made of fake polished wood.

Jesse doesn't respond, and the voice I felt blow through me is gone. Whatever that was, it's over.

She wants to find you, Azrael says.

Azrael is my height with shoulder length black hair. It's fluffy like a shampoo commercial. Voluminous. Her eyes are gray like Lake Michigan in January. They're practically silver with the weird moonlight that flickers through them.

She looks the way I remember her. Shiny breastplate. Big sword. Her wings are dove gray and white underneath. Some have blue at the tips.

Azrael's eyes fix on Dad. On his bloody clothes and brutalized neck. Then she flicks up her eyes to meet mine. "Do you want her to find you?"

I'm about to blurt, *Duh. I totally want her to find me.* It's not as if I went with Mom willingly. I want Winnie Pug. I want to know our friends are okay. I'd even like to see Gideon's stupid face and maybe pull out one of those little hairs growing on his chin.

I want to hug the hell out of Jess.

She could use a hug. She saw the love of her life get murdered by her best friend. Then watched her best friend get killed. I brought Ally back, but I couldn't save Rachel.

I recall Jesse's hands reaching out to me, begging me to escape Mom. *"Jump! I'll catch you!"*

"Why wouldn't I want to see her?" I ask

"You are protecting your mother," Azrael says.

My shoulders slump. "You think I'm a moron."

She blinks at me.

"You think Jesse *should* kill her."

Azrael lowers her sword. Its tip brushes Dad's boot, and for a second, I wonder if she's going to lop it off at the ankle.

"I felt someone die," I whisper. I can't look at his jagged neck any more. The sight of all that muscle and junk makes me feel sick. I cross the living room, giving the angel, coffee table, and dead dad a wide berth. I plop down into a high back chair with a fuzzy blanket thrown over one arm.

The blanket is itchy and an ugly lemon yellow. I push it off the chair. It hits the floor without a sound.

"Who died?" I ask Azrael.

She doesn't answer. I'm not sure if it's because she doesn't want to or if it's because I'm supposed to be able to discern that for myself.

It's lame, but I don't know much about my superpower or how to use it.

"I can feel them die, but not how," I say. "Am I supposed to know how they die too?"

I feel death for a reason. So I can save the person if I want to. And I've used my gift that way a few times. If I can get to them soon enough after the death, then my three-breath trick is all it takes to bring them back.

"I did not hide you from her," Azrael says, bringing me back to the moment, and the corpse on the floor. "She will find you."

I can't decide how I feel about it. I want Jesse to find me. But I don't want her to find Mom. What if I run out of the house right now? What if I run into the desert until I find Jesse? Can I call out to her the way she did me?

I stand up from the armchair and stare at the back door. *I can run*, I tell myself. *I can run right out of here and never look back.*

"You are safer with your sister," Azrael says. "She will not harm you, unlike him."

Him. My eyes slide over the corpse on the floor before returning to the desert. Hurt me. That's one way to put it. My fingers instinctively fall to my thighs, scratching at the denim. The fabric is too thick to feel them, but the scars are there, underneath.

The front door pops open, and I jump. Mom bursts in with an armful of plastic bandages. Azrael is gone, forced out by my Mom's aura or polarity or whatever we're calling the weird mojo following the partis around. But I don't need to know what Azrael was going to say.

Him. My dad.

I'm safer with Jesse than with Dad because Dad *will* hurt me. Again.

It's only a matter of time.

"I ditched the truck." Mom kicks the front door closed with her foot. "She won't be able to track it."

Jesse's following me, not the car, I want to say. More lame stupidity. But I want to warn her. I want her to let me go.

"So are we leaving now?" I don't want to be in Sam's house. The urge to leave is like an itch on my back I can't reach.

"I want to sew him up first. He can't heal with his neck like that."

Instead, I blurt out. "What've you got?"

"Bandages."

She drops to her knees beside Dad's body and starts ripping open plastic packages. Her cherry red fingernails shred everything. The right index nail is broken off, jagged along the top instead round like the others. She doesn't seem to notice.

Ace bandages and cottony clumps tumble onto the carpet. One bounces off Dad's pale face. Mom frowns at him. She brings up a hand and touches his cheek before leaning in to kiss him.

I look away, heat burning in my cheeks. It's too weird to watch.

"I'm right here, Eric," she whispers. Her voice trembles. It makes all the muscles in my stomach knot up. These weird tender moments between them always make me feel that way. But my parents being into each other doesn't even make it to the Top Five Problems I Have Right Now list.

My eyes stay focused on the checkered recliner and the big wooden handle at its side. I imagine if I pull it, the footrest will pop up. Someone likes to come home and plop into this chair, yank the handle, and then spend the rest of the night watching television.

God, what a life!

I don't look up until I hear cabinets opening and closing. Wood slamming against wood.

Mom pauses in the doorway reading the label on a big brown bottle of peroxide.

"Help me." She drops to her knees beside dad, twisting off the cap of the peroxide.

I join her beside him, but I hate being this close. For one, the smell. The A/C is on full blast which seems to minimize the grossness, but when I'm this close to a rapidly putrefying corpse, cold can only do so much.

I turn my head away, and Mom clucks her tongue. "Don't go wimpy on me now, Maisie. I need your help."

She slides one towel under dad's head and another over her shoulder, to wipe her hands on as she goes. Then she pours the peroxide over dad's sliced throat. The open wound bubbles and hisses. It's like a mouth full of Pop Rocks.

The bloody pink foam and the rot of roadkill make me turn my head away. I suck in a breath and try not to vomit on Dad. Mom would be pissed if I did.

"I want you to hold his head in place while I sew." Mom opens a black canvas sewing kit on the floor beside Dad's skull. She unzips it, flipping the cover open. It falls flat. A dozen bright needles shine in the lamplight. Along with threads of all kinds. Mom's fingers pass over the thin sewing threads, red, green, gold, and white. And she grabs a thick piece of twine instead. It could be burlap maybe. Then she selects a large hooked needle.

"Jesus." I pinch my eyes closed, but I was too slow. The crazy needle flashes on the back of my eyelids. "Is that what you're going to use?"

"I need to get through the muscle too." Her voice is muffled as she pinches the twine between her teeth and tries to thread it through the hooked gold needle.

The muscle too. God, why are bodies so gross? My stomach turns. I look away, fixating on the clock on the wall. My eyes trace the octagon frame. I should be in school. Or if not in school, at least on the computer watching my favorite TV shows or texting my friends. I should not be holding a head to a neck so my mom can *sew* it on.

I thought looking away would help, but it doesn't. Not looking at the head makes it heavier in my hands.

"Maisie," Mom scolds. "Watch what you're doing."

I put a knee on either side of Dad's temple and take his head in my hands again. It's cold and slick with—oh, I don't know and don't *want* to know. Juice? Dead body juice? I push the head down onto the stump of his neck as Mom bends over with the needle. When the needlepoint pricks the flesh above his sliced throat, I pinch my eyes closed.

Parties. I tell myself. Some girl crying over a stupid boy who doesn't love her enough. Getting into trouble for drinking with my friends. When my beloved dog dies after a long and happy life. Getting a B on a test I studied hard for. That should be the worst of it. Not this.

Jeanne d'Arc was but a child when she was called, Azrael whispers.

She was nineteen when she was burned at the stake. She had three years on me.

She had a life of poverty, hardship, and war, Azrael argues. *Child warriors fill this world.*

She's right, of course. I shouldn't whine. There are people in the world that have it way worse than me right now. As horrible as holding a head between my hands is, it's a guarantee that right now someone somewhere is going through worse. Kids even younger than me.

"Maisie! Come on!" The head slides away from the neck. I readjust, connecting flesh with flesh and add more pressure.

When I close my eyes again, I can still see the puckered flesh pulled tight between the thick twine. And gristle. White gristle protruding through—

I inhale, but it smells like a corpse.

I turn and vomit onto my shoe. And it's like breaking a dam. Once I puke, puking a second time is much easier. If Mom is bitching about it, I can't hear her. Not over the wet sounds coming from my throat.

My nose burns and I groan. A third convulsion tightens my stomach, but only hot bile comes out on the third heave, stinging my nose. On the fourth, only air.

One benefit, oddly enough, is now the air smells like vomit—acrid and sour—instead of a corpse. Small mercies.

On the downside, my sneaker is warm and soggy, chunks of vomit caked into my laces. Awesome.

"Better?" Mom asks.

I nod and resume holding his head in place. It goes on and on. The sewing. The pressure. Dad's head wobbling in my grip when Mom tugs the twine tight.

"Help me turn him over," Mom says. "Prop his head on your knee. Just like that. Perfect."

Mom starts on the side of his neck, working her way toward the spine.

"You're doing great," she whispers. Her eyes cut up to mine. "Very brave."

I snort. "The puking was extraordinarily brave."

Mom spares a half smile. "I'm sure you haven't slept well. That always upsets my stomach. Add a few adrenaline spikes, everything else that's happened, and the smell..."

She pulls the string tighter with her teeth as if it hasn't just been through Dad's corpse flesh.

"Don't be embarrassed," she finishes, once the needle is out of her mouth. "That's all I'm saying."

I nod. *Thanks* doesn't quite make it out of my mouth.

"There," she says, rolling Dad back onto his back. She lifts the opposite side to add a few more stitches, and Dad's head comes to rest on my other knee. "All done."

I slide back from the body. "I'd kill someone for a shower."

As soon as I say it, a strange feeling rolls over my skin. I can't say things like that. Not in this family. Someone might take me seriously.

Mom points toward the dark bedroom where she'd emerged with the sewing kit. "There's a shower through there. I'll look around for some clothes that might fit you."

My heart throbs. "Thanks, Mom."

She smiles and for the first time I get a good look at her face. She's sweaty and dirty and puffy purple circles droop beneath her baby blue eyes. Her ponytail has come undone. She seems to realize this the same time I do. She reaches up and pulls the hair tie out, letting her hair fall to her shoulders. It's the same golden hue as mine.

The urge to hug her wells up inside me. It does that sometimes, even when I'm mad.

"Go on," she says, using the arm of the recliner to pull herself up. "We won't be here long."

I limp into the bathroom on my swollen ankle and find a shower stall adjacent to the bedroom. The en suite bathroom is tiny. The stall and the toilet sit in a closet-sized room, with two vanity sinks outside, a stone's throw from the bed itself.

I step into the shower stall before I strip out of the grubby clothes. I throw the clothes on the bathroom rug. I keep the shoes in the stall with me.

Naked, I turn on the hot tap. Cold water hits my back, and I hiss. Slowly it warms, and my shoulder blades stop trying to grab on to one another.

I start with my shoes. No point in cleaning myself and then tackling the vomit. I squat in the stall and pull out the laces. I use bar soap on the canvas and then on the laces themselves. I rinse them until no soapy suds ooze out.

Then I tackle my hair.

I'm moving slow. On purpose. If Mom wants to hit the road, I've got to slow her down.

Dad can't wake up. He *can't*. And yet, I didn't do a damn thing to stop Mom from sewing him up, did I? And why not? It isn't like Dad doesn't have it coming.

I look down at my thighs. Scars crisscross the flesh from mid-thigh to knee.

What happened to the carnival glass bowl, Maisie?

I don't know, Daddy, I don't.

Liar liar pants on fire. Do you know what I do to liars, Maisie? I hurt them.

I angle the shower head, turning it toward my face. I push Dad out of my thoughts with each scrub, each scrape under my nails until there's nothing left for me to do but let the water run cold.

Mom put clothes on the double bed while I showered. Jeans and a belt. A T-shirt and socks.

Everything's a little big. And the style says *boy*. That's probably what the belt is all about. I dress, detangle my hair, and brush my teeth with an unopened toothbrush from a spare drawer. The only deodorant I find is this musky male deodorant that smells like someone's grandpa. I skip it. I'm done with strong smells for the day, thanks.

I also find a bandage I can wrap my swollen ankle in. I do, and the pressure feels great. It gives me a peg-leg kind of walk, but the tender muscles stop throbbing.

I'm pulling a comb through my hair when I step into the living room, wet sneakers in hand. "Mom?"

"In here," she says.

The vomit and the blood's gone from the carpet. The carpet's soaked, and a bowl of soapy water sits by the coffee table, off to one side.

"I'm in here," Mom says again.

I step over the wet spot and follow her voice into another

bedroom. This one has only a twin-sized bed pushed up against a wall. It's Sun Devils everything. Posters, bedding, yellow curtains, and a team flag.

This is Sam's room, the sweet boy from town, probably wondering where I ran off to before he could return with the soda. It's probably a local thing, this whole ASU Sun Devil fandom. Like the Cubs in Chicago. On certain days, a sea of red and blue floods the subway.

Dad's on the twin bed, Sam's bed, his hands laced over his chest, looking more like a corpse than ever.

"I want you to sit with him while I shower," Mom says. She's frowning at her nails.

I'm about to argue sitting with a corpse is not my idea of a good time, but she's out the door before I can speak up.

"If you get the urge to wake him up that would be *great.*" She's mad again.

I stand in the middle of Sam's room, my dead father lying on top of an old comforter until I hear the shower turn on.

What happened to the carnival glass bowl, Maisie?

I don't know, Daddy, I don't.

I take a seat at the desk beside the bed. The chair wobbles when I sit down, and my arms shoot out to balance me. The desk doesn't look super sturdy either.

There's a copy of *Never Quit: The Michael Jordan Story* on the desk beside a laptop. But the laptop is password protected. Bummer. I could totally lose myself in some cat memes or a good internet spiral right now.

"I'm not waking you up." I spin the chair toward Dad. I fall back against the chair and prop my bum ankle on the bed. The elevation is supposed to be good for swelling, and I should probably do all I can to get fighting fit as soon as possible. If I thought the fighting was over, I'd be a moron.

"Jesse's coming," I whisper to him. "She's coming, and she's going to kill you."

Dad doesn't open his eyes. He doesn't even blink. The gross sheen of unknown fluids gives his skin a waxy look.

"She'll kill you and then we're going to be okay. Me, Mom, and Jesse. We're going to be fine without you. Better than fine. Freaking *great*. Enjoy your nap because I'm not waking you up."

If I keep saying it, it might come true.

CHAPTER EIGHT

JESSE

"What did *I* do?" I try to sound innocent and surprised. This is a small town. They might recognize Donnie's truck and think I'm a common thief. Or I'm a suspicious person who isn't from around here, hovering outside a crime scene.

I let the officer who tore open the door pull me out of the cab. Innocent people don't struggle, so I keep my hands up and eyes wide until I'm sure I can't sweet talk my way out of this.

"Jesse Sullivan, you are under arrest. Anything you say can—"

Jesse Sullivan.

Well, there goes my innocence.

If they know my name, they aren't arresting me for killing the people at this hotel. Or if they are, those deaths are simply part of a long list of crimes already laid against me, thanks to Caldwell. When we managed to rescue Maisie from his crazy ass, and Caldwell couldn't find us, he used his mind control mojo to manipulate half the world. Damn the news and all its cameras. You can't believe anything you see on television these days.

"You cannot let the police take you." Gabriel's wings hunch with his irritation.

You think? I groan inwardly. I can't talk to him aloud unless I want to freak these guys out. *I thought they wanted to go for coffee, and maybe if things go well, a bit of kissing.*

The police officer wrenches my arm behind my back. Hard. Way too hard considering I'm practically a spaghetti noodle in his grip.

"Hey!" I yell. "I might need that arm someday."

"Shut up."

"Shut up?" My temper flares. Heat floods my neck and face. "Shut up? How's that professional?"

I get a look at my dirty face and messy hair in his aviator glasses before he says, "Shut up, or I'll make you shut up."

"Uh, no." I ignite.

Blue flames engulf me, blazing from my navel, over my abdomen along each limb. The heat, and no doubt surprise drives the cops back. I erect my shield as soon as they're clear of me, and none too soon either. A second later, bullets ping off the outside of the shimmery purple barrier. I let the flames die. They shrink, quiver, and then completely disappear like a faltering gas fire.

One cop, the one right in front of me has emptied his clip, but his finger keeps pulling the trigger. The cop beside him is holding his gun, pointing it at my head, but it dips as his mouth falls open. He's gawking at my shield, trying to process how little ol' me is doing all of this.

I want to fire bomb their asses. I want to see arms and legs fly in all directions.

You murdered eight people on live television. Ally's scolding tone burrows into my ear.

The woman I love already thinks I'm a monster. No need for her to wake up and see how much carnage I've left in my wake while she lay dead. Dead, because of me.

Gee-*zus*. Guilt is such an impediment! It should be counted as a disability!

I dial it down and throw sparks on the pants of the officer who roughed me up. He jumps back, cursing, his pants burning like flash paper.

I can't suppress a giggle as he undoes his buckle and tries to tear them off. He falls out of his pants into the street, his butt bouncing on the ground, wearing only briefs.

Ewww. Not something I wanted to see today.

His utility belt, or whatever they're called, hits the pavement with a crack. The handcuffs clank to the sandy road with his gun, Taser, and mace.

The other cops are looking at me, unamused by my Abracadabra no pants trick. I ignite their pants too. That gets them moving, and I widen my shield the moment they're gone, giving myself some breathing room.

A radio buzzes to life, and I catch my name blasted over the intercom.

Shit.

If the feds get a lock on my location, they'll come out and blow this tiny town to smithereens. I doubt they'll hold back since they think I'm a terrorist responsible for bombings in Chicago. According to reports, I left dozens dead and hundreds wounded. All of this on top of the accusation we kidnapped Maisie, a Church leader's daughter, as part of our anti-Church statement.

If I let the feds come out here, this will get ugly fast. Ally would argue to save the town. I'd have to be the one to remind her the government doesn't give a shit about a town with only one Quick n' Go and no stoplight that I can see. If they come here for me, guns blazing, the causalities will be a lot higher.

No way in hell am I leaving this place without Maisie, or without Caldwell's head on a platter.

Fight it is.

Sorry, Al.

I throw a blast of flames out across the street and strike the police car right in front of me. All four tires lift off the ground with an audible *whoomph*. Flames eat its rusted under-carriage, and the windows explode as it climbs higher into the sky. Then as the flames turn black and the smoke rolls out of the busted windows in corded waves, it sinks back to Earth.

Once the tires hit, the screech of crunching metal rico-chets off the buildings. Glass bursts through the air like confetti.

"Holy fuck!" Someone shouts. The men scatter like mice caught in the dog food bag. They dart for buildings and parked vehicles and rock facades to hide behind. The problem with this is they are taking their radios with them.

"Listen!" I scream at the top of my lungs as a dozen eyes fix on me. I count the pairs of aviator glasses.

Gabriel confirms, *fourteen.*

"Take off your radios and throw them into the street. If you don't, I'll have to kill you, and I don't want to do that."

Four radios clank onto the concrete without hesitation. A low mumble hangs in the air. They want to discuss their options before handing their connection to the outside world over to the firebombing monster. I get it. Unfortunately, I don't have time to keep this democratic.

Maisie doesn't have time for it.

Every second I waste is a second closer to Caldwell's resurrection.

"Not good enough!" I hope I look pissed and not petulant.

"You can't shoot me." I point at the shield. "But I can kill you no problem. Give me the radios. *Now*."

Eight more radios tumble onto the pavement. A minute later, a shot rings off and a bullet pings off my shield.

I turn toward the young cop who fired it. "Really?"

He gives me a good ol' boy shrug like he knows he fucked up.

"Radio." I wiggle my fingers at him.

He rips it off his uniform and throws it into the street giving me a total of thirteen.

I unleash another fire bomb on the second cop car. And I blow up the coroner's hearse too.

"You're making me mad!" I warn. I refrain from tearing my clothes off and doing a Hulk smash because it won't help my street cred.

A scuffle draws my attention as one cop rips another's clothes off. Well, hey! That got sexier than I expected. Until I realize he only ripped the other man's shirt off to get the radio he refused to give up. The shirt and the radio hit the pavement.

"You saved his life," I say. "Feel free to remind him of it next time he gives you shit."

I ignite the radios lying in the sand. I watch the black cords and mouthpieces sizzle and pop in the hot sun, their heat easy to overlook in the inferno of the burning vehicles.

Now I have fourteen cops and a small crowd standing around staring at me. Shit. What the hell am I going to do with them?

Stupid Ally and her stupid don't-kill-people ideas.

She isn't here, Gabriel whispers in my ear, and he's right. I'm carrying Ally and her code of ethics around all by myself.

And why?

Because I got her killed. Again. Man, I suck.

I don't need my therapist Herwin and his psychobabble to tell me so.

I can see her motionless on the tiled floor of the military compound, deep in the belly of the testing facility where Caldwell was held and tortured for years. Where he met the woman who would become Maisie's mother. Where he discovered what he was and what he could do.

But despite all his cruel intentions, it hadn't been Caldwell who'd killed Ally. It was Rachel.

Rachel, my own best friend. The first friend I ever had once I woke up from my own suicide and learned what I was and about the job Brinkley had waiting for me.

And whose fault was it that Rachel got away with murder? Mine. I trusted her. Even when Gloria and Ally, and hell, Brinkley too, told me she was lost, I still believed she wouldn't hurt me.

Hurting Ally is definitely hurting me.

You cannot be blamed, Gabriel says.

"Oh shut up." I shrug off his attempt to soothe the confusion saturating my thoughts. "Tell me what to do with these people."

The cops nearest me shrink back in fear. I said that aloud, huh? Oops. I suppose it doesn't matter if they think I'm unhinged. That can't possibly be bad for my badass reputation, right? All the best girls are unhinged.

Distract them.

Gabriel's right. If I distract them, I can slip away.

I search the area for something to blow up. There's the corner store. The saloon. Large, orange boulders were worked into the landscape as part of the town's charm. A few fences made of wood with old-fashioned hitching posts. I haven't seen any horses, so perhaps it's only for historical significance.

Over my right shoulder, a building looms. It's old, and

falling apart. That might work. It's big enough it would need immediate attention, lest the fire spread to more vital parts of town.

The building reminds me of the kind of place you'd put farm equipment back in the Midwest where I grew up. If it comes down to blowing up some random equipment or cars versus buildings with people in them, I'll choose the structure that's half collapsed already.

I throw a fire bomb near the top, and a chunk of roof flies off into the sky. Burning shingles rain down on the crowd, and they scurry back. The cops try to put distance between us.

I blast again, and more of the roof explodes upward before blowing inward. A chunk lands on the roof of the old saloon hotel, and it catches fire.

Oops.

The men scatter. In a town this small, I wouldn't be surprised if some of them are also the local firefighters.

I throw another blast through the middle of the building, and dried and decaying wood explodes out into the street—if I can call this sandy corridor where we all stand a street.

The fence is broken where a giant beam blasts through it, splitting the wood in two. Then the debris starts to smoke.

"One more should do it." I draw in a breath, feeling the sweat trickle down the side of my face and drip off my jaw onto my shirt collar.

I unleash the last blast and the building caves. Wood boards explode outward. Flaming shingles erupt into the sky like Cape Canaveral rockets. More glass explodes raining down on our head like glitter.

I turn back toward the hotel and store to find all the police officers that had been waiting for me with baited breath. Only, they aren't waiting for me anymore.

I stand alone in the middle of the road.

Some of the officers are working to put out the hotel fire.

Others are dodging the flames engulfing the cars which are also spreading to adjacent buildings. The wind.

Fuck. I hadn't thought about the flames traveling or how dry everything is. This place is going to burn fast.

Shit.

I wanted a distraction, but I didn't want to burn us alive! Maisie's in this town somewhere. And those flames leading dangerously toward the adjacent building will be charred cinders in no time.

The cops are running and shouting, giving orders to one another as they try to prioritize the damage. Two men with a giant wrench begin to open a red hydrant outside the convenience store. A group of people stands behind the glass window, mouths covered, watching the carnage unfold.

If I'm going to run, now's the time to do it, when everyone's looking the other way.

I turn to bolt, and there's a cop, a young one whose uniform barely fits him. His pants are hiked up a little too high and his utility belt hiked a little high as well.

"Freeze," he says.

"Can't," I tell him. "I've got a sister to save."

"Freeze!" he says again, as if he shouts at me loud enough I'll actually listen to him. His back is to one of the orange boulders. It gives the impression this town was carved right out of the desert.

"I'm sorry about this," I tell him, and I mean it.

His brow furrows. I run at him, keeping my shield up, and his eyes double in size.

When my shield slams his body against the boulder, and I hear his head bounce off the stone, the gun falls from his hand and hits the sand with a *poof*.

I step back as he falls unconscious at my feet.

"Sorry," I say again, knowing his head is going to hurt like hell when he wakes up. I've been conked like that myself a couple of times, and it isn't fun.

"We are running out of time," Gabriel reminds me.

"Yeah, yeah. Don't get your feathers in a twist."

I cast one more look over each shoulder, searching the wreckage and town for eyes. But no one's looking my way. They're watching the cops scurry like ants trying to reassemble their crushed ant hill.

I run.

CHAPTER NINE

MAISIE

"*Y*es, this is Georgia Caldwell," Mom says into the phone. She's pacing in the small white kitchen of the house we *commandeered*. And here I thought that was only something you could do to pirate ships. "Trace this call and use the coordinates to come get us. Now."

She listens. I'm not sure who she's talking to, but I can guess. Dad has about a dozen personal armed guards. They follow him around like an entourage. *Followed*. I don't know if he'll ever have a use for them again. Who needs an entourage when you're dead?

I pivot in Sam's desk chair. I try to imagine explaining to him why I'm wearing his jeans and his boxer briefs and my face floods with heat. Hopefully, he'll never see me like this and I won't have to worry about it. And me borrowing his clothes is probably the least of Sam's worries.

How would he feel knowing a dead monster is in his bed?

It sounds like some twisted Goldilocks story. *And a sadist jerk has been sleeping in my bed...*

I like stories. In my fantasies about the college life that's never going to happen, I often imagine myself as an English major, with awesome homework like reading books all the time. Or I could save time and get my stories from television or movies. I bet I could write an amazing paper on *Supernatural*, analyzing the story arc and everything.

Or I'd major in art. I'd love to know more about dimension and shading and color and just about everything really.

"Lieutenant Perry, we do not have much time," Mom says. "Hurry."

Lieutenant Perry is the head of Dad's security team. He'll have the helicopter in the air in ten minutes. And then the whole team will he here in Arizona.

Jesse. Hurry.

A tingle flutters in my chest. Followed by an explosion.

Boom. Boom. Bang.

"Come prepared," Mom adds and disconnects the call.

I lean over the bed to look out the kid's window. I place one hand on Dad's cold boot for balance and raise the blinds by yanking the pull cord with my other hand.

Smoke blooms in the distance. Maybe eight or ten blocks toward town where the houses are closer together. Thick black plumes billow into the sky, rolling like ink in water.

Mom bursts in. The thin bedroom door and brassy doorknob bounce off the wall behind her. "Wake him up."

My stomach knots. "I'm tired."

Her lips press into a thin line, and she stalks across the room, her hair wet from the shower. She's wearing a man's shirt and sweatpants that drown what Dad calls her *chicken legs*.

She wrenches me out of the desk chair by the elbow. I gulp down the pain without squealing.

She thrusts me toward the bed, but steps on the hem of my jeans.

I fall forward, elbows catching the edge of the mattress. My knee connects with something metal, and red explodes behind my eyes. White hot pain bursts from my knee to my hip. I bite my lip to keep from crying out. But she heard my sharp intake of breath.

I try to understand what happens. When I engage my brain, my emotions pale.

My brain tells me my knee hit the metal bed frame holding the mattress up. The edge of the frame slipped into the crevice beneath my knee cap perfectly. That's why it hurt so bad. Body. Pain. Natural.

"We're all tired!" Mom screams. "Stop fucking around!"

"I don't want to," I say again as tears pool in my lashes. I try to even out my breath and loosen my clenching throat. I picture Winnie Pug. I imagine pressing my lips to his wet nose.

Mom yanks the blinds open. Only one side is ripped up, giving the slats an uneven and assaulted look. She jabs a finger out the window. "Look what she's doing! She's destroying this place. She'll destroy us with it."

"Not me." It comes out more like a wish than a certainty.

"Don't be stupid." Mom snorts. "She wants your power like the rest of them. She'll kill you too."

"She should."

Silence stretches between us, filling up Sam's room. I finally dare to look at her and instantly wish I hadn't. Tears stream down her cheeks.

"Why are you doing this to me?"

If I say a word, I'll start crying. I don't even try.

"She's going to kill me, Maisie. You understand that, don't you?"

Yes, I do. My guts clench again, and I start to worry I'll have to run to the bathroom.

"Are you going to let her murder me? Your own mother?"

I look away. It's not her tears that tear me apart. It's the utter look of betrayal on her face. Like I'm the one person in the whole world she should be able to count on. I'm her baby. She brought me into this world. If anyone betrays her, it shouldn't be me.

I want to leave the room, get away from her, and breathe some fresh air. My arms and legs feel like sacks of sand. Wet sand.

"After all I went through to get you back," she chokes out, and I sink completely to the floor, giving up my hope of escape. Hot tears spill onto my cheeks.

"We had to send you away so you'd be safe, but I got you back."

I can't imagine it. I can't imagine what it was like giving birth inside a torture camp and then giving up your baby so it wouldn't be experimented on by greedy military scientists.

You're all I thought about. You're the only reason I survived that place. It didn't break me because I had you. Knowing you were okay was enough.

How many times had she said these things to me when I was little? How many hundreds of times?

She crouches down in front of me, taking my hands. I can't pull away. I'm pinned on three sides: her in front, the bed on my left and the desk drawers at my back. I can't leap right either, or I'll only launch myself into the desk chair.

I'm trapped.

"Have I been such a terrible mother?" she sniffs.

"No." I choke on the word.

I remember her on Navy Pier, shoving an ice cream cone into my face, soaking my nose in. Her laughter as she dabbed it off before kissing the tip of my cold nose. Her walking me to the library to check out books, my hand loosely clasped in hers the whole way. Her arms enveloping me in the night when I woke screaming and afraid. Her bringing me a glass of water and rubbing my back until I fell back asleep again. Her bright laugh. Her lips on my forehead. How completely she hugs me, squishing me to her like she'll never let me go. No one else hugs me that way.

"No," I say again. This time it sounds like the word. "You weren't a terrible mom."

"He's the only one who can protect me from her," Georgia says. "You have to wake him up. For me."

I'll protect you. I want to say it, but she'll only laugh at me. I can't protect her. I don't have fancy powers like Jesse and Dad. Mom can protect herself better than I can.

"She would spare you if you'd just stop fighting. She only wants Dad."

Mom's anger explodes. She launches to her feet, her face red. Her elbow clips my jaw accidentally, and my ears ring.

"*Just* Dad! Maisie, listen to yourself! He's your *father*!"

Anger starts to burn in my chest, hot in my cheeks and throat, but the clenching muscles in my lower gut win out.

What would I say anyway?

I could remind her how many people he has killed.

I could remind her how many lives he's destroyed.

I could pull down the baggy jeans cinched in place with Sam's belt and show her my scars. But if I dare to go there, she'll only defend him. The only thing worse than my mother's manipulative tears is listening to her justify Dad hurting me.

He's been through so much.

And that makes it okay he hurt me? That he locked me in a tower? The impenetrable fortress he'd had built with no entrances or exits, suspended above Lake Michigan. Perfectly inaccessible except for him with his teleportation abilities.

He locked me away like a freaking Rapunzel, and my imprisonment had been a *compromise*.

I had to give up my bedroom, my friends, my school in Chicago. My freedom.

Why?

Because when Monroe's son died, and I inherited his partis power. I tried to hide it. I didn't understand what was happening to me, but as soon as I felt the change, I knew it was big trouble. Dad had felt the power overtake me too.

I'll never forget the feral look in his eyes. The hungry, crazed expression.

He'd said, *special delivery. Right to my door.*

He'd almost killed me on the spot. He'd snatched me off the floor, my feet dangling in the air. Mom had pleaded, begged for him to spare me.

If I don't take it from her, someone else will, Dad had said. He wanted to rip the power out of me then and there. I didn't think anything Mom said was going to stop him.

We can send her away. Please, Eric. Please. You know what I'm like without her.

I was moved to the tower. Alive, but knowing perfectly well Dad is going to kill me, sooner or later. *Do you know what happens to bad girls, Maisie?* A knife glints in my head, and I squeeze my eyes shut as if I can block out the memory.

"You leave me no choice." Mom's sadness morphs into anger like it always does.

Kill me. Shoot me and end it. Maybe it'll be easier for everyone if I wasn't here in the middle.

"I'll kill her myself." Mom storms out of the room, and a moment later I hear the screen door bang against the wood.

I lean over the twin bed and strain to see her cut across the front yard. She crosses the sparse lawn, if one could call the dead clumps of grass and sand a lawn, and heads out the gate. She's barreling toward the black smoke.

I should be scared for Jesse, but I'm not. As long as her shield is up, Jesse can't be hurt. And since Ally's back at the compound, she'll be fighting fit. She's more than a little dumb with Ally around. Without Ally around, Jesse's focus will be better.

If I'm scared for anyone, it's Mom.

You leave me no choice, she said. Yeah, well, she isn't leaving me any choices either. All she's leaving me with is heartache. I want to help her. It's stupid and psychotic, but I want to protect her. I want to protect Mom even though she's wrong.

I pull a dental mirror out of the deep pocket of my baggy jeans. I stole it from the bathroom right after I wrapped my ankle.

A small circular mirror sits angled at the end of a thin piece of white plastic.

I put the mirror under Dad's nose and wait. I count to five super slow. The mirror doesn't fog. His chest doesn't rise or fall.

I lean over and look at the pinched flesh knotted together by twine. The skin is less red. The pucker is softening.

It's healing.

Once it's healed enough, his heart and brain will kick back on.

How much longer do we have before the monster is awake?

I slip the mirror back in my pocket—Sam's pocket—and frown at the darkening sky.

CHAPTER TEN

A kick in the gut stops me. I duck down between two houses and lean against its exterior. It's hot and unforgiving even through my layers. It takes me a minute to position my body against the rock in a way that doesn't scald my skin.

I wipe at my face with the bottom of my T-shirt. I'm sweating like crazy.

The kick comes again. *Jesse.*

It's Maisie. I don't hear her voice in my head exactly, but her presence is unmistakable. As unique as any fingerprint.

Is she in danger? I ask Gabriel. I ask with my thoughts because running half a mile has left me winded. Okay, maybe not half a mile. Maybe a quarter-mile. Or half a quarter-mile. The point is, athleticism has never been my strong suit. It's no surprise why I developed a shield—an ability that requires me to mostly be in one place—rather than something like super speed.

"The mother is coming," Gabriel says. Despite his dark suit and wings, he hasn't broken a sweat. His skin is flawless.

I straighten, breathing through the cramp in my side. "With Maisie?"

He cocks his head as if listening to something. "No. She comes alone."

"Where the fuck is Maisie?"

"Close," Gabriel says. But he's turning in all directions like he's not sure. If I'd asked a guy for directions and he'd turned a circle like this, I'd be more than a little worried.

"Okay, where's Georgia?"

"Closer."

"That's very specific." I groan and straighten. My back keeps cramping. God, I'm getting old. "Thanks for letting me know I could be attacked. Somewhere. Sometime."

I peek around a building, looking back the way I came. No one seems to be following me. No aviator glasses or spies bobbing and weaving around the buildings headed my way.

I'd give about anything to look up and see Gloria or Gideon right now. A friendly face. A comrade in arms. Anyone who can talk me through this, offer advice, or hell, look in the opposite direction so I can stop craning my neck.

My throat tightens. If I die today, they'll die without them knowing how much I appreciated their help.

"We need to send thank you notes," I tell Gabriel.

He blinks at me. "Now?"

"I guess not, but remind me to send notes if we make it through the day."

Smoke rolls through the street as the blaze I started grows. The fire is getting out of hand. Oops. I'm sorry about that, but those man-handlers didn't make it easy. That guy shouldn't have threatened me. "Why were they so mean? I was sitting in my truck minding my own business!"

"Donnie's truck," Gabriel corrects me. Black feathers from his wings flutter in the hot air.

"Okay, I stole a truck. Big deal! I'm trying to save the world!"

"You do not need to justify your actions to me."

"Don't I?" I snort.

But he's right. Why am I explaining myself to him?

Habit, I realize. Because if Ally was here, I would have to explain my every move to her. Gabriel's serving as her proxy, forced to listen to my every rationalization. Poor thing.

I reach out for Ally. Part of me is curious if I can feel her the way I can feel Maisie. I pinch my eyes closed. I let the darkness, the steadiness set in as I try to forget about the hundred aches and pains all over my body.

Nada.

I don't feel her.

"She is alive," Gabriel assures me. His cold hand touches the back of my neck. God, it feels good in this awful heat. "You have drawn the danger away from her."

And she's got Gloria and Nikki with her. And I haven't seen Gideon nurture anything but his bank account.

Imagining Nikki cooing and coddling Al irritates me to no end, but I let it go. Obsessing about Nikki's eternal quest to steal my girlfriend is the least of my problems right now.

"They are coming." Gabriel's eyes fix on the blaze. "You should hide."

He doesn't have to say it twice. I dart through the back door of the nearest house. The latch pops open with one hard shove of my shoulder. I stumble into the house and shut the door behind me.

Unlocked?

That's practically an invitation! I can hardly be frowned upon for ducking inside. There's a door, and the door is unlocked. What says *come on in* better than an unlocked door?

Thank goodness for small town folk and their trusting ways.

I squint through the low light. Why is it so dark in here? All the blinds are down. To keep in the cool air probably. I can only imagine how hot a house gets in the desert during the day. Keeping the blinds down probably saves a million dollars a year on their cooling bill.

A pang of remorse hits me in the chest. I used to have a house. I used to have utility bills. That was before I burned it down. I was trying to murder Caldwell, not destroy my shit. And it wasn't the first bit of damage my house suffered. The local church members vandalized it every other week the first time I was outed as a death replacement agent. Later, they upgraded from eggs and toilet paper to throwing bricks through my window.

Okay, my house wasn't a paradise or anything but it was mine. It had a big bed and soft pillows and a great shower with a rainfall shower head. A big couch I liked to nap on and a deck where I could drink root beer and stare into the trees.

I can't help but move through the kitchen, past the sturdy oak table and laminate countertops of this house and miss the evenings when I came home and kicked off my shoes after a long day.

Will I ever have this again?

A home?

A peaceful place where I feel safe?

I press my fingers into a loaf of bread until it leaves indentations. Then I feel bad and eat the bread I smooshed. The owner of said bread loaf will never know. I'm munching on crust and fluffed wheat as I meander down the hallway stretching from the kitchen to the living room. Photos line the wall in a makeshift gallery. Mostly it's a woman and two boys, smiling. Well, in one the youngest boy looks rather grumpy. Obviously not his best day. But in another a woman and a man are dancing on their wedding day. Unless they went as husband and wife for Halloween.

"Am I ever going to have a wedding?" I ask Gabriel.

He says nothing, leaving me to my thoughts.

I turn away from the pictures and finish off the smooshed bread.

People live here. Love here. Feel peace each night when they come home and dump their bags by the door here.

I'm going to try really, *really* hard not to burn it down.

The living room sits in the front of the house. Three pieces of soft pink furniture: a sofa, a loveseat, and a chair, point toward a ridiculously large television. Sports fan, I guess. What else would a person watch that looked best in blown up high-def?

I grin. I guess I could think of a few other channels.

The room smells like cinnamon and orange. Potpourri? Or one of those plug-in air fresheners.

Car doors slam outside. I whirl on Gabriel. "Shit! Are they home?"

"No." As he shakes his head, he rains feathers onto the soft pink chair. Lucky for the owners, they won't be able to see them, what with Gabriel being incorporeal and all. "Look out the window."

I do as he says. I cut wide around a coffee table with six issues of a knitting magazine fanned beside a remote. I move the standing lamp and peek through the side of the curtain. I try to keep my body hidden by the wall rather than stand in plain view.

Real subtle.

After my entrance into Cochise, I'm not sure why I'm even trying for subtle. Dousing half the town in flames is far from subtle.

I pull back the curtain and see a cop car pull into the driveway across the street. Two armed cops enter the house, guns drawn. Then at the next house, another police car swings into the driveway, and the car doors open.

They're on my trail. I wonder how long I have before I'm found.

CHAPTER ELEVEN

MAISIE

"Azrael," I whisper. My voice breaks. I lick my lips. *Why do we love the people that hurt us the most? Or is it because we love them the most, they hurt us?*

Light shimmers in the corner of my eye and I look up. Azrael stands leaning against the wall, her wings dragging along the carpet. Her arms hang ready at her side.

I do not love, she says. Her face is smooth and unreadable. It makes me think of Jesse. Not because Jesse's ever unreadable. As if. Her face is super expressive and whatever her face doesn't give away, her mouth does. I'm pretty sure my sister has zero filter.

Even though Azrael seems super serious and Jesse's a huge goof, there's something about Azrael that reminds me of Jesse.

"She's coming," Azrael says.

I feel her. Her fear for Ally's safety. Her hurt and confusion over Rachel's betrayal. Her guilt over Brinkley. Like with my death-sensing ability, when we're far apart, it's hard to notice, but it doesn't disappear completely. The connection's there, thrumming inside, if muted.

"I should help her." Only a loser would sit here and wait to be rescued.

"No," Azrael disagrees. "You are safer here."

I laugh. It's a bitter, sour gurgle in the back of my throat. "You think I'll be in the way. I'm always in the way."

"You must not lose hope," Azrael whispers. "She is coming."

I turn to Azrael. She's watching me with those bright silver eyes. Her big eyes sparkle. Something about her eyes makes me think of deep water. A reflective surface which hides unfathomable depth.

I look around Sam's room. It smells like him. Like boy. "What should I do?"

"Wait," she instructs in her husky voice. "It will not be long now."

"Before the end of the world?"

Azrael regards me with her heavy gaze, but I manage to meet her eyes. Mostly because she's pretty. It's hard not to stare. I mean, I'm not into chicks like my Jesse, but some-times girls are so beautiful I can't help staring. I wish I had Azrael's hair. Thick, dark and wavy. It's the exact opposite of my thin, straight hair.

I wish I knew more than the few pieces I've cobbled together about Azrael and the angels like her.

Why would the Reliance choose you? Why? What does your angel say?

Daddy, I don't know! I don't know! I don't have an angel.

I rub a hand on the back of my neck and sigh. I wasn't lying. I didn't see an angel at first, not until Mom begged him to move me to the tower. Not until I was alone. Then Azrael came and explained she isn't always there, but she's accessible. Whenever I'm with my parents, her voice is drowned out. If I'm with Mom only, I can hear Azrael's whisper, but that's it.

"Are you always here? Even when I cannot see you or hear you?" I ask her.

She pauses. "No."

"Where do you go? Back to the Reliance?"

I've never asked about the Reliance. I thought Dad was out of his mind when he accused me of being some spy for a secret angel organization. Oh, make no mistake. He *is* crazy. But maybe there's some truth in his ramblings.

"No. You do not remember?"

I sit up straighter, my hand brushing Dad's. Goosebumps break out on my arms. "No."

She huffs. It's something Jesse does all the time. And there it was again. Something about Jesse looking back at me in those gray eyes and black hair. Though Jesse's eyes are hazel like Dad's.

"The demands of the flesh never cease to amaze me," she murmurs, looking away, giving me a view of her profile. She's got a strong jaw for a girl.

"Are you actually an angel?" I ask, hoping that while she dismissed my direct question about the Reliance, maybe she won't dismiss me entirely. I'll take anything.

"I am many things, across much of space and time."

I'm not sure where to go from there. "So you are an angel...and a lot of other things."

"Yes."

"Why do you care what happens here? We're morons. I can't imagine we're worth saving."

She doesn't say anything. I catch myself staring at the soft, downy white of her under feathers, where it meets dove gray. I bet the wings are soft. I want to touch them, but I don't dare. If some weirdo came up to me and started petting me, I would freak out.

"The Reliance," Azrael says. She watches my face, her eyes darting the way Mom's does when she's searching for a word. "It is not as you imagine it."

"What is it then?"

She looks at the ceiling. "You would call it an *ideology*."

Confusion oozes into my thoughts, making everything sticky like peanut butter.

"No," she says, her eyelashes fluttering. "That wasn't the right word. A philosophy?"

"A belief?" I offer.

"This is not religious."

"Beliefs don't have to be religious." I prop my head in my hand. "I believe BBQ potato chips are the best. Jesse believes plain potato chips are the best. Ally voted for cheddar and sour cream."

Azrael flashes a smile. "A belief then. Those who are part of the Reliance, we hold a shared belief."

She doesn't say anything else. The chair squeaks and I realize I'm leaning forward, straining with anticipation to hear what she'll say next.

"A belief about...?" I encourage her with a wave of my hand. "Potato chips?"

"No."

I make a serious guess. "Humans?"

"Yes."

Whew. We're getting somewhere. I wonder if Jesse's ever this frustrated with Gabriel.

"What do you believe about humans?"

She doesn't answer. And she won't. She has that faraway look in her eyes again. I'm not ready to give up.

"Are all the angels part of the Reliance?"

"No." Her gaze sharpens. "We war with one another."

"And here I was hoping there was a civilization out there that existed without war. I should've known better."

"You created us," she whispers, her gaze distant. "We are no better."

CHAPTER TWELVE

JESSE

Two more patrol cars fly through the neighborhood. They plan to search every single house I bet. Who knew a tiny town like Cochise could afford such a well-staffed police department. Hell, at this point, every citizen in this county must be a police officer. I've seen more uniformed cops than civilians today. Maybe even Donnie himself was a cop. Good thing I knocked him out, or he would have been more trouble than he was worth.

Another disturbing possibility, and a more probable reason for all the cops whizzing down the streets and bombarding all the houses is this:

Reinforcements.

Either the news story broke, and the wanted terrorists have been found, or Georgia herself has called for help. It's crossed my mind. I mean, *I* wouldn't go crying like a little girl if I was stranded in the desert—but I imagine *some* people would.

I run up the carpeted stairs in the house to find a front-facing window in one of the bedrooms. I crouch down and crawl past a queen-sized mattress and storage ottoman. Slowly, I pull myself up and peek over the sill into the street below.

I have a much better view from here. The height of the house allows me to see in all three directions, not to mention through the spaces between houses.

I gulp. Shit.

Gabriel materializes beside me and gazes through the window in full view. Sure, if I was an invisible man I could stand in front of windows too, instead of hunkering down and looking ridiculous like I am now.

"There are many officers," Gabriel says.

"You think." I roll my eyes.

Every fiber in my body's screaming, *get down!*

"They can't see me," Gabriel says, blinking those green cat eyes at me.

"I *know*," I grumble. It's stupid to worry since no one can see him. But he's real to me and instincts are hard to override.

I scan the streets and see the cops everywhere. They give the distinct impression of an ant hill, restless at dusk, devouring the lawns and houses now the birds have gone to sleep.

I slide down the wall facing the door. The mattress is higher than my head. I stare down the hallway, at the cold light illuminating the carpeted floor from some window I can't see.

"You are stronger," Gabriel says, standing beside me.

I reach out and place a palm on the back of Gabriel's calf. The fabric is soft like cotton. The calf firm as any boy's calf I've ever touched.

I sigh.

"You can easily destroy them all. You are untouchable within your shield."

"I know," I say because I want him to stop talking.

"What troubles you?" He kneels beside me, his face close to mine. If he were a real boy, I'd expect him to kiss me. But he isn't a boy, so he only stares at me.

"She's going to wake up," I whisper, searching those green eyes for answers he doesn't have. Green, the color of expansive fields running along the highway. Green, like untilled land in spring. Bright with rain.

"That should please you."

I cover my face. "It does! I want Ally to wake up. I'm glad Maisie was there to save her."

So fucking glad.

He places a cool hand on my leg in turn. Here we are, holding each other's legs. Me and my imaginary friend. Weird.

"When she wakes up, she's going to see what I've done. If I leave this enormous body count..."

I can't even finish out loud. *She's going to think I'm a monster.*

She's well on her way to believing that already. But there's more. I know Ally. I know if she wakes up and I've exploded a whole town, she's going to blame herself. She's going to think she should've been alive. She should've been awake to stop me.

If I succeed in this mission, if I finish Caldwell and save Maisie, that means I will have absorbed his power.

I'm not stupid.

Rachel lost her freaking mind when she absorbed one power. *One.* What do I think is going to happen when I absorb all of Caldwell's powers? And then let's throw Georgia's abilities on top of those.

Once I absorb all the power, I don't know who I'll be, *what* I'll be.

By the time this day's over, I might very well be the monster of Ally's dreams.

Do I want Ally to wake up to a world where I'm out of my mind, and all Ally has to remember me by is a heap of corpses in the desert?

Gabriel squeezes my leg. "You are stronger than you believe you are."

"She won't understand." My voice cracks.

"You must focus on the task at hand," Gabriel says.

He's right. If I get myself killed by doing something stupid, that won't make Ally happy either.

I huff and pull myself up to look out the window again. They keep shouting something to each other. Here? *Here.* What kind of game is this?

They rush in the houses, guns drawn, sticking to a formation recognizable in any action movie.

"Clear," an officer says. Clear! That makes more sense. Clear, as in no one is in the house. I watch them do the work for me. If they find Maisie, they'll drag her out. But they don't. House after house. *Clear. Clear.*

Where are you, kiddo? I close my eyes and reach for the connection inside me, the power tethering me to Maisie.

Ping. It's like echolocation. I get a sense of the general direction, but nothing specific. No exact *I'm here!* No signs appear in my mind. I'm not psychic like Gloria. I'm not getting any information but the echolocation.

I tilt my head and push again.

Ping.

I do it for the third time.

I open my eyes and look at the wall straight ahead. But it's a closet. Beyond that is east. Further east of all these houses. Perhaps on the edge of town. If that's true, the cops aren't going to find her right away. If they keep sweeping town the way they are now, it will be one of the last places they look.

If I were Georgia, I'd want a place out of the way to hole up while Caldwell recuperates. Further east it is. Now I need to get out of this house and make my way to that side of town without getting caught.

A door bangs open downstairs.

The rush of feet makes me suck in a breath. Fuck.

Of course, they're going to check my hideout now.

Who said it would be easy?

I leap up from the floor and duck into the dark closet. I shut the door behind me and turn on the light. I search the closet for an exit. Nada.

A door in the ceiling looks promising. I reach up and pull the cord. A ladder slides down, and I start climbing without wondering where the hell I'm going. Halfway up, I realize I left on the light. Fuck.

I clamber down, turn off the light, making sure the door is pulled closed and start up again.

The air above is hot. It's worse than stepping out into the desert afternoon again. Immediately sweat begins to bead on the back of my neck as I lift the ladder as carefully as possible, pulling it back into place slowly. Quiet-as-a-mouse slow. That's all I need. To bang a door shut and let the cops hot on my ass know exactly where I am.

I tiptoe across the attic looking for a place to hide.

Use the shield, Gabriel advises.

My heart pounds in my chest. He's warning me the cops are about to wrench me out of the attic space until I realize what he means. The shield would soften any footfall. Probably not eliminate all sound completely, but it would help. Can sound be trapped inside a shield too?

I'd totally be set in a horror movie. No madman would hear me breathing in the closet.

I shield myself, making my way toward the back of the attic.

Cardboard boxes sit to the left and right of the space, and even as short as I am, I have to hunch, or I'll hit my head on one of the crossbeams. I'm at the very back wall when I spot another door. If you can call a square cut out of the wood a door. I stick my fingers inside and work it apart. There's a 3x3 crawlspace behind it.

The bedroom door squeals beneath me as the cops open the bedroom. Heart pounding furiously, I duck into the space without another thought. I drop my shield long enough to push a couple of the boxes closer, hoping to better block this door. Then I pull the door closed on me. I have no idea if it's making an audible noise. For all I know, it sounds like I'm murdering a cat up here.

The light from the closet comes on, shining through the floor. I freeze in the darkness. On impulse, I cover my face and nose and steady my breath, as if they're going to hear me huffing and come up here. I open my eyes to make sure my purple shield is shimmering safely around me.

Hangers screech on a metal pole.

The clatter of the stairs tumbling down freezes my blood. I shrink deeper into the shadows with only the purple glow of my shield visible in the dark.

Boots mount the stairs. They groan under the weight of what I imagine is a big man.

Take a look. See nothing. Move on, I pray.

I don't want to kill anyone today. If they yank open the door to my crawlspace, I'll have no choice. My back is against the wall. Literally. What can I do if they burst in? Explode through the roof? I imagine the wood splintering and chunks hurling themselves in all directions as I tumble down. If I keep the shield up, it'll be like I'm in a hamster ball, a hamster wrecking ball.

Then I remember the cute pictures in the hallway downstairs and the bread loaf downstairs.

I renew my promise not to destroy their home.

Boxes slide along the attic floor, and I hold my breath. My flames are close. It's as if they're crawling under my skin, ready for me to call them up.

I hold my breath.

A shadow passes, darkening the trim of the crawlspace. I raise a hand, ready to throw flames into the face of whoever opens the door.

One moment stretches into two. My heart pounds hard. I'm certain I'll pass out from lightheadedness.

"Clear!" someone shouts, and I jump, startled by the proximity. Right there. The man's right there on the other side of the door. But not crouched down, peering into my nook. His voice travels right over my head.

Boots sound on the creaky ladder as the men, and maybe women, cops file back into the closet.

I don't move. I don't dare.

Even after I hear the door snap closed, I keep every muscle still. I breathe as quietly as possible as I strain to listen in the dark.

That's the thing about having a father like Caldwell. Deception. Mindfuckery. It can happen at any time. I can't shake the image of some cop waiting on the other side of the door with a *boo*, a pair of handcuffs, and a bullet to the brain. I'd have to drop my shield to open the door.

Despite the awful heat, and the sweat dripping down my neck, and the hairs matting themselves to my forehead and temples, I don't move.

I'll wait a little while longer. Let them search all the houses. Let them think I got away.

Then I'll head east, house by house, until I find Maisie.

They are watching the house, Gabriel whispers. He can't materialize in this nook, and that's fine. That's what our awesome mindphone is for. *One man believes he saw you in the window.*

I'll have to wait them out. See who has the better attention span.

There is not much time.

I huff, unable to help myself. Does he think I want to stay in this cramped, hot as hell attic? Does this look like my idea of a good time? *I know we are out of time. I don't need you to keep reminding me we're out of time.*

Every second we waste is a second closer to Caldwell waking up. Waking up and jumping halfway across the country, destroying any chance I'll have of finishing him off.

But he's right. No matter how I slice this, he's right.

We're running out of time.

CHAPTER THIRTEEN

MAISIE

I search the desk drawers. It's something dumb to do to keep my mind and hands busy.

One drawer is full of photographs. The kind printed on paper. It's weird. They're relics, what with everyone using digital cameras or their phones now. When you can upload photos to the Internet, who has time to make paper copies? But here they are, honest to goodness paper pictures.

I shuffle through them, enjoying the sound of the glossy squares rubbing against one another. Several pictures are of a very cute beagle. Big brown eyes like Winnie Pug and large floppy ears. I didn't see a dog dish, bed, or toys in the house when we came in. Even Winnie Pug, who's a fugitive, has a stuffed moose and a food dish. This puppy is probably dead. The fact the photos range from puppyhood to a muzzle full of gray tells me his whole puppy life has come and gone.

I hope I get to see Winnie Pug grow old. He'll be cute with a wrinkly old man face and a stiff old man shuffle. I'll give his little shoulders a massage at night for his doggie arthritis and everything.

Here I go again, making promises to the universe. If I see my eighteenth birthday, I'll be super busy for the next seventy years. I've promised the powers that be just about everything: *If I survive this, I promise to build houses in poor countries. I'll deworm orphans. I'll invent a cure for cancer. I'll raise money for some debilitating disease. I'll discover some cool techno gadget that'll purify drinking water for millions.*

I've heard bargaining is one of the stages. How pathetic.

Kids starve to death before they're five. Or get cancer. Or hell, they're *murdered*. Don't you think they wanted more time? And I'm begging for days like I deserve it. As if I'm special.

I'm not.

I swallow the lump in my throat and pick up another stack of photos.

A few of the pictures focus on a group of kids in red jerseys. Basketball team pictures. Big surprise. Sam eats and breathes ball. He must be tall enough for it, given the length of the pants I'm wearing. I had to roll them up four times before I stopped stepping on them. I'm looking for Sam in the photos. I try to guess which of these kids are his friends. Are they still friends? Do they spend their mornings playing ball together before the desert gets too hot?

I sit the pile of photos on the top of the desk and open another drawer.

My breath hitches.

Scissors, scotch tape and a shiny boxcutter with a yellow plastic sheath sits in the drawer. I pull out the cutter. An inch of the blade protrudes from the plastic. The metal catches the light from the open window. The plastic is cold and bright in my hand.

I pivot in the desk chair toward Dad's lifeless body.

I should kill him. I couldn't do anything super morbid like plunge the cutter through his eye. I have a weak stomach and a super vivid imagination. The thought of his eyeball oozing out of its socket makes me want to puke, and I've done enough vomiting today thanks.

But maybe I can cut through the stitches, reopen the wound, and slow the healing. It would buy Jesse more time.

Or woman up and plunge it into his heart. Then I'll have his powers. And I won't be a weakling anymore. I could help Jesse.

But help her do what? Kill Mom?

Like that's going to happen. I can't do that anymore than I can protect Mom from Jesse.

I lean over the bed, and the mattress creaks under my palm.

I climb onto Dad's chest. He doesn't smell as much anymore. It's the NRD. It's putting him back together from the inside out. Decomposition is reversing. His cheeks gain color.

I put the edge of the shiny blade against one of the thick stitches and push. I don't have to push hard. The blade slices right through with a POP. The stitch splits, popping open like a busted guitar string. The skin parts like a red mouth. No blood. No gristle and bone now. Most of his flesh has fused back together.

I cut through another stitch. *POP.* The skin peels farther apart, revealing marbled meat like a cut of sirloin in the supermarket. I turn away and suck in a breath.

Maybe if I'd had a normal adolescence with high school science classes, I'd have dissected a frog or something. Then I wouldn't be so queasy and I could do this.

Tears sting my eyes.

Great. Now I'm crying. Not only am I too weak to kill a

guy who totally deserves it, probably saving hundreds of thousands of lives in the process, but I'm going to sit here and wail about it like a big baby.

Stupid.

The cold spark of death flashes inside me. Ice chips spray across my skin. I look up, blinking until my vision clears. I don't see anything outside the window except for the burning town. A layer of gray fog hangs in their air, blurring out the desert beyond that.

Someone died.

Not Jesse. I can feel her. Her adrenaline. Whatever she's doing, she's got her hands full.

I wipe my eyes and a shadow darts past the window. I jolt upright. Through the glass, a bike sits in the yard. Overturned, one wheel spins in the air, the plastic reflector going around and around in the sunlight.

It wasn't there before.

A door bangs open and someone bursts into the living room.

Not Mom.

The footsteps are all wrong. Their weight. Their rhythm.

I grip the box cutter tighter in my hand. Every muscle in my back goes rigid, freezing me in place.

I look down and see the boxcutter shaking. Beneath me, there's a dead guy. *I* know it's my dad, but whoever burst through the house doesn't know that. They're going to see girl plus blade plus dead body.

I only have a moment to consider whether I should keep the boxcutter to defend myself, or hide it. Holding a knife beside a dead body sends the wrong message, you know?

At the last second, I slide the blade back into its yellow plastic sheath before hiding it in my pocket. I clamber off the bed and stand there, shifting from foot to foot.

My hand is in my pocket clutching the boxcutter when a boy rushes into the bedroom and skids to a stop. His hands go out at his sides for balance. His mouth opens in a surprised *O*.

I recognize him instantly even if he's much taller without his bike. "Sam."

I breathe his name. It's a relief to see him. I'd hoped it was him, but it could've been his dad or a sibling.

"Hey," he blinks as if he's trying to process me. Is it because I'm a girl—a strange girl—standing in his bedroom? Or because I'm wearing his clothes? Or is it the dead guy in his bed?

So many considerations.

"Hey," he says again, this time calmer. His eyes slide off me and fall on Caldwell. "What're you doin' here?"

Friend or foe? I ask Azrael. She's close, listening and watching. She won't leap between us and save me like Gabriel does for Jesse—or at least what Jesse says Gabriel does—but she has her own ways of protecting me if it comes to that.

A breeze blows through the room. A chill slides up the back of my neck like a wet tongue.

Friend, she whispers.

Sam's eyes soften. I've seen this before. Azrael reaches into minds the way Dad does. Not to control them the way Dad does, but certainly to influence them.

He is afraid, Azrael whispers.

He should be.

Soothe him. He wants the truth.

I'm not sure how soothing the truth is. All of this is pretty screwed up.

Tell him, Azrael insists.

"I'm here because we're in trouble, and we were looking for a place to hide."

"In trouble," he repeats, his lips slightly parted.

"So," I hold my breath as Sam's eyes refocus. His full pupils constrict. "How bad is it in town?"

"There's this crazy b—" He stops short, and chokes on the word. He stammers. "Crazy person blowing things up."

"That's my sister."

He stiffens. "Your sister?"

"Yeah," I shrug, but my hands shake in my pockets. "She can firebomb stuff with her mind."

His eyes widen. "Yeah, that's just how she does it. No blowtorch. No accelerants. Nothin'." He clips the end of his words as his excitement grows. He barks a short, sharp laugh. "What the hell's going on?"

"I can explain." I lick my lips. My heart is pounding so hard I'm totally going to pass out. Then I'm sitting, rather *sliding* down onto my knees.

"Hey, are you okay?" Sam's face screws up with concern. He reaches out and grabs my arms before I go down all the way. I stiffen under his palms, and he's quick to let me go.

"Sorry," he mumbles. His gaze studies my face. He isn't looking at Dad. That's got to be Azrael's doing. Who doesn't stare at a dead body in their bed? I've seen her manipulate people like this before. She can make someone overlook something. Or she can make something serious seem minor.

It's better on the floor. I'm more grounded. I fold my legs. "I'll explain, but it's going to sound weird."

He exhales. "Okay."

No smile, but he doesn't look ready to choke me either. His eyes search mine. At least he's curious and not mad.

He shrugs one shoulder. "After what I saw, I'm prepared for weird."

So I tell him. "My parents are maniacs. My sister saved me. But they found us, there was a fight, and I was kidnapped back."

"—by your own parents?" he asked.

"Don't interrupt."

"Sorry." He gives me a heart stopping pout.

I try to explain everything that's happening in town and why Jesse is trying to get me back.

"Then go to her," he says, shrugging again and takes his cap off his head. He crushes the bill in his palm, rounding it out. "Your mom isn't here to stop you. Don't you want to get away?"

"I do. It's—" It's what?

Sam's words make sense, and yet my first thought is *no way*. Why?

With horror, I realize I don't want to leave Dad behind. The reason I didn't run away and find Jesse the second Mom left was because I'm guarding him. I believe Azrael. Jesse will find me, and when she does, I want Dad to be right here. He's like a boogeyman. If I take my eyes off him, he's going to disappear, only to drag me screaming into the closet once the lights go out.

"I thought your sister was the one who kidnapped you. That's what they're saying on the news." He runs his fingers through his hair, before turning the cap backward.

Cute.

My face burns. "It's more complicated than that. Do you want the super weird part?"

He looks at me for a full minute, chewing on his bottom lip. "Yeah. I need to understand this."

I explain about the dead body in his bed, how he's my dad and if he wakes up he's going to keep killing people, keep destroying the world. I explain that my mom's no better. I can't explain the death ribbon thing to him. Jesse described it as ribbons to me once and later as smoke. That's what they look like to me too. Sometimes solid. Sometimes wispy. But only the partis can see them come out of Mom's torso and strike people dead. He's never going to understand if he can't see it for himself, so I tell him Mom kills people with her mind. She looks at them, and they fall dead.

"So she's the one who did it." He looks away, and I can see his jaw working. The muscles jump under the skin.

My stomach cramps. *No. Please. No.*

"There wasn't a mark on him."

My palms begin to sweat with my spiking adrenaline. I know I'm about to hear something very *very* bad.

"Who?" I ask even though I don't want to.

"My dad. Your mom killed my dad and our janitor, Billy."

My mind is already presenting evidence before Sam finishes speaking. The hotel. The rushing into the truck and speeding away. The license and searching for the house. The bullshit story.

I'm blubbering. I pull my knees up and throw an arm over them, hiding my face in the crook of my elbow. This way he can't see me ugly cry. Or god forbid, see snot running out of my nose.

"Hey, it's okay." A large hand engulfs my shoulder, squeezing gently. "It's not your fault."

The only reason Sam can bring himself to say something selfless is because of Azrael. She's pumping happy juice into his head. Without her, he'd be having a level-ten freak-out right now. And I want him to. I want Sam to get mad. I want him to scream and cry and blame me for bringing my screwed-up family life into his town.

I'm the one that pointed at the hotel. I'm the one that asked mom to get a room.

"It's my fault!" I shove the heels of my hands into my eyes as if that's going to stop the tears. *You pointed the hotel out to me,* I accuse Azrael. *Why the hell did you do that?*

Azrael says nothing in her defense.

"I'm sorry about your dad."

"You didn't kill him." He holds onto me and I wonder

how long I have before the angel-ease wears off and Sam's anger and fear rain down on me. "And it's not like you can bring him back."

My head snaps up, heart hammering against my ribs. "Actually, I can."

CHAPTER FOURTEEN

JESSE

"*J*ess, wake up."

I grumble and swat the hand away.

"Baby, wake up. We'll be late." Ally pulls the covers off me, and grabs my ankles. She tugs. I play dead. My bed is soft, and it's Saturday. I want to sleep. If I don't move a muscle for long enough, Ally might give up and crawl in beside me. That would be nice. She's the best cuddler. It's probably her boobs. You never can have too many pillows.

Damn Brinkley for giving me two replacement jobs close together. My neck and shoulders still hurt from the last one.

A soft hand brushes my face. "Baby, I've got coffee for you."

My eyes fly open.

I reach out to grab the coffee Ally offers me and swipe empty air.

There's no Ally. No queen-sized bed from my burned

down house back in Tennessee. No pressing replacement job to do. And damn it, no coffee.

I'm in the crawl space, in a house in Cochise, Arizona. It's hot, and sweat soaks the back of my neck, matting my hair to my skin. My clothes cling to my body too.

I'm going to boil to death in here. Super fun.

A sadness socks me in the gut as I try to move my stiff muscles. This part of the dream is real enough. I can barely move after sitting crouched in the same position for so long. No wonder I fell asleep. The heat. The inability to move. Either one will do it.

I run a sweaty palm over my face and huff. Gross. It's supposed to be February. Didn't this town get the memo?

The sadness doesn't ease up.

I want my old life. I'm longing to wake up and find Ally in bed with me. I miss my old house with my deck and river trail. My programmable coffeemaker. Overstuffed sofa and unlimited channels. My rainfall showerhead. A freaking bag of Cheetos and a Dr. Pepper. Hell, I'll take the shitty replacement jobs if it means I'd get to see Brinkley's gruff face again.

I'll take it all back. The good and the bad. Every little thing I didn't appreciate about that life.

Wow, how fast life can change. Seventeen months ago, I had it all and didn't know it.

I scoot on my knees up to the crawlspace door.

I hover there, listening to the house. Creaks. Moans. Hushed whispers. Anything at all that might suggest the cops are waiting to jump my ass.

But I don't hear anything except for the ringing in my ears.

I push open the crawlspace door, and it hits the tower of cardboard boxes. I get the boxes to slide out of my way by pushing with my feet. I can't stand until I clear the low frame, but then I'm up. Full height. All sixty-three inches of me, baby.

The attic is empty.

I tiptoe across the space to the trap door, trying not to announce my arrival to anyone below. I wait at the exit, but I hear nothing. Man, I keep waiting for the horror music to cue and someone to jump out and cut my Achilles heel. Ouch.

I take a breath, release the latch, and shield myself. Tense, I wait for the cops to spring out, guns loaded.

Nothing.

Well, damn. Don't tell me my plan worked.

Leaving the shield in place, glowing faintly around my body, I creep down the steps one at a time. I lean my butt against the wood for balance.

No one's waiting to pounce in the closet either.

The bedroom is quiet.

I lean against the curtain and survey the street below. Black-and-white cars line each side of the street, but there's no people. Are they inside the houses searching? Are they having a pep talk in the street? Clearly, I'm going to have to choose another window if I want to find out.

I sneak down the hall, one hand on the wall, walking as quickly as possible on the tippiest-tip-top of toes. I'm sure I look like a cartoon villain.

I want to hurry out, but I don't want to be caught unaware by some sneaky cop waiting to put a gun to my head. Not that anyone could grab and shoot me. The shield would prevent any actual grabbing or shooting.

I make it all the way to the back door when I smell something sour. Like vegetables rotting in the trash or garbage disposal.

Sadness wells up inside me again. I even miss the stinky trash and the half-ass garbage disposal I used to have. My old life. My own level of normalcy. *Baby, I've got coffee for you.*

What the hell is wrong with me? All this over the smell of rotting produce? Really?

Pull yourself together, Sullivan.

The living room and kitchen areas are as empty and silent as the rest of the house. Where the hell is everyone? What if this is going to be like one of those movies where I fall asleep and wake up and everyone in the whole world is gone?

The back door has a curtained window. Peeking through the curtain, I have the partial view of a blue Crown Victoria car, and the side of the next house. That's it.

I take a breath and twist the handle of the back door, easing it open.

Fresh air hits my hot face and cools the back of my neck. My sweaty skin tingles as it begins to dry. Ah, fresh air. It must be at least twenty degrees colder down here. I slip into the backyard, searching the airways for Maisie as I do.

Maisie?

I reach out for my sister, hoping to hone in on her signal.

Ping.

Maisie?

Ping.

I freeze, leaning against the neighbor's Crown Vic. I reach my hand out to steady myself. The house's exterior is scalding under my palm.

Maisie?

Ping.

Shit.

I have a problem. The first echolocation I got from Maisie was east. The second and third were south.

She's on the move.

Why?

I peek around the corner of the house, letting my gaze rove over the cars, porches, and pavement for signs of the police hunting me. This is the most intense game of hide-and-seek I've ever played.

One group of officers is clustered in front of a house near the end of the street. They appear to be discussing strategy. A man issues orders while the others listen, hands on hips.

The shield around my body cracks and hisses.

"What the hell?" I hold up my hands and see the shield trembling.

The cracking hiss comes again, and I catch a glimpse of darkness in my periphery. I whirl as black snakes strike my shield for a third time.

"Gee-*zus*!"

Georgia lashes out at me. Her face hardens, angry that my shield is in place. Didn't she see it? Or was it too small to notice?

"Die, you bitch!"

"Tell me how you *really* feel." I huff. "Where's Maisie?"

"Wouldn't you like to know?" Georgia's snakes stop striking, and their muscular bodies soften into smoke. The smoke begins to conform to my shield, and I can feel the pressure rising as if it plans to squeeze me out of hiding. Fat chance. But I've got to say, crushing darkness does create a certain claustrophobia.

"Did you leave Caldwell with her?" I ask, searching her blue eyes for the truth.

Georgia doesn't answer. She's playing it close to the chest. Fine. I can be devious too.

"Did you call for help yet?" The second worse thing to Caldwell waking up and jumping halfway across the country would be his reinforcements showing up to whisk my enemies to safety. They'd bring the big guns, as they have every time before. Haven't they learned? Big guns are only good for body count. "I mean, you're getting into trouble with the police already. If you didn't have reason to call for help before, you do now."

"Drop your shield," Georgia hisses, red-faced. Is she mad or hot? Maybe a little sunburnt. Scratch that. Why the hell do I care? Stray hair has fallen out of her ponytail and lays stuck to her sweaty forehead.

"Nope," I say. "How about I blow your ass up instead?"

"Maisie said you wanted to strike a deal. To become—" She bites her lip. "—to become friends."

I snort. "We both know 'friends' is stretching it."

The first time I met Georgia, she had arrived to escort me to the toilet, so I wouldn't pee on myself while waiting to be tortured. Later when one of the guards broke my ribs, she essentially told me to walk it off. Her coldness hardly encouraged affection.

Uncertainty flickers in her eyes. "Will you spare my life?"

You cannot, Gabriel whispers.

My heart contracts. Not because I give a damn about Georgia. But because I was truly hoping there was another way, for Maisie's sake.

Georgia's gaze wavers. Wow. She must be desperate without Caldwell around to serve as her private instajet. "You'd never spare my life. I can't trust you."

"You're the one who tried to kill me when I wasn't looking," I remind her. "Do you think I didn't notice that?"

"Forget it." She takes a step back, ready to run.

"Wait," I say. Wait, what? Wait right here so I can kill you? I guess I *am* tired of running.

Georgia shifts her weight. Her gaze falls on something over my shoulder. "We can't talk here."

I turn and see what she's looking at. The huddle of cops in the front lawn have broken formation, and are dispersing like a flock of birds.

"Let's go inside," she says. "We can talk about this. Come to some sort of agreement."

"Take me to Caldwell." *We can discuss me severing his head. Again.*

"No!" Her nostrils flare and eyes dilate. Then as if realizing her crazy is showing, she says, "Maisie's with him. He's safe. He's protected by an armed guard. You'll never get to him."

I don't want him to be safe. I want him to be dead. But I send another search beam out, to see if Maisie is with Caldwell.

Ping.

Maisie's farther east than ever before. I assume she's on her own. A sixteen-year-old girl isn't dragging around a dead body. Not alone. Did she run as soon as Georgia turned her back? If she did, then where the hell is Caldwell?

Unguarded?

I hope so.

"Maisie isn't with him." I throw it out there. I want to see if she knows. If she does, then this is some sort of test. She's luring me to my death, and Maisie is being dragged off by the armed guard. All of this is some elaborate trap to kill me while they can. Caldwell seems to have lots of traps. I never know when one will pop up.

"She's protecting him from you," Georgia insists and she looks irritated that I'm questioning her. If her jaw works any harder, some of her teeth are going to crack.

"Test your connection."

"Excuse me?"

There's an opportunity here. It's a gamble, but it might throw Georgia off balance, but it also puts Maisie at risk. The payoff would be worth it though, if I get Georgia to lead me to Caldwell's body.

She's not in danger. Yet, Gabriel assures me as I frantically search the emotional connection for a sign of Maisie's wellbeing. I don't sense any fear or pain, two things I'd felt when Rachel had her face blown off.

"Test your connection," I say again, reassuring myself this gamble is worth it as long as Maisie isn't at risk. I visually measure the distance between the cluster of cops and me and Georgia. They're getting closer. I lower my voice. "If you're connected to her emotionally, you'll feel her. She's on the move."

Georgia looks ready to spit in my face. But then her gaze slides down, and to the right. Seconds later, her brow creases. Then her eyes spring open, and her lips part.

"She—" Her gaze flicks up to mine, her cheeks going red.

"Yep," I say with my best told-you-so grin. "She totally ditched him."

"Freeze!"

My shield, which I'd kept at a polite smallness while talking down the hell bitch, flares to life. I whirl to find cops with their guns raised. Damn.

"Settle down, boys," I begin. They can't shoot me no matter how many clips they empty. They can only draw a bunch of attention and make a big freaking mess.

I place my hands up in front of the group creeping forward. They get close enough I can see the eyes of their guns, the black chambers where bullets would eject straight into my head if given the chance.

It's too close for comfort. And apparently, Georgia agrees.

Black ribbons snap past me and strike the officers. They all collapse on contact, eyes rolling up into their heads. Their necks roll and knees give. All five hit the grass like cotton dolls tossed aside.

"Freeze!" Someone screams. "Hands in the air!"

Really? You're going to keep saying that? Because it was *so* effective the first time.

I whirl on Georgia. "You sure know how to keep it low-key, don't you?"

Only I'm not bitching at Georgia. I'm bitching at thin air. Georgia's gone.

I take off down the only narrow path between the two houses. I burst through the gate at the end of the passage and spot her. Or I spot the back of her blond hair whipping behind her as she vaults over a fence. She's heading west, the opposite direction of Maisie.

Bam!

Now we're talking. Her reaction tells me everything I need to know.

He's still dead.

Her reinforcements aren't here yet.

Most importantly—I still have time.

If Caldwell is surrounded by a guard, Georgia would've stayed and finished me. Or at the very least, she would keep me busy so Caldwell has time to wake up. If she's running back to him, it's because she thinks he's vulnerable.

Time to chase her. Time to find Caldwell. Time to take out the sadist trying to destroy the world and everyone I love in it.

I sprint after Georgia.

CHAPTER FIFTEEN

MAISIE

I can't keep up with Sam. It's harder than it sounds. My ankle feels a million times better now that it's wrapped tight, but it's still sore. And Sam's got ridiculously long legs. I can see why this boy wants to play basketball. His body moves in a way that's more animal than person. Very fluid. I shamble after him. It's like I've suddenly got six clumsy legs all vying for the same space.

If my inadequate body wasn't bad enough, he's got us going through playgrounds and back alleys.

"They called a curfew," Sam explains as I struggle to get my second leg over a hip-high wooden fence. He reaches back and grabs me by said hips.

A boy's hand on my hips nearly kills me.

Okay, not *kills* me. But if I wasn't motivated to keep my girl parts from getting impaled on a wooden fence, I'm sure I would have melted to a sack of jelly when his thumb brushes that sweet spot just below my hipbone.

One day, I whisper to myself as he lifts me like a box of feathers and sets me down on my feet like a baby kitten. *One day these hormones will pull themselves together, and I won't be such a nonsensical loon.* The internet says the teenage brain isn't fully formed. Lucky me. How can I be expected to live like this?

Assuming I live at all.

My shirt slides up, and his warm palm brushes my bare stomach, which would be much sexier if I wasn't sweating like a pig.

"If we get caught outside our houses, we'll be arrested. I had permission to get my stuff while they waited with my dad. The paramedics."

He seems totally unaware of the effect his touch has on me. Or his dimples. "Are you going to tell them who I am?"

"I'll say you're..." He stops walking. "Maybe they won't recognize you. I didn't with all the blood."

"Yeah, blood. It'll stump you every time." But I've showered since then. Is he trying to politely tell me I still look like hell? Uh, thanks?

"*The* Maisie Caldwell. Wow."

"I told you who my parents were. You saw them on the news. Don't act surprised."

After a pause, I add, "You didn't even guess it was me?"

He shakes his head. "I don't like to assume. You know what they say about assuming."

"No. What?"

He picks me up and puts me on the other side of the next fence like nothing. Seriously? How tall is this kid?

"It makes an a—"

He freezes.

"What? It makes what?"

"It makes, uh, something."

"Sam." I offer my upturned hand so he can balance

himself as he lifts his own long legs over the fence. "Can I tell you something?"

His hand stiffens in mine. "Okay."

"You know, I *have* heard curse words before."

He grins. A sheepish, part shy, part embarrassed grin. "My dad says it's rude to curse in front of a lady."

A lady? Am I a *lady*? Despite the offensive image of myself in a Victorian skirt and parasol, my heart swells.

"Well, let me tell you. My sister has a very *extensive* vocabulary. There's nothing you can say that I haven't heard before."

Sam's grin tucks into the corner of his mouth again, but he never finishes telling me what assuming makes a person. I've heard the joke before though. And it's a good thing, or my curiosity would be killing me right now.

Sam's hand seizes mine. His fingers close and I'm totally prepared to swoon.

Okay, yeah, I've had a lot of time to imagine my first real kiss. I've kissed. But a casual snogging and a real kiss aren't the same thing. Everybody knows that.

I wish I was a little less sweaty, but I could be dead by tomorrow the way my day is going. So I'll take whatever I can get.

I come up on my toes, trying to help close the distance between our mouths. You're supposed to keep your eyes closed when kissing, but I peek mine open to make sure our mouths are lined up.

Sam isn't looking at me.

I sag.

"If you can't..." he begins. He looks at me and the corner of his lips tug into a deeper frown. "If you can't bring him back, it's okay. I don't expect—I—"

I turn to see what he's looking at. His eyes are fixed on the ambulance parked on the adjacent street. The back doors are open and inside the ambulance, a gurney sits. The distinct shape of a body rests under the sheet as a paramedic sits perched on the step, smoking. Vapor rises around his head, mingling with the heat.

Smoking? A paramedic!

Aren't medical professionals supposed to know better?

"This will work." I squeeze his hands. *Please Azrael, let that be true.*

Sam squeezes my hand again. "There they are. But I'm not sure how to get you over there without you being seen. The second they see you, they're going to bring the police down on us."

He falls back against the building, shielding us from view. The smell of campfire lingers in the air. I turn peer around the corner and see a forest of charred buildings.

It's practically a big *Jesse was here* sign.

It looks like most of the emergency crews have managed to stop the blaze. A few buildings are smoking, but the flames have gone out.

Why did Jesse have to blow up the town? I thought she was going to be more careful with her fire stuff. She'd promised Ally. I can't believe she'd break a promise to Ally without a really, *really* good reason. So, what happened? Was she trying to reach me? Surely it was for her own protection. She can't possibly believe I'm important enough to burn a town down for.

I tell myself not to be stupid. I'm not that important to anyone. Yet I can't help but feel a flutter in my chest. I replay Jesse reaching out to me, begging me to jump out of the speeding truck.

She made me feel important then.

Maisie.

Jesse calls out to me. I want to go to her. I do. But there's something I must do first. Sam needs his dad.

Azrael's power flares. It's the smell of metal. The smell of blood and cinnamon.

I turn to Sam, expectant, knowing whatever he says next will be her influence talking.

"I've got it!" His eyes brighten. "I know how to distract them, and draw them away from the ambulance. Once the coast is clear, go in and do your thing."

Do my thing. Wow. My superpower sounded much cooler the way he put it. It's like I have a highly specialized technical skill, one honed after years of hard work and craftsmanship. In reality, I blow into someone's nose. That's it. It doesn't require a medical degree.

"Ready?" Sam asks.

I squeeze his hand back. I'm getting used to the fact that he's a hand squeezer. Every time he pumps my hand with his, it doesn't mean he's about to French me. Sad face. "What if they arrest you or something?"

Sam shrugs. "I'm not going to break any laws. And I'm fast."

Not what I want to hear. "Don't run. Only guilty people run."

"Can you do it or not?"

"Yes," I say, feeling defensive.

"How much time do you need?"

"A minute tops." With the whole conjuring the power part, it doesn't take long to huff into a couple of nostrils. Sam's dad should start breathing right away, and breathing is what Sam needs to see. When Ally died, it's what Jesse needed too...and probably anyone who has ever lost a person they loved. If they can see the person breathing again, that's when they start to believe everything is going to be okay.

"Here we go." Sam steps out from our hiding place between the buildings and approaches the ambulance.

His head is down, and shoulders slumped. He slips his

hands into his pockets and kicks a rock in the road. The smiley, hopeful boy holding my hand is transformed.

The smoking paramedic sees him first and straightens, flicking his cigarette away.

Sam stops short of him and gestures into the back of the truck. I'm waiting to see what he might say. What crazy line he might use to get the paramedic to leave his post and give me access to the body...to Sam's dad.

Sam's shoulders suddenly hitch, and he begins to cry. I can see the tears glittering on his cheeks from here. He's pointing at something down the alley adjacent to ours. He's touching his chest and flailing his arms. The paramedic's mouth parts in surprise, his lower lip going soft.

Wow. Either Sam's drawing on his honest to goodness sadness, or he's a great actor. Hey, if this whole ball player thing doesn't work out, then maybe he can take up acting.

The paramedic and Sam start hurrying toward the alley—if that's what you want to call the narrow passage between a row of charred buildings. I can't help but think of alleys in Chicago, which are three or four times larger than these little pathways.

I wait, breathing heavy in the mounting heat as I watch them hurry away. The ambulance sits there, completely unguarded. I can see straight into the back of the vehicle, and the lumpy form under the white sheet.

Sam's eyes flick to mine before he turns down the alley, and he flashes me a wicked grin.

Naughty boy.

The second the paramedic and Sam step out of view, I move. I give the area one good look, searching for anyone who might stop me. Seeing no one, I dash toward the open door. I'm like one of those power-walking grannies as I hustle to the back of the ambulance and heft myself inside.

I have to lift my leg pretty high to clear the first step and then hold onto a silver handle by the door to pull myself up all the way. Grit from my sneakers grates audibly against the platform.

No one stands in the sandy street. No cops or bystanders are rushing to yank me out of ambulance. If anyone saw me, they don't care enough to stop me. I quickly reach for the door handle and pull it shut. I don't want anyone to look inside and see me molesting a man's corpse. I duck down and keep my head below the window. I don't want anyone to see me through the back window of the ambulance either.

With the door shut, the heat doubles immediately. And with it, the rate of decomposition. If I don't hurry, Sam's dad is going to stink.

A little creeped out to be shut into the back of the ambulance with a dead body, I keep breathing, trying to calm down. But the air is stagnant and thick, giving me the feeling I can't quite draw a full breath. Or it's the anxiety of, you know, hanging out with a dead guy.

"This is fine, totally fine," I say as I kneel beside the sheet. "It's not like he's going to pop up and eat you. This isn't Dawn of the Dead."

The body twitches, and I scream. I clamp a hand over my mouth and leap back, slamming my head on the edge of a cabinet. White hot shock and pain spiderwebs through my skull. I swear again, placing a hand over the burning wound.

Every swear word I can think of pours out of me as I stumble around, eyes pinched shut, viciously rubbing the new hole in my head.

"Christ on a cracker! It was a twitch!" I scold myself. Dead bodies twitch. Dead bodies move. Dead bodies fart. Quit acting like a wimp and do this!

I'm not sure if my pep talk is working because while I do manage to open my eyes and stop rubbing my head, I am not able to approach the lumpy dead guy right away.

I lean forward and yank the sheet off his face in a single swipe.

I exhale. Whew. That's better. No ghastly wounds. No horrific gobs of blood or brain to contend with. Just a man, lying there, looking like he's enjoying his afternoon nap.

"Hey," I say, because it's only polite to say hi. I'm kind of interrupting. "I'm Maisie."

He doesn't say anything. I'm not sure if I need someone's informed consent to bring them back from the dead, and it feels a little weird to be thinking about it now.

I lean in and peer into his face.

He's older than I expected him to be. I'm not sure if it's because I compare all parents to my parents, and my parents look young. It's the NRD and dying. We age differently. When we die and come back to life, our cells remake themselves, all brand new. It's like the perfect anti-aging spa treatment. If you can get over the whole pooping on yourself when you die thing, it's the best anti-aging option on the market.

Even though they don't look alike, our parents are probably the same age. Sam's dad has bushy gray eyebrows and wrinkles at the corners of his eyes. The stubble on his jaw and upper lip is gray too, with lots of little lines around his mouth. Dad's barely got some crow's feet.

I run a fingertip across one of the lines.

Is this what Mom would look like now? If things were different? Would she have gray in her hair? Lines by her mouth?

I can't help but wonder if I'm screwing with fate by bringing a person back. What if someone as old as Sam's dad is supposed to be dead and I bring him back? Am I threatening the very fabric of existence? What if Sam's dad wakes up, and it causes an earthquake to rock the other side of the world and kill a hundred people?

I wonder if I'm naturally paranoid, or if I'm so used to crazy things happening that my anxiety is conditioned.

But if I'm not supposed to use this gift, then why do I have it? Why give me the ability to feel someone die, and the power to reverse it, unless I'm supposed to help people? I'm not the one who broke the rules. Someone else did when they gave me this power in the first place.

I lean over his bristled face. "Hope you don't regret this. Mr..." I fail to recall his name. "Mr. Sam's Dad."

I close my eyes and reach down inside of me. There's a cold stone in there. It sits near my belly button. It's always there, waiting, but when I concentrate on it, it grows hot in my belly. I inhale and the stone glows like an ember. The power emitting from it swells with the oxygen I pull inside myself. Air slides over these coals, catches fire, and burns. As I exhale the air into the man's nose, it's not my air. By passing the air over the warm coals in my guts, the air is changed. It becomes infused with magic and life somehow.

I inhale again and the ember brightens. My chest and throat grow hot with it as I expel a second breath. By the third inhalation, my insides feel alive, like a fire eater who's stuck a flaming stick down her throat. But I breathe anyway and release it into his nose.

I feel the spark.

The stone in Sam's dad reignites with my borrowed sparks and begins to burn again, he's alive. This life swells, the ember glows with flame. The flame swelling to something substantial enough to burn on its own.

I lean back, a little light-headed. I always lose my breath during this.

I sit for a second, waiting for the dream-like quality of the ambulance to refocus into something resembling real-time reality.

Then the idea of time hits me. I've been in this ambulance way too long. Holding onto the handle of the cabinet door, I pull myself up. The cabinet door swings open under the strain of my weight, and I glimpse bandages and breathing equipment wrapped in plastic.

I let go of the handle and the door swings shut on its hinges.

Sweat slides down the back of my neck and the overwhelming heat of the enclosed cab rushes in on me again. I've got to get this door open, or Sam's dad is going to bake to death.

I don't see anyone in the street, hovering near charred buildings, or lingering on the sidewalk in front of the store and hotel. The townies must take their orders seriously, staying inside like they were told to do.

I throw open the door and jump down. Cool air rushes over my skin, and I suck in a deep breath. Relief washes over my skin and face. I swallow and realize how incredibly thirsty I am. I could use that soda Sam promised me. I could use ten of them.

Trying not to run and look guilty, I walk away from the ambulance toward the narrow alleyway where Sam and I were. I keep my head down and act like I've got somewhere to be. I count my steps, fifteen, seventeen. I'm going to make it. I'm about to step into the alley, when a hand clamps down hard on my shoulder, spinning me around so fast I lose my balance.

"What the hell are you doing here?" the man demands, and refuses to let me go.

CHAPTER SIXTEEN

JESSE

She is not in danger, Gabriel assures me as I stand there, torn between chasing after Maisie and tracking Georgia.

As soon as I'd felt Maisie's fear, I'd stopped dead in my tracks, giving Georgia a greater lead.

She is safe, Gabriel says again. He wants me to forget about Maisie and chase Georgia. Is she really safe? Or is he lying to me because we're so close? Because so much is hanging in the balance and if I don't find Caldwell before he reboots, the danger is to us all.

"You better not be lying," I warn him, and bolt after Georgia. The muscles around my tailbone ache. My thighs burn. I make it all the way down a tight alley and don't see her. Then as I burst from behind Kenny's Pizzas and Pies, I saw the blond ponytail bobbing.

Gee-*zus*, she's booking it.

I skid through the dirt, heading in the opposite direction. I'm moving so fast I lose my balance and stumble against the house. It stops my momentum, and I'm able to correct course.

The stench of trash rises from hot cans. I weave around them the best I can, keeping my eyes on Georgia. But she's obviously the more athletic of the two of us. She keeps getting smaller and smaller as I dodge bicycles and flower pots and more parked cars. A bunch of urban crap crammed in these pseudo walkways between houses.

Then she cuts another corner and disappears. Oh, come on.

A cramp in my left side begins to form between my ribs. Every breath is sharp. I become aware of how much of a mouth breather I am as my wheezing intensifies.

I burst out of the alley.

I don't see Georgia.

"Where. Did. She. Go?" I ask between breaths. Gabriel's right beside me, looking collected and calm. Yeah, well, we can't all just float around like pretty princesses in our expensive suits now, can we?

"There." His wings twitch. I follow his finger over the shiny hoods of cars lining the street.

There's another narrow space between houses.

I groan and start running again. As I cross the street, Gabriel yells, "Shield!"

I throw it up the same instant a bullet flies past my head, and hits the house in front of me. Splinters fly off the building. Debris hits the shield, sizzling.

My shoulders hunch instinctively as my head tucks, and I whirl to see cops behind me.

"Not now, boys," I say. "I'm busy. Come back later."

I lift my left hand and throw a fire bomb at one of the cars in the street. A white hatchback lifts off the ground in a ball of flames. The cops fall back, hitting the dirt and covering their heads. Before they get up, I'm gone.

I follow the passageways Gabriel points out one after another until the rows of tightly knit houses end. I step into a wide-open street with only a vast desert stretching across the other side. To the right, a playground belonging to a one-story school sits. Bright plastic tubes and ladders and rope swings stand unused in the hot sun. What child is going to use the swing when the rubber seat will surely burn his ass off?

To the left, two homes sit far apart from one another. Both are one-story ranch houses with fences and modest yards.

Apart from the one flowering cactus by the three-way stop across the street, lumpy grass and gravel seem to be the extent of the landscaping out here.

My shield crackles and I whirl. Surprise, surprise. Here's Georgia trying to kill me with her death ribbon dancing. Again.

"You know." I groan, but it doesn't sound like a groan. I'm panting. My face is hot and sweaty. Beautiful. I'm sure I'm pulling off the unconquerable badass look right now. Dry heaves and all. "I promised Maisie I wouldn't murder you outright, but if you keep ninja attacking me, I'll have every excuse to destroy you."

"You think self-defense is going to make her feel better about the murder of her mother?"

Good point.

Yet, she seems to have no interest in self-preservation. Her ribbons strike me again and I welcome it. I start walking toward her, hand on my cramping side. "Stop that!"

She strikes one more time, backing away. I hate the hiss and pop of it, like grease in a too-hot pan. It's a sound to put your teeth on edge. I cross the street after her. She backs away but keeps striking.

"Stop being such a twat!" I throw sparks on the leg of her pants like I did to the cops earlier.

She does stop then. It's funny how setting someone on fire does that. She growls, swatting at her legs.

Then I'm on her, pinning her back to the fence. I can't touch her. Well, I can, if I open my shield, but that's sort of like sticking my hand into a basket of pissed off snakes.

Instead, I position myself over her legs, knowing my shield will trap her from the knees down.

"Get off me!" she screams. "Get off me this instant!"

"Uh, no." I'm kind of surprised she thought such a command would work. Even the people I love and respect have a hard time getting obedience out of me. A command from Georgia will get a snort at best.

She starts to scream.

"Yeah, that's a good idea," I mock her. "Get the cops over here so they can arrest you. Worst Mother of the Year here folks."

"They won't arrest me!" She squirms. Geez. It's like trying to sit on a mound of baby pandas without any of the cute. "I'm the victim. I'm the distraught mother who had her child taken."

"Yeah, Caldwell might have been able to sell that story, but I doubt you're as good at the mindfuckery."

She finally stills.

"That's what I thought." I lift some of my weight off her body, but I don't give her enough room to get up. "Listen, for the sake of time, let's be honest here."

She glowers at me. If her big blue eyes, the exact replica of Maisie's, could shoot their own firebombs, I'm sure my face would be *so* melty right now.

No, not the exact replica of Maisie's. Maisie's eyes are full of kindness and empathy. In sad movies, she's the first to cry when the actor does. In Georgia's eyes, I see only calculation. Strategy. She measures me, looking for the best place to sink the dagger even as I try to work in her favor.

A spike of fear coils my guts. I try to push Maisie's feelings away again, but I'm silently begging Gabriel for reassurances that she's okay.

She is not in danger. Finish what you started.

I could argue that I didn't start any of this. Caldwell did. But okay, I can be the closer.

"I'm going to kill him, Georgia. There's not a person in the whole world that's going to stop me. I'll do it today. Or tomorrow. Or next week. Whatever it takes. But it's happening. Caldwell is dead."

She snarls. "I won't let you."

"For the sake of argument let's pretend it's a done deal. Are you ready to give up on Maisie too?"

"Maisie's a child!"

"She's sixteen! Last I checked, she's old enough to drive." Not that anyone in this family has taken the time to show her how to use a car. Or keep her in school. Or teach her the basics of self-sufficiency. Hell, we're all failing Maisie in about a thousand ways.

"You're her mother." I try to keep my temper in check. But the longer I look at this crazy sociopath, the more I want to slap her across the face.

I'm sure I'm projecting. I've got my own mommy issues. Our mothers look nothing alike except that my mom had blue eyes too.

But it's easy to spot the similarities between the women when it comes to their personalities. Both are selfish. Both are neglectful. My mom didn't woman up and protect me from her pervert husband when she was supposed to and I hated her every day for it. And I don't need to convince anyone that Georgia has also left Maisie vulnerable and defenseless in a way that a mother never should.

Yet, somehow, Maisie loves her despite the fact the woman puts her life at risk every day. For each insult, Maisie provides an excuse. Any wrong is forgiven. It blows my mind that she manages to have only love in her heart for her mother and I don't want to change that. I'd never want her to be as hard-hearted as me.

But I can't look past Georgia's neglect. Or my mother's.

So I'll be angry enough for the both of us.

My throat constricts with emotion. "She's a great kid."

Georgia stops squirming.

"She needs you and you're throwing her away." I'm grinding my teeth so hard that my jaw hurts.

Georgia looks me dead in the eye. "Kill me."

"You're not the one I want. Where is he?"

"Fuck you!" she hisses and spits onto my electrical shield. The saliva sizzles and burns away instantly.

"*Rude*." I'm keeping my tone light, but I want to reach up and crush her throat so bad I can't see straight. "Of course, look at the monster you're in love with. I can't expect you to have manners."

"Drop your shield and fight me," she says and lifts her chin. "Fight me fair."

I snort. "Because you're the picture of fair, you wannabe ninja."

"You're scared of me," Georgia taunts. As her lips move I can't help but stare at the red lipstick smeared in the corner of her mouth. It gives me the creepy impression of clowns. I want to wipe it off with my thumb, but that'd be super weird.

Instead I roll my eyes at her. "I can burn you and your pretty pantsuit to a crisp."

No fear. She hardens as if she's preparing for an attack. "I dare you."

Indignation rises inside me, rearing its head.

Jesse. Gabriel's voice is faint. Very far away, but his tone of warning is recognizable.

I say, "I wanted to do it for Maisie. I wanted her to have you. I didn't have my mom when I needed her, and I didn't want to be the one to take you from her. Now I don't see a way around it. You'll kill me the second my back is turned and then it'll be the two of you. I can't trust you to protect her."

Her smirk falters.

"I'd rather Maisie be alive and hate me than stuck with you until one of you decide to finish her off."

"Kill me," she says again. But it isn't as hateful. Why? Why would her hate falter now?

Do not be deceived, Gabriel warns. The scent of rain washes over me, clearing my head.

Where's the string?

Where's the pull tab that springs this trap?

She's trying to distract me, but from what?

She will sacrifice herself for him. Gabriel's voice whispers through my mind. The option of materializing is impossible if I'm sitting on Georgia's legs in the dirt, but I consider what he's saying. She's sacrificing herself and I'm being deceived.

How is she sacrificing herself?

If I kill her in the street, I'll be dead. Absorbing her powers will kill me. And I'll wake up stronger, but by then Caldwell will be awake, Maisie will never forgive me, and every power makes me a little more insane.

Because again, I'm vulnerable if I kill her. Because it will buy him time to resurrect. He must be very close to waking now. And what if I'm still dead when he resurrects?

Clues click into place.

I grin down at her. "Tricky."

I stand, getting off her legs.

"Kill me!" she shouts. But the smirk is entirely gone. Her eyes aren't hard squints anymore either. They're round with desperation and fear. Tears start to shimmer in the milky white orbs.

"Which house is he in?" I ask her.

"He isn't even here. He's in town. I lured you away from him."

"No you didn't. You would've run slower." I turn and look at the two houses on this street. There are only two. He's got to be in one or the other.

Georgia took a step back. When I first saw her, she kept walking *backwards*.

One house she stepped toward and one she stepped away from.

If I was hiding Ally in one of these houses, and Caldwell showed up to murder her, would I step toward Ally or away from her? I'd run toward her.

But I'm not Georgia. Or rather Georgia isn't *me*.

I start toward the house she walked away from.

Georgia screams, full on Viking battle roar, and charges. I brace myself for the impact that never comes. Instead, she yelps and drops to her hands and knees.

"What the—?"

Blood soaks through her shirt and trails down her arm. I stand in shock. Did I spontaneously develop a new power? Instant bleeding for all my foes? That'd be awesome.

Another bullet flies and I realize what's happening. I didn't develop a new skill on the fly. Georgia got shot.

"Arizona State Police! Get down and put your hands on the back of your head."

Georgia flicks her wrist and the men are thrown back. I can see the bottom of their black boots as they sail away from me. It's an immediate reminder she has Rachel's telekinesis.

Why hasn't she used it on me? But Rachel didn't use it either. Not against my shield.

Rachel. Just thinking about her hurts. I see her tilt her head and wrinkle her nose. My best friend—once upon a time. Repairing our relationship became impossible the second Georgia murdered her.

Anger swells inside me. I'm ready to attack Georgia again, but more bullets fly.

I expand my shield, trying to cover as much of myself and the worthless jerk as I can. It works. No, I haven't suddenly changed my mind about this horrible creature. If they shoot her in the head, her powers will be dispersed to the next partis to catch. One or more will be called and we'll have to hunt them down again. There's a chance that a power could land with someone even worse than Caldwell.

No thanks.

Bullets ping off the shield and fly in all directions.

In a moment of panic, Georgia's eyes flick to the house down the street.

"I knew it!" I turn and look at the house myself. Nothing remarkable. One-story white wood and a bicycle in the yard. Man, I hope Caldwell's body is the only dead body I find in there.

This is taking too much time. He lives.

Gabriel's words are a kick in the gut. He lives? Caldwell's breathing?

That won't do.

I throw my arm up, and a spray of fire leaps toward the cops. I close my eyes. I don't want to see it. I don't want to see their eyes as they die. I don't want to hear them screaming as they are burned alive. As if I could block out the sound.

I hesitate, wondering if I could find an alternative. Could I use my shield to knock the police back? They'll keep coming. Could I burn them only a little? Not really. Once I kill Caldwell, I'll be dead myself. I'll be as vulnerable as I can be in those moments my mind and body reboots. And if something happens to my body then what about Maisie? There's no one to protect her.

I have no choice.

I must kill these people. Five or six more police is nothing compared to numbers of dead left in Caldwell's wake. Sacrifice a few for the whole.

If I keep saying it, maybe I'll believe it.

I pinch my eyes shut and pretend there's nothing but a scary movie on.

But all I can see is Ally's hurt face. Her hand over her mouth. The tears in her eyes.

I'm sorry. Forgive me.

I peel my wet eyes open and find charred bodies in the street. No more guns. No more screaming. I whirl on Georgia who leans against the fence. Two more bullet holes, either direct shots or ricochets from my shield, have nailed her in the gut and the leg. No headshots. She tries to get up, but she can't.

But her brains are in her head and that's what matters. That's what'll keep her powers locked safely in her body for now.

I turn and run toward the white house at the end of the lane, the one with the upturned bicycle in the yard. I don't look back.

"No!" Georgia screams after me. "He's your father!"

"No. He's not." I call back as I struggle to draw a breath.

My father died a long time ago.

CHAPTER SEVENTEEN

MAISIE

"Hey!" The hand on my shoulder whips me around. It's the paramedic from earlier, the one who escorted Sam away on the pretense of whatever lie he told him. "What the hell are you doing here?"

"I—I...?" My mind flatlines.

"You can't be here." His hawk nose wrinkles in disapproval. "There's a curfew." He's scolding me like I'm five.

"S-sorry," I say.

I hate it when I stammer. It's ridiculous.

"Roy!"

The paramedic, Roy, turns without letting go of my wrist. I wiggle it, trying to let him know he's hurting me without straight up whining. His hold loosens. If this were Dad, he would have crushed it harder.

"*What?*" He yells to the paramedic calling him, but Roy doesn't look away. His eyes are fixed on me. His face scrunches in confusion. I definitely look familiar but he's not placing me. Good. Hopefully he won't until hours or days from now.

Please don't recognize me. Please don't recognize me. Azrael?

"He's breathing! Let's go!" The other paramedic is in the back of the ambulance, working on Sam's dad. The sheet has been ripped off, sliding off the back of the ambulance into the dirt. He's cutting his shirt. I don't know why. I'm not a medical professional. But if I have to guess, I'm sure it's to prep him for the trip to the hospital.

It's not necessary, but I'll let them do their thing and save myself the explanations.

Roy turns back on me, torn between two opposing civic duties.

"Get inside." He lets go of my wrist. "It's not safe out here."

I nod. He's already jogging back to the ambulance. He climbs into the cab at the same moment the other paramedic jumps up to close the back doors.

"Are you coming? Now or never!" the paramedic in the back shouts. He's yelling at Sam.

Sam looks at me, and then back at the ambulance. He chews on his bottom lip.

I wave him on. I mouth, *go on stupid. Go with your dad!*

If it were my mom, I'd go to the hospital in a heartbeat.

What in the world is he waiting for?

My heart fumbles when he leans into the ambulance and says something to the paramedic. Then he shuts the door and the ambulance speeds off. The tires leave a dust trail in the smoky air.

I assume they're headed for the hospital fifteen minutes away, the one Sam mentioned when he thought I'd been in a car accident.

Sam stops in front of me.

"What the hell?" I ask him. "Don't you want to—"

I don't finish.

Sam wraps his arms around me, lifting me off my feet into the air.

He kisses me. His mouth is sticky and hot. I smell his sweat and cologne. It's like the magazines in waiting rooms, with the perfume inserts you can rub all over your wrist or neck, or maybe your boobs, if you're not easily embarrassed.

I melt in his arms, each cell turns into a grain of sand and tumbles to the earth.

When he lets go, I suck in a sharp breath.

"Sorry! Sorry!" He puts me back on my feet as gently as if I'm one of those creepy porcelain dolls.

"Why didn't you go with him?" I say again, waving at the dust trail the ambulance left in its wake. The ambulance itself is long gone.

"He's alive," he says as if this answers my question. "He's *alive*."

I smile, feeling a little squirmy under his intense stare. "It's the least I could do to compensate for a dead guy in your bed." I mean it as a joke, anything to lighten the intensity of this moment...and that kiss. I've never been kissed so...*hard* before. Hard isn't the right word. Excitedly? Exuberantly?

Am I blushing?

Sam doesn't seem to notice. "You're amazing. You're..."

"Hey," I say, stopping him. I put my hand out in front of me only to discover a super firm pectoral muscle under my palm.

I pull my hand back. Yes, okay, I'm blushing.

I feel super weird now. I can't tell if it's because this boy kissed me or because he's heaping on the praise. "My mom killed him. I was doing damage control. I don't deserve a medal or anything. I owed you."

Because if I'd let Jesse kill Mom back at the base, when she had the chance, Sam's dad would have never lost his life in the first place. Or if I'd never suggested the hotel to Mom at all, for that matter.

He scoops me up again and holds me. I can see the sweat gleaming on his tanned neck.

"You're going to squeeze the life out of me," I tell him, trying to get away. But I'm not trying that hard.

"I'm sorry. Sorry." He releases me again, but he looks like he's going to bolt, arms spread, and screaming. He's practically bursting. "But you saved my dad. I don't understand how you did it, but you did! He was alive! I saw him breathin' myself."

His happiness is infectious. I can't help but smile, shielding my face from the sun with my hand. "He'll be okay. The hospital is far enough away that he should have plenty of time to recover."

Assuming my parents don't destroy the world and kill us all, I think. I decide not to say this. No one likes a pessimist.

Sam's brow crinkles together. "That's why I stayed."

His response confuses me.

"Because he's going to recover?"

"You're in trouble." His brow is still scrunched. "I want to help you."

He takes my hand and presses it against his chest again. My heart flutters. "You should've gone with your dad. It's not safe here."

Sam doesn't have any powers. Okay, I'm not Wonder Woman or anything, but at least I have NRD. If something happens and I die, I can resurrect if I hold onto my head.

"You don't get it. I owe you," he says. "My dad's everythin' to me. I can't thank you enough, Maisie."

Maisie.

Hearing him say my name makes goosebumps rise on my arm. I feel strange again. Like I'm floating above my body. What's wrong with me?

"You're welcome. But you shouldn't come back to the house with me. I'm not kidding about it being unsafe. My mom—"

"I know what she did. I get that she's like you." His face hardens. He looks way older when he scowls like this. "But you need help and you deserve help. Let me help you."

She's like you.

My stomach turns. Am I? Am I like my mom?

I think of Dad lying in Sam's bed. The healing neck. The lack of time.

He's wrong. I'm weaker than both. Half the time I don't know what I'm doing or what I want. Mom and Dad are battering rams in comparison.

Mom would kill her own father if she had to. Jesse can do it too. I'm the weakest one out of all of them.

I search Sam's face, looking for the deceit. It wouldn't be the first time someone takes my feelings and uses them against me. Jesse's right not to trust people. It's better that way.

But I don't see anything dark in Sam's face. I see big earnest eyes and a determined jaw.

And if I'm honest with myself, I want him to stay.

It isn't the kiss or him rubbing my hand all over his beefy chest—god help me. It's the fact he doesn't want to leave me. I can't remember the last time I had a friend. Someone my age. Someone who didn't treat me like a freak, or like I was a kid the way my sister and her friends do.

If anything happens to Sam, I'll never forgive myself. He has to know that.

"I don't think you understand how danger-ous this is. The—"

Sam doesn't let me finish. He places his hands on his hips and grins. "I've got skills too, you know."

His grin is ruthless. Oh man. Am I falling for this guy?

"Do you?" I ask, unable to hide my grin.

"I do, but if I fall short, I've got you," he says and offers me his hand. "You can bring me back like you brought back my dad. I'm not scared of dying. Not if I'm going to wake up to you."

My face is on fire. It's got to be. Maybe all this sunshine is making me slow and stupid.

My chest vibrates. The ground under my feet shifts.

"What the hell?" I turn and look back down the alleyway. "What's that?"

"Gunfire," Sam says. "And...bombs?"

Jesse. As soon as I think about her, her emotions flare to life inside me. Focus. Sadness. And whole lot of...regret? Without thinking, I start running in her direction. Toward the fighting.

"Hey! Wait!" Sam says. "Wait up!"

I can't wait. She's fighting Mom. My mother's fear is like ice in my veins.

Please. Please don't hurt her.

A minute ago, I could acknowledge that Mom was evil. She hurts good people like Sam's dad. Now I'm begging for her life again. Why can't my head and heart ever agree?

My legs grow heavy, but I can't quit. I run as fast as I can in the direction of the explosions. I hit a gate and Sam's there, picking me up and putting me on the other side, proving his helpfulness right away. Or at least, proving that he's got some freaking long legs.

The firebombing stops. A horrifying silence fills the air.

I'm too late.

I run harder.

Jesse responds. Not in words. I'm not sure this new emotional tether works that way. But with her spirit...for lack of a better word. Or maybe consciousness. Some essential part of her, it acknowledges me. I reach out to Mom. I beg, *hold on! Hold on! I'm coming*, but I don't feel anything back. Her fear is all over me. It makes my limbs weak and stomach sick. But I don't sense her acknowledgment the way I felt Jesse's.

It's one-sided.

I don't have time to consider what this means as Sam launches me over yet another fence and a cluster of trash cans.

Then something else. Thunder rattles the bones in my chest.

I slow, trying to understand what I'm hearing.

Recognition dawns.

The distinct whirl of blades cutting through the atmosphere.

A helicopter in the distance.

They're here.

CHAPTER EIGHTEEN

JESSE

The front door to the last house on the lane is already open. I close it so I don't have to listen to Georgia scream and cry behind me. It's like listening to a cat being skinned alive. It's wretched. No matter how I feel about that hateful bitch, it doesn't change how heartbreaking her pleas are. Or maybe I don't have a stomach for begging.

Somehow, she loves Caldwell. Whatever happened in the camps, whatever brought them together, it solidified a relationship I'll never understand. Because of that, she doesn't want him to die any more than I want Ally to be dead.

Don't think about that, I warn myself. *Don't start humanizing the monsters now.*

It helps to remember how many times Caldwell and Georgia have hurt Ally. Every bruise. Every stab wound. All of it piled on top of the emotional trauma. That makes the line between good and evil more clear.

I find myself in a kitchen. The floor is standard linoleum,

coated in dirt and blood. I follow this trail into the living room.

By the coffee table, there's a red stain on the carpet. It's blood but the wetness is from something else. I bend down and press my fingers to the moist fibers. I sniff it. Hydrogen peroxide.

So they stitched him up here.

"Where's the body?" I ask.

Gabriel places a hand on my back. His fingers push, turning me toward a door on the right.

I hold my breath and brace myself for whatever I might see on the other side, and cross the threshold.

I'm assaulted by a splash of yellow. Sports paraphernalia soaks the walls. Against the left wall is a cluttered desk with a landslide of photos on it.

Caldwell is in the bed.

My whole body tenses.

A piercing and vivid memory surfaces from somewhere deep in my brain-damaged mind.

I was eight years old, had to be, because I came into the living room, proudly displaying my math test with a unicorn *good job!* sticker beside the A-. Unicorn stickers were a Mrs. Yu thing, Mrs. Yu being my third-grade teacher.

"Look! Look!" I wailed. I'd run all the way up the driveway from where the bus had dropped me and into the house, desperate to show it to my parents. Instead of being instantly proud as I expected, my mother's face twisted up in a rage.

"Hush!" she hissed. She turned with a knife in her hand, a red bell pepper laid on the cutting board. "Your father's sleeping."

I screeched to a halt in the kitchen where she'd intercepted me.

"He's exhausted. Let him sleep."

"Okay," I whispered. "But look! I got an A!"

"A-," my mother corrected, turning back to the stove. She didn't look at the sticker.

Dejected, I crossed the kitchen into the living room, as there was no real barrier between the two. I saw Dad's white socks propped up on one arm of the couch and his head on the mauve throw pillow.

He wore his dark blue mechanic's uniform, his eyes closed and mouth parted in sleep.

Knowing my mother was going to yell at me, I crept toward him anyway, slipping off my backpack and stopping at the side of the couch, leaning one hip against it.

His lips curled into a smile. Then one eye peeked open mischievously.

"You're pretending!" I whispered.

He reached out and pulled me onto him, snuggling me into the small space between the cushions and his side. He stank of sweat, oil, and the strong orange-scented soap that all the mechanics used. I loved it.

I thrust my crumpled test into his face. "I got an A-!"

"A-!" he said, his face lighting up. "That's amazing! Did you study hard?"

"No!" I said.

His mouth rounded in surprise and he snorted. "You're a genius."

"Look at the sticker!" I pointed at the sticker, now curling at the edge and threatening to fall off the page from the stress of my abuse.

My dad smoothed the sticker down with his fingers. The whites of his fingernails were blackened out with grease. Then he kissed my forehead, holding me tight against him.

"Good job, baby. I'm so proud."

"Jesse! Did you wake your father?"

"Quick!" Dad had said, his eyes big. "Pretend you're asleep."

And we did. I laid in the crook of his arm until I fell asleep there. I'd slept curled against him like that until dinner time.

I exhale and blink away the memory and the tears that've collected in the corners of my eyes.

It's hard to look at Caldwell and not see my father.

My eyes start at his black boots, dusty with sand, and travel up his pants legs to the bottom of his blood-stained shirt, over his stomach and chest to his brutalized neck. I linger here. There's a lot to take in with the Frankenstein-esque stitches and pinched flesh.

It's amazing how something as simple as sleep can transform the polished church leader, the charismatic demagogue, into the family man I knew long ago.

His lips are parted, showing the tips of his front teeth.

But he isn't the same man, I remind myself. Eric Sullivan died and as Caldwell, he's done more terrible things than I can count. The kind and attentive father who carried me in his arms, doted on his wife, and worked hard to support his family, *that* man was a good man.

The man that crawled out of my father's ashes murdered hundreds of thousands of people. And he *will* destroy the rest of world if given the chance.

I tell myself this over and over again. I repeat it, hoping to drill it into my heart. He tried to stab me to death only hours ago.

I feel the temperature change in the room. I turn toward Gabriel, who's tucked in his black wings to accommodate the cramped space. Now he looks like a man, wingless, in a suit worthy of an Armani model.

"Did you feel that?"

Gabriel flickers. His body bleeds to transparency, and I can see the ASU poster on the wall behind him as if looking through an opaque water glass. The yellow brightens with each second.

"What the hell?"

Then I rush to the side of the bed where Caldwell's body is stretched long. I stare down at his placid face, looking for any signs of life.

My fingers brush the stitches, and I'm horrified by what I don't see. Death. Decay. The line is healed, the flesh holds no red tinge of infection.

"Shit," I say. "Shit. Shit. Shit."

As if to make this point, Caldwell's chest rises with his first breath. The soft whisper of exhalation slips past those parted lips.

"Fuck!"

You must hurry, Gabriel whispers. He's whispering because that's all he can manage as he flickers and fades beside me.

I turn on the desk, shoving the pictures into the floor. I yank open drawers. There's nothing.

Unless I want to bludgeon Caldwell to death with sports memoirs or papercut him to death with old photos, I'm screwed. There are no weapons here. I need something to destroy the brain with. The idea of bludgeoning him with a blunt object is a big fat *no*. I could burn him to death, but that will probably set the bed and then the house on fire too.

My heart broke when my house burned. I can't do that to someone else.

I run to the kitchen. I cut the corner too close and clip my hip on the edge of the counter. A ping of pain shoots up to my collarbone as I rifle through more drawers.

Soup ladles, cheese graters, measuring cups and spoons. What the fuck? I am not shoving a soup ladle up this man's nose. Where are the knives? I throw a rolling pin and give up on that drawer in favor of another.

Bingo!

Long shiny knives with black handles lay in a drawer all their own. I grab one about half as long as my forearm.

I stumble back to the room half expecting to find Caldwell gone, the bed empty, and another whirlwind adventure on the horizon. It wouldn't be the first time I've gotten this freaking close only to have the devil slip through my fingers.

But he's there. The same sweet and sleeping face turned toward the wall.

Jesse.

I'm back on the bed, crawling on top of him. I place a knee on either side of his body and look down into that calm face. The carving knife in my hand shines in the sunlight pouring through the window.

I raise the blade to Caldwell's throat and hold it there against the stitches. It strikes me as some sort of bizarre Cut-Him-Yourself template. Follow the pre-drawn lines!

I press the tip of the blade under his nose. I point up.

It's one thing to stab a man who's actively trying to tear you apart. The lines are clear, the battle obvious. You or me, buddy.

But finishing off a man while he's in a coma, sleeping like a swaddled baby, feels unfair. It feels cheap. Like I'm cheating.

It's worse that I'm about to stab him through the nose, straight into the skull matter, all to be sure he freaking stays dead this time.

I look ready to plunge the tip of the blade into Caldwell's nostrils. My reflection gleams in the metal and my heart pounds harder. I hope I don't faint. Real smooth, Sullivan.

I have to ask. "What's going to happen to me?"

I hope there's enough of Gabriel left to answer me. It's my fear of what this death is going to do to me that's holding me back.

I'm brave enough to kill someone who threatens my

friends. But Caldwell isn't just anybody. If I kill Caldwell, I'll absorb all his powers. His mind reading, his teleportation, his control over the earth and water. Not to mention the gift of darkness he took from Liza when he murdered her. That's five abilities in all. Add that to the powers I already have: Jason's healing, my control of fire, and by proxy electricity, and Monroe's power over the air that I shared with Maisie.

Why the hell am I counting them? Why am I doing this obsessive compulsive, let's count it all out thing? Is it going to change anything? Somehow lessen the effects?

No.

That's a lot of power coursing through a single person. I'm going to go from 2.5 abilities to 7. There's no way I'm *not* going to be insane when I wake up.

If I wake up.

"What's going to happen to me?" I ask him again. In the past, I feared being confined to an asylum, eating mashed bananas for the rest of my days.

Now my fear is no asylum can hold me. There would be no place on Earth strong enough to would make sure the people I love stay safe.

From me.

I will be with you, Gabriel says. *I will be with you until the very end.*

I snort. "Shouldn't be long now."

I exhale and steady my hand against Caldwell's throat. With the other hand, I press the blade down harder and the skin dividing the nostrils starts to split.

Whatever happens, I beg Gabriel as Caldwell's flesh begins to give. *Don't let me hurt them. If I'm not myself just keep me far away from them.*

Ally. Maisie. Gloria. Gideon.

I have coffee for you, baby. The feel of Ally's lips brushing mine. A beautiful dream. A beautiful dream that I can take with me.

Don't let me be the reason for their death. Or even an ounce of their suffering.

Warm blood washes over my knuckles. Caldwell's eyes fly open. They're the same hazel green as my father's.

His lips pull back in a hissing snarl and both of his hands clamp down on the hand holding the knife. I only push harder and more warm blood soaks my grip. His eyes widen, and his eyebrows arch.

He sits up, slamming me into the wall. My head echoes and my grip on the knife weakens. It drops through the crack between the bed and the wall.

Fuck.

"You just won't die, will you? Like a fucking cockroach. Every time I turn around there you are."

His forearms are corded with his efforts. A vein in his forehead bulges as he squeezes harder. The tendons in my neck burn.

I can't open my mouth. I can't breathe. I must resort to insulting him telepathically. *I was just thinking the same thing about you.*

"You have so much fucking power and you don't know what to do with it. I would have made your death easy. You think you know what's best for this world? Do you think you grasp the situation or have the nerve to do what has to be done? Never. You're a child. A stupid child who doesn't know when enough is enough."

He shoves himself into my mind. A wall of fear and pain washes over me.

Jesse, Gabriel calls to me. I feel him reaching inside me, turning up my own juice. My body thrums with it. I'm going to pass out in seconds and he knows it.

He sneers. "Die already and let me handle the rest."

I throw my weight against him, pushing him upright away from the wall. I cast my shield, enveloping us both, pinning us to this time and place. I ignite.

Flames leap up his arms and neck. It scorches his hair and eyebrows. He's screaming, trying to jump away or extinguish himself. I tighten the shield. I draw our bodies closer and burn even harder.

"You don't understand what you're doing," he cries out.

"Just die already," I tell him. "And let me handle the rest."

I plunge my thumbs into his eyes, searching for the brain matter I must destroy in order for this to really be over.

The warm tissue under my nails is the last thing I feel before we're both consumed in blue flames.

CHAPTER NINETEEN

MAISIE

I'm running so hard I have a cramp in my side. Sam's long legs are made for athletics. I have half his height and even less of his speed. He could run a whole lap around this town in the time it would take me to finish my warm up stretches.

I finally recognize Sam's street. He pauses in the middle of the road to look back at me.

"Coming," I pant. "Right behind you." A hundred yards or so.

Sam freezes the way bunny rabbits freeze when they catch me walking Winnie Pug. Ears up. Nose twitching. Ready to run like hell at the slightest hint of chase.

So I freeze too. "What's wrong?"

I look up at the sky and see the helicopter. The advantage of a barren landscape is we can see the helicopter long before it arrives. Nothing blocks out the sound of its whirling blades.

Despite the distance, it'll be here in no time. Ten minutes tops.

But Sam isn't looking at the sky. He's fixated on the road in front of him.

In the middle of the road is my mom. She's dragging herself through the dirt toward Sam's house. A bloody trail follows her in the sand.

"Mom?"

She reaches out her arm again and uses it to drag herself another inch or so. Her arm is shaking from her efforts. She cradles the other arm against her body.

"Mom!"

Sam reaches her before I do, and turns her over gently. As soon she sees him, she shoves him away. But not with her hands, with her mind. The power she absorbed from Rachel flares to life and lashes out. Sam's struck, thrown through the air as if hit by a massive fist. His body arches back comically as he sails.

"Mom! Stop! He's a friend! He wants to help!"

I sound stupid and desperate, but I'm not above begging for Sam's life.

Mom groans and I kneel beside her, but I can't take my eyes off Sam. He hits the dirt and falls into a fit of coughing on impact. He doesn't look seriously hurt, though. He's opening and closing a fist and he can pull himself up to standing. Mostly okay then.

Mom's face is red with her efforts.

"Mom?" I touch her cheeks. They're hot. "Mom, what happened?"

She's bleeding from her shoulder and side. She's been shot. Is that why she's cradling her arm against her body?

Mom's hand grabs mine and squeezes so hard I cry out. "Go! Stop her before she gets your father."

I look up at Sam's house and dread washes over me.

Is Jesse in there? *Now?* Ready to kill Dad?

She's supposed to wait for me. We're going to share the power so it doesn't overwhelm either of us and make us insane like it did Rachel. That was the plan.

"She's going to bleed to death." Sam's impossibly large eyes are fixed on Mom. He's never seen something like this. Jesse's firebombing. A person bleeding to death, or even someone being shot. Or maybe he's surprised to be tossed through the air by a woman who didn't lay a finger on him.

Shock runs through me. There are people out there, people like Sam, who go their whole lives without seeing the things I've seen. They never believe this stuff is real. Never encounter it. I can't imagine what that must be like.

Anger rises in me. I want that kind of blindness.

Sam saw his dad's body though. That's something of an education.

"She'll live," I tell him, my anger softening. I'm looking at the house again.

Has Jesse already done it? Is she already dead?

"Leave her." Sam's voice rises. His anger matches my own. For a second, I'm confused. Then I realize Sam's finally face-to-face with his father's murderer. Of *course,* he'd be pissed once he processed his surprise.

"Help me move her over here." I grab her wounded arm. She cries out when I start to drag her out of the road. "You're going to get run over."

Sam looks at me.

"Sam, please." I beg him. I can't drag Mom by myself. "She's my mom."

His jaw works furiously, but he bends down and grabs her arm like I do.

With a final hoist, we get her back up against a fence.

"Eric!" she screams. "Eric!" Her blue eyes are unfocused.

Pain will do that do a person. Mental and physical, and it looks like she has both in spades. "I'm coming!"

She turns her head toward Sam's house without seeing it.

I turn too. Sam's open gate slaps against the wood, caught in a soft breeze.

Please don't let her turn into Rachel. Azrael, please.

I'm begging Azrael for a promise she can't make.

Rachel traveled with us for months. She was grumpy and dramatic but nothing about her screamed "escaped mental patient." Even the fact she was *literally* a person who left the mental hospital without permission.

In New York, Rachel killed a girl and absorbed her partis power. She wanted to be strong enough to fight Dad. But this strength came with an awful price tag.

I was the second partis Rachel tried to kill. Probably because I'm the weakest in our group. When we confronted Rachel in the military base, she fought Jesse trying to get to me. Thankfully, Jesse protected me inside her shield. But Rachel was like some crazy animal, foaming at the mouth, whose only goal was to get her jaws around my throat. She's the reason I had to wrap my ankle. And she would have torn me apart, devouring my power too, if not for Jesse.

It's stupid relying on her. Why does it matter if my sister has a cool shield? I should be stronger. I should be more able to defend myself. But I've never been good at protecting myself. The scars on my thighs are proof enough.

My mind flutters back to Jesse. If Rachel lost it when she absorbed one more power, how in the world is Jesse going to overcome all the juice coursing through Dad?

Wait, Jesse! I try to shout to her through our connection. If she's in the house now, sizing Dad up—*please wait! I'm here!*

"Don't move!" I shout to Mom.

Mom's hand reaches out and seizes my forearm.

"Mom, we can't carry you! Do you want me to stop her or not?"

Her nails bite into my forearm. She doesn't believe me, doesn't think I'll stop Jesse from killing him. And she's right. But I have a very good reason for Jesse to wait. I don't want Jesse to do it without me, to take on all the madness alone. Nor do I want her to do it with a helicopter full of men loyal to my father bearing down on us.

If Jesse dies absorbing his powers, she'll be defenseless. They'll put a bullet in her head the first chance they get.

"Please," I beg and try to tug away. I'm going to have to pry her fingers off one by one. And Sam, sweaty and red-faced, looks ready to help me.

Mom lets go.

I run. Without looking back to see if Sam follows, I sprint for the house. Okay, sprint is an exaggeration given my pitiful ankle. I'm surprised the bandage I used to wrap it is still holding up.

Sam catches up to me like it's nothing, and like a total showoff, vaults over his fence. He tucks his legs to one side and using the ledge as a balance beam, launches himself over. I run through the open gate after him.

I slow at the sight of the front door partially ajar.

"Jesse?"

The sound of helicopter blades grows louder, and my heart kick starts into action.

I tiptoe through the kitchen and stop dead in the living room.

Ice cubes slide into my stomach and melt there. My heart's rhythm wobbles. The hairs on my neck rise. Sam bumps into my back and apologizes.

I don't move, stuck in the entryway to his house. He says, "What's wrong?"

Blue light flashes from Sam's bedroom.

And the ice in my stomach solidifies.

How do I tell Sam we're too late? How does one casually mention I'm waiting to see if my sister explodes from his bedroom like some horror movie beast to rip our heads off?

Then I blink, the shock dissipating.

No. She would die first. Reboot. Her brain and body would adjust to the powers they've absorbed.

I creep to Sam's bedroom and peek inside.

My stomach bucks.

His bed is covered in black ash. It coats his pillows and coverlet. It's splashed up onto the wall like a mini volcanic eruption. The powdery black stuff covers his desk and window too in a fine layer.

I walk to the side of the bed and put my hand in it. By *it*, I mean one of the highest mounds. One of three or four heaps resting on top of Sam's bed.

I barely touch it with my fingers. It's soft. Like baby powder.

I sink my fingers into the powder harder and harder until the compacted ash is hard enough to withstand my pressure.

Jesse lies in the ash. It coats her face and nostrils. It's weird how still she is. Every muscle is unmoving.

"She's dead," Sam says.

"Yeah." I don't look at him. I can't help but rub my fingers together. "That's what happens. If we kill another person like us and take their power by force, they burn up. Then we die as that juice integrates with what we've already got. She'll come back."

Unless you're like Monroe. And you're kind enough to give your power away. Then you don't burn up like flash paper.

"She's a zombie?" he asks. "No, wait. I'm sorry. Sorry, that's not the right word, it's—um—"

"Necronite," I remind him, knowing he's spoken volumes about his small town and their views of people like me. They don't even know our proper name, only the bad one. Zombie. The derogatory term for NRD-positive people like me. "And yeah, she's got NRD. So do I. We all do."

"You all have superpowers too?" he asks. He can't hide his shock.

"No, that's different," I say. I don't want to explain the partis to him or the angels or how weird this gets. If he struggles with the idea of my neurological disorder, the rest would be way too much for him.

He doesn't say anything.

I can't look away from Dad's remains. I lift my fingers out of the ash, and my fingertips are black.

Is he really gone?

"You're free." I feel Azrael beside me before I can see her. A cold shadow at my side. Then dove gray feathers with their blue jay tips bloom in the corner of my eye. I don't turn my head to look at her. Not in front of Sam anyway. "He will never hurt you again."

"I'm free," I whisper. I bring my ash coated fingers up to my cheeks and drag them across.

My cheeks are wet.

Free. With my father's ashes on my cheeks like war paint.

I turn toward Sam, and if I look ridiculous with ash on my tear-stained face, he's nice enough not to make fun of me.

I kneel beside Jesse.

I place a hand on either side of her face. Her freckles are brighter than usual. We're getting so much sun out here in the desert. There's a smudge on her face where I touched the skin.

You're free too. She is, from Dad at least. But the war isn't over for any of us yet.

Burn scars on both sides of her face look like melted wax paper, but they're evaporating before our eyes. I was going to use my breath to wake her up, hurry her along. But I'm not sure I need to.

And when she wakes up, what's left?

To murder Mom?

Me?

"Have faith in her," Azrael says. Her voice is as steady as always. "Gabriel is seldom wrong."

If only I could be as confident. Even with both my hands blackened in his remains, I can't believe I'm free of Dad. I'm waiting for the other shoe to drop. For the next horrible thing—because there's always another horrible thing—to happen.

"He serves her well."

Who? Gabriel? I ask.

Azrael hasn't told me much about him, only that he isn't one of the bad angels.

I bend down and place my mouth near Jesse's nose. First, I kiss it and find the tip cold. The ash is bitter on my tongue.

Then I blow into her nose, dragging the air across the embers inside me and sparking life again. Sam's watching with intense curiosity but he's smart enough to keep his mouth shut.

When it's done, I sit back, dizzy.

"Now what?" Sam says. His eyes are huge and he keeps bouncing his knee, an obvious nervous tick, but at least he isn't screaming and running away.

The sound of blades whirling grows louder.

Our wide eyes meet over my sister's body.

"Help me," I say, already trying to lift Jesse up by the arms.

Sam leaps to his feet. "Help you do what?"

"Hide."

CHAPTER TWENTY

JESSE

I'm drowning in a lake of fire.

Intense pressure crushes my chest. I can't breathe. I keep trying to draw air into my lungs, but they won't fill, won't expand.

My chest, neck, and guts burn. I keep trying to step out of the fire but I can't.

Gabriel!

I'm here.

Do something, for fuck's sake! I'm not above begging. Some people might think it's weak, asking for help. But I'm sure these people were not suffocating while their body was burned alive. So they can bite me. *Please!*

Cool hands wrap around my stomach. My bare stomach. I must be naked or somehow able to feel skin on skin through my clothes. Gabriel's arms enclose me. His chin tucks into the corner of my neck. The whole of his body conforms to my back and legs. The scent of rain washes over me.

His cold skin lessens the heat rolling through me, through the black fire killing me. Or keeping me dead. It's hard to tell what's going on. This place has a dreamlike quality to it. A disconnect with time.

Wings envelop me, fully cocooning me against the warm man holding me.

Are you ready? he asks.

For what?

Before I can answer, another spark of fire explodes inside me. My back arches—if I can call it my back. I understand on some level I'm dead right now. Some part of me is in a house in Arizona, lying dead in Caldwell's incinerated remains. But my body is only part of me. The rest is here, submerged in the lake of black fire. Engulfed in pain unlike anything I could have imagined.

Gabriel holds on to me tighter, whispering sweetly in my ears.

What's happening? I beg. I'm panting as if air exists here. As if the sweat on my brow is a real symptom of my distress and not some physical representation of an experience. The dream of living. The dream of death.

Do not fight it, Gabriel suggests, dragging an icy hand across my brow. *Resistance only erodes your will more quickly. You will need your will for this. Embrace it.*

It hurts!

Only resistance can cause you pain.

And if I'm resisting, then yes. He's right. It hurts like hell. Did Caldwell murder me? Am I burning in hell like all those church jerks said I would?

Let go, he begs me. *I am here.*

I can't.

You can, he argues. *What are you afraid of?*

Becoming the monster she knows I am.

Ally with tear-filled eyes says, *you murdered eight people.*

I can't. I can't hurt her. I can't become a monster, and if I can't stop from becoming a monster, then I can't let her see it. Oh how easily our hard limits prove soft in times like this. First I said I'd never get her killed, then I got her killed twice. Then I said I'd never hurt her, but I've seen enough tears to know I botched that too. Then I promised I wouldn't become a monster...right before I littered a street in New York with bodies.

I keep making promises, and I keep breaking them.

I want to say I'll never go insane. I'll never give over to the power the way Rachel did or Caldwell did. Everything I say *won't* happen *does* happen.

You are stronger than you believe you are, Gabriel says, bracing me against him.

You keep saying that. I groan. Or at least I think I do. It's hard to tell in the suffocating darkness. I would call this place the bottom of a lake, far below where the sun's rays could reach, if only it weren't so damn hot.

There's also the fact I'm not wet.

I don't think.

And yet, I have that feeling of being suspended in water. The resistance gives the distinct impression I'm underwater because of the lazy and useless way my limbs move.

But the pain—

Another bolt rips through me and fire races up my spine.

Gabriel, please!

He holds me closer. *Let go. Jesse. Let go, I have you. You are free to be exactly what you are.*

No. I beg, writhing in the burning dark.

Please god, no.

CHAPTER TWENTY-ONE

MAISIE

Sam blinks his big eyes at me. "What?"

"Hide her!" My voice comes out like a hissy squeak.

The windows vibrate with the force of the helicopter's growling engine. The whole house trembles as I stoop down and grab Jesse's arms. But Sam isn't moving.

"Sam!"

"I'm thinking." His eyes are cast down and to the side, his leg bouncing a mile a minute.

"Can you think and move at the same time?" I wave my hand as if this is going to hurry him up. "Somewhere hidden? Somewhere they won't know to look?"

Because they will search the house. Once they find out Dad's dead, this will get very, very ugly. Very quick.

Sam snaps his fingers. "I've got it!"

He bends down and takes Jesse into his arms. He scoops

her up like she weighs nothing. Thank the Lord of Kibbles and Bits he's got muscle. It would be better if he had a fancy superpower, but I won't hold that against him. Mom, Dad, Jesse and I all have superpowers, and look where that's got us. Superpowers are way more trouble than they're worth.

He carries her through the house, her long dark hair swinging over one arm. The carpet squishes as he steps on the mess we made sewing Dad up.

Dad's dead. The truth hits me in the chest again and a void opens in my mind. It spreads. It's like not knowing what to say, but for my brain. I don't know what to think.

Dad is *dead*. The emotions swell. Relief. Regret. Sadness. Excitement. Pure bliss.

I want to run my hands over the scars on my legs and scream. Scream until I collapse into laughter. I could throw my arms open and spin and spin and spin.

Will it be like it was before I got my power? Friends and school and nothing to worry about but my homework and how dumb my outfit is? Will it be Mom and me in Chicago with ice cream and skates and a whole city to lose ourselves in?

Mom.

My elation ebbs into fear.

Mom. She's going to freak out when she finds out he's dead. She's going to lose her shit. What am I thinking? How stupid can I be? Mom's never going to be like *oh your dad is dead? Let's get ice cream.*

This isn't over.

The partis stuff. The powers. The angels and the world ending.

None of that is over now just because Jesse murdered Dad.

This is happening.

And I have my power. Things aren't better. They're about to get a lot worse.

"Can you get the door?" Sam asks.

Like a robot, I reach for the back door, grabbing the silver knob below the small curtained window.

"No, wait." He adjusts Jesse in his arms. "Look outside. We've got to make sure we can make it to the shed without them seein' us."

I open the door slowly and poke my head out.

Sam's backyard is empty. The grass—or lack thereof—is like the front of the house. Only clumps here and there rise out of the red dirt. I'm guessing he doesn't spend his weekends mowing the yard. Maybe he doesn't even have to pull weeds.

The white fence stops halfway around the house. I'm not sure what that's supposed to do. In one corner of the yard, there's a metal shed.

"Wait," I tell him.

I step out of the back of the house, pulling at the top of his borrowed jeans so they sit higher on my hips.

I ease myself into the yard, looking over each side of the fence. No helicopter parked in the red dirt. Nothing in the blue sky either. Keeping my eyes on the horizon, I wave to the boy hovering in the doorway.

He runs across the yard to the shed. I keep sweeping my eyes across the horizon for any sign of the reinforcements. Nobody yet. At the shed, I reach for the handle, wanting to open for Sam.

"No!" he hisses, and I freeze. "It'll burn you."

He turns his butt toward me.

I arch an eyebrow.

He grins automatically. "There's a bandana in my back pocket. Take it and open the door."

His eyes slide over my shoulder to the desert.

"Hurry."

I do as he says, finding the white strip of cloth in his pocket. It's smart. And I wonder if it's standard for anyone living in the desert. Where temperatures get above 100 every day, people can't walk around opening knobs and car doors without burning their hands off.

That's also why I haven't seen any black cars.

It's all starting to make sense now. There's a desert logic.

I place my wrapped hand on the silver handle and shove down. It groans, swinging out. Sam ducks inside and I do the same, peeking out one last time to make sure no one sees us.

Nada.

I pull the door closed, leaving a small crack of light for us to see by. Shelves with boxes and tools hang on the walls, and something that looks like a leather belt. Car parts maybe. The shed smells like oil and god, it's so hot in here. I feel like we stepped into a sauna only I'm too filthy to be at the spa.

The shed is small. The ceiling isn't far above Sam's head. He could reach up and touch the wooden planks, and his elbows would still be bent, if he wasn't holding on to Jesse.

"There's a trap door." He taps the wooden floor under his foot.

It doesn't look like a door. It looks like nine wooden tiles lying flush with one another, creating the floor of the shed.

He taps it again. "Pry it up."

I drop to my knees by his foot, tracing the groove on the wooden slat with my fingers. To my surprise, it gives. The wood lifts and reveals a black hole underneath.

Cool air washes up from the dark. Cool because it's underground, I realize.

He bends and sets Jesse on the edge, with her feet hanging into the darkness like she's chilling by a pool. It's weird. I snort before I can help it.

Sam waves me forward. It's hard to see him clearly in the shed without the light.

"Hold her up until I get inside," he says.

I place my hand on her back, and when she starts to pitch forward, I put a hand in front too. Only it's not quite enough. I lean her back to keep her from tumbling inside, on top of Sam.

"Got her?" Sam asks. He's got a reason to question my stability, I guess. I'm fumbling around quite a bit. But Jesse's as big as me. I don't have Sam's size advantage.

"Yeah." It's also hard to pay attention to what I'm doing. My focus wanders as I strain to hear feet. Guns. The helicopter. The reinforcements must be close now. I can't be in this shed when they get here. If I'm missing, they'll search for me and probably find this place. I'm going to have to convince Sam to hide here.

My legs shake.

"Okay." Sam pulls Jesse toward him and my pulse skyrockets when she slips from my hands. But Sam catches her, rolling her into his arms like a lumpy sack.

I'm not sure if he's partly on the ladder, or if the bunker is shallow enough for him to stand in and still have his head above ground.

He must be on the ladder. Because he descends into the dark with Jesse, leaving me to hover in the shed alone.

I crawl toward the door again, straining to hear. Nothing. It's an eerie silence with only a faint whistle of a breeze through the crack. Except, I don't hear the helicopter anymore and I don't feel its vibration through the ground. It's got to be landed by now.

My heart pounds so hard I'm going to pass out. It's the hot shed and my fear and this horrible uncertainty about what's going to happen.

Not even the cold air wafting out of the bunker is enough to calm me.

I hear a click, and I lean over the side and peer into the not-so-dark. A Coleman camping lantern illuminates the room in white-blue light.

On my stomach, I lean over into the hole for a better view.

Jesse's on a cot in the far corner. On the opposite side are two milk crates overturned. The milk crates are made of black plastic and look shiny in the artificial light. On one wall are wooden boxes. Is that where he got the light? Are those boxes full of supplies?

He must be reading my mind because he says, "This is an emergency bunker. Dad built it in case anything happened, like a natural disaster or a meltdown at the military base."

"Cool," I say, but apart from the actual temperature, it isn't very cool at all. It's claustrophobic and very end of the worldsy. Sam can only take about four steps in any direction with the ladder in the middle of the room.

I open my mouth to say more, to thank him for helping me, but before the words are out, a bucket of ice water pours into my chest. My guts tighten along with the muscles low in my abdomen.

At the same moment, my tether to Mom winks out. The silence is sudden and shocking.

"She died," I say. I blink, sitting up on my knees.

"Who?"

"Mom died."

Sam comes to the ladder and climbs the first two rungs. "She probably bled out."

I nod. I'd seen her wounds too. He has the decency to look sympathetic for my sake, though I can't blame him for hating my mom. Not after what she did.

But at the same time, I make up my mind to ask something first, however embarrassing.

"What's it?" Sam asks. He's on the ladder, his face even with mine. And he's got a cute pensive pout.

"When you kissed me," I begin and my mouth goes dry. "Did you kiss me because you like me, or were you thanking me for saving your dad? It's totally cool either way, I was just wondering."

He leans forward and kisses my lips again. This kiss is slow and deliberate and when he opens his mouth it forces my mouth open a little too. It's hard to say which kiss I like best.

He pulls back but not much. I can feel his hot breath on my face. "What do you think?" he whispers.

My face is uncomfortably hot. "Both?"

His grins. God, help me.

"You have to stay here with Jesse."

He gives her a look and then turns back at me. His smile has lost some of its shine. "Okay."

And he doesn't sound like it's okay.

"I don't want them to find you. I don't trust them, okay?"

He frowns.

"Promise me," I tell him. "Whatever you hear, stay here."

"What if she wakes up?"

I don't want him to be boiled alive by my half-crazy sister either.

"Try to talk to her. If she seems..." What? How in the world to finish that sentence? "If she seems crazy, give her space."

"Give her space?" he snorts. He gestures to the room. "Okay, *sure*."

I scoot back and start putting the floor tiles in place. "It's better than the alternative."

"The alternative?" he asks before the wooden tiles click into place, sealing him inside.

"I use my power for the third time today."

I stare at the shed floor until I'm convinced no one can see the edges. I tap on the top and Sam echoes my rhythm playfully.

It's all the reassurance I'm going to get.

"I'll be back," I say and step out into the sunlight.

CHAPTER TWENTY-TWO

MAISIE

I run through the back door, past the living room and kitchen, and out the front door. I think it'll be quicker to cut through the house than to try to go around. I hesitate on the stoop.

Beyond Sam's white fence and upturned bike, a cluster of men with guns—very big guns—stand over my mom. They aren't wearing their usual head-to-toe black. It's desert fatigues this time, cloth the color of sand except for black combat boots.

They're looking down at Mom and saying things. One looks up and I see his mouth move. No voices though. A second scans the area, craning his head as far as his neck will allow before he pivots toward the other side of the street.

He spots me and nudges the man beside him. I don't need to know what he says next. I get the gist of it. They all turn and glance my way.

Azrael?

I don't want them to find Jesse or Sam, so if I can use Azrael's influence I will. I'd do anything for my friends. I consider it one of my better qualities. It'd probably get me sorted into Gryffindor.

I am here. A cool breeze slides up the back of my sweat-soaked neck. Boy, I can't wait to get out of the desert.

I start walking toward the men, hoping to meet them more than halfway. I should have already been outside. I should have led them away from this house entirely. But they would have wanted to see where Dad died no matter what I say or do here.

Azrael's power hums in my mind and electricity glides along my skin.

"Maisie," a man says when we're about four feet apart. "Are you hurt?"

"No."

Lieutenant Perry has always been kind to me and Mom. I'd even say he loves her, but Dad would've murdered him if he'd harbored any thoughts like that. Unless Dad was the kind of person to rub a person's obsession with his wife in a guy's face.

My stomach turns as the gun resting across his chest dips. He's bending down to look into my eyes. I don't know if he's looking for shock. As he grabs my arms and begins to run a hand over my skin I realize he's looking for a wound.

"I'm not hurt."

He lets go of me and steps back. "What happened here?"

Azrael shifts inside me.

"They were fighting," I say.

He wants me to elaborate.

"Mom, Dad, and Jesse."

"She's alone?" Because of course he'd focus on the threat above anything else.

"I think so," I say. "I haven't actually seen her in action yet." A half-lie.

"She blew up half the damn town," a second guard says, pulling at the collar of his shirt.

Perry holds up a hand to silence him, and for a moment, I'm struck by the sight of blood on two of his fingers. It's drying on the flesh exposed outside his fingerless gloves.

"Dad's dead," I say.

Perry's jaw flexes. "Did she hurt your mother?"

"No. The police shot her." I can't help but notice his lack of reaction to Dad's death.

Perry doesn't look happy or convinced by this. Azrael's breeze blows through me, sliding over Perry's body like a ghostly sigh. I watch Perry's eyes glaze as his mind is forced to accept the truth.

"Mom died from her injuries." He's got to know this since Mom didn't disintegrate into an ash cloud. But then again, Lieutenant Perry's just a guy. He's head of team, sure, but a guy. How much did Dad tell him about all this crazy partis stuff?

Perry kicks at the ground, his jaw working furiously.

"I told him to take me with him!" he kicks the dirt again and swears. "Where is she?"

I glance at Mom and scrunch my brow. I'm playing dumb on purpose.

"Your sister," Perry hisses. He's not mad at me, but having an angry man with a gun growl at me is enough to make my pulse jump.

"She killed Dad. She must have because he's gone."

"Where were you?" Perry says, grabbing my upper arm. His fingers bite into my arm. "When your mother was attacked, where were you?"

"In town!" I squeal. My arm burns.

I say nothing as he drags me into Sam's house.

"Is she fully conscious yet? Or is she still dead?"

"I don't know!" This rings true because I don't know. Jesse could have woken up. She could be out of the hole by now. But she was breathing when I left her with Sam.

I turn to glower at Perry. "You're hurting me."

He pulls me into the house. My sneakers squeal on the linoleum as he drags me up to full height. "Which room?"

I point at Sam's bedroom. No point in trying to lie now.

Perry drags me into the room, his fingers digging into my upper arm. He has to turn his body and duck his head to get through the doorway. As he crosses the threshold, he finally lets go of me.

The second time around, it looks worse.

The wall behind Sam's bed is scorched black. His bed is soaked in ash, and particles of it hang in the air above the bed, dancing in the light coming through the window. It's like a chimney exploded, vomiting soot all over everything.

And there's the blood. A spray across the wall. A destroyed pillow. The pillowcase could work as a Trick 'r Treat sack, but not much else.

"He's dead." Perry's mouth falls open.

"I wasn't lying!" Because I didn't have a choice.

He surveys the grimy room for several heartbeats more. I'm counting by heartbeats because mine are pounding in my ears. I'm praying he doesn't see all the footprints. Mine and Sam's and the mark we left in the soot when we dragged her away. All the evidence is right there.

"Where are her friends?" Perry glares at me. "The crazy bitch, the so-called psychic. And that whore with the nose ring. Where are they?"

I can't speak. My mouth hangs open. I've never heard Perry talk about people like that before.

He nudges me hard and I fall back a step.

"Spill it. Where are they?" He points at the tracks. "They helped her get away."

"You can't talk about people that way." My face burns. "You can't even *think* about them that way!"

"Donovan," Perry says, turning back toward the door. Until he does it, I don't realize there's another guard so close. "Send Black Hawk Four to the military base."

"No!" I scream.

He smiles.

"She's not there!"

"If they're at the base, then who helped her get away?" he asks, with an arched eyebrow.

I don't say anything. Hot tears fill my eyes and spill over my cheeks. Here I am again, choosing. Choosing between people I love. If I don't give up Jesse, they'll go to the military base and find Gloria, Ally, and Gideon.

If they're even awake, they're weak. They can't possibly win against another attack so soon after the battle they just endured. Jesse isn't there to protect them. And she might not be there in time.

Give up Jesse or let the others die?

Don't give up Jesse and watch her kill my mother.

"Did you hide her?" Perry asks.

"No."

It's the only word I have. It's small and pathetic, but it's all I got.

"No."

Perry knocks me back. Azrael's there. She places a hand on my shoulder to steady me as I face Perry.

He speaks without blinking. "Donovan?"

"Yeah, boss."

"Send the Hawk in."

"Sure thing." Donovan gives the order. "That it?"

"*No.*" His word is a mockery of my own refusal. "Search this place."

CHAPTER TWENTY-THREE

MAISIE

*P*erry grabs me by the arm again, and I grit my teeth. I don't want to cry out like a baby, but he's holding on to me so hard. The skin under his fingers is ghost white where he's squeezing, and the surrounding parts turn redder by the second.

Guards flood Sam's room. They tear clothes out of his closet, flip his mattress. When they realize Jesse isn't in here, they start tearing apart the living room. Something hits the ground, a large piece of furniture probably, and the whole house shakes. I hear something break and pinch my eyes closed. It's hard to listen to, them tearing apart every room of Sam's house.

I bite down on my hysteria. I want to scream at them. Throw myself at them.

But what good will that do?

I'm so sorry, I think at Sam, like he can hear me. This is probably the worst day of his life. His dad died, his house is ransacked, and all because I came to his town with all my bullshit.

Tears sting the corners of my eyes.

The first round of "Clear" rings through the house as men continue to search and continue to find nothing.

"I told you," I say through gritted teeth. "She's not here."

As if the sound of my voice infuriates him, he pulls me forward, dragging me through the door, through the living room—which looks absolutely demolished—and out the front door. I can't walk as fast as him. I trip, but Perry keeps hauling me forward.

There's nothing in the road. No bodies. They've already begun to clean up the cops' bodies. Good. The sooner we get out of this town, the better Sam and all his friends and family will be.

Perry drags me over the sand toward a helicopter. It sits in the middle of a wide-open area. A few boulders and dry trees litter the landscape, but that's it. It's probably why they landed there, a nice big open space to put a military helicopter.

As we get closer, I can see through the open doors.

Mom's lying there. They'd put her on a blue tarp, her hair spread around her head like one of the mosaic saints common in Dad's cathedrals. Someone has removed her shirt and cleaned the wounds on her arms. The black stitches are thin and they're shiny like plastic.

Perry shoves me toward the helicopter, and I slide on the sand. My hands fly out in front of me to catch myself. I grab onto the lip of the doorframe before I face plant it.

"Do your thing," he says. Only it doesn't sound like a polite suggestion or request. He's talking to me the way he talks to the other guards.

"My thing?" I ask, pivoting to face him.

He puffs out his cheeks and huffs, in and out, in and out.

He looks like he's preparing to give birth. "Your freak thing. Do it."

"You've never been mean before, Perry." I frown at him.

"Did you think we'd still be friends after you ran off with your sister and got your mother killed?"

I don't immediately hop up into the helicopter and blow into Mom's nose, so he nudges me with the butt of his gun.

"They're monsters," I say.

"You chose your side. Live with it."

Is that how he sees this? That escaping the tower where Dad forced me to await my execution was a betrayal? Do prison guards feel betrayed when an inmate runs for their lives?

"If you don't get into that helicopter and revive your mother, I'm going to show you a real monster," he says. Perry snarls and snaps his teeth at me to make his point.

I pull myself up into the helicopter and scoot across the floor to Mom.

I reach down and brush a lock of blond hair off her face.

I don't want her to wake up.

I don't want her to know Dad's dead because I can only imagine what she'll do next. She wasn't the most emotionally stable person before his death, and this is going to send her right over the edge.

"Hurry up." Perry glances around at the town and encroaching desert.

He's looking for Jesse. He thinks she'll come back any second and that's why he wants Mom awake. Mom's abilities are his only chance to get out of the desert alive. But he's a fool if he thinks Mom will protect him.

I don't see a way around it, so I bend down like I'm going to kiss Mom on the nose. I draw breath, ready to reignite her life and set the clock in motion.

Or I could *pretend* to do it.

Before I decide on my plan of action, Mom's eyes fly open.

She blinks once, then twice like a sleepy kid. She jolts upright so fast I sit back before I get head-butted.

After a confused stare at her bra and bare arm, her gaze goes to Perry. Perry stands at attention, his back straight and gun in position.

"Mrs. Caldwell," he says, and the only thing missing is the salute.

"Where is he?" she asks.

Perry doesn't speak. He only licks his lips.

"Is he dead?"

"Yes, ma'am," he replies, his voice soft. That's the Perry I know. The sweet one. The kind one. The one who followed me down the sidewalk in Millennium Park, trying to keep my handlebars straight because I wanted to ride without training wheels. Perry who always brought me a little something from his assignments. A plastic pony. An apple shaped eraser. A Chinese finger trap.

I've known him all my life. Could two months away from him change everything?

All because I went with Jesse? Because I chose to protect myself instead of be murdered? What kind of friend is he if he expected me to stay behind?

Mom's face screws up. She hiccups once, and then the floodgates burst. Tears stream down her cheeks. A low cry snowballs into a full-body screech. Her whole frame shakes. She grabs fistfuls of her own hair and pulls until strands rip free.

I'm shoved out of the helicopter as if by a giant invisible hand. I hit the ground and the air is knocked out of me. I skid across the desert floor, inhaling sand.

I choke and spit, unable to breathe.

Mom did this. She used Rachel's power to throw me out.

This is all I'm able to process as I tumble along in the dirt. As I slide to a stop, the impact makes my back muscles seize. A coughing fit overtakes me. I push myself up on my knees and elbows. I try to spit out as much grit as I can. The dust in my eyes feels like sandpaper. They're watering like crazy, but it isn't clearing my vision fast enough. I can't see.

Between fat droplets, a menacing shadow pulls itself out of the helicopter.

Mom.

And her fury hits me like a tidal wave.

Ready or not, here she comes.

CHAPTER TWENTY-FOUR

JESSE

*J*esse.

Gabriel calls to me through the pulsing darkness. It contracts and relaxes like the warm body of a desert snake. To think the darkness is a void, an empty space, is so wrong. If it were, then what's sliding against me, squeezing me, then releasing me? I keep my eyes pinched shut because I don't want to know the answer to that question.

Jesse, let me in.

So we're back to this again.

And here I thought I'd made progress. I've grown into my powers. I can use the firebombs and shields with mere thoughts. When Monroe died, I'd shared his control over air with Maisie. No fuss.

No kicking. No screaming.

What are you afraid of? Gabriel whispers in the dark.

His breath slides across my cheek and a part of me realizes he *is* the darkness in this place. And if I open my eyes, I might see him for exactly what he is. Enormous. Serpentine. And as ancient as creation.

You're not an angel. And you're not my imagination. You're—

—some gargantuan beast I can't begin to fathom.

Horror ices my skin. Panic spreads in my mind, pushing all rational thought against the walls I've constructed to make my existence small and manageable.

Look at me.

I can't. I can't open my eyes. The dark presses against me, ready to swallow me whole, and I can't lose myself in the crushing madness. I can't lose even the smallest part of myself, because I love a girl named Ally, and everything I do has the potential to hurt her.

I can't let her see me that way.

If you want to save her, look at me.

He's getting better at his ultimatums. I open one eye.

Gabriel's standing there. On *what* is the question. We're suspended in this pitch black place. There's no above or below.

I'm in his arms. If I can call them arms. Even with his human body, his pretty face, I can see right through it. The serpentine dark coils around me. It's only given me something comprehensible to look at.

I am your ally, he says. His lips are at my ear again and I smell the storm on him. Rain and lightning. And a sound like thunder rolling in the distance.

I can feel my mind stretching to its limit. One wrong thought and it might rip at the seam.

Like Rachel.

In my memory, she sits on the floor of her living room. She's taken a knife to both of her arms, let herself bleed all over the expensive carpet. She's drawn unintelligible symbols which she claimed would keep the bad angels *out*, whatever that meant. The blood drying brown was meant to be a protective circle, but she'd gotten as much of the blood on herself as she had on the carpet.

When she'd turned her wide vacant eyes on me, rocking and muttering through her shattered reality, I'd known she'd lost herself.

Lost herself, because some—*thing*—like Gabriel had pushed itself inside her and broken her mind.

Do not be afraid, Gabriel says, letting his lips kiss my neck. He kisses me again, and again, moving toward my ear until hot breath warms the tender lobe.

I'm waiting to have my throat torn out.

A cool breeze blows. As soon as it touches my skin, something sparks inside me. An ember glows. I feel Maisie. This wind smells and tastes like her—bubblegum and soda pop.

I chose you for your strength. You will bend, not break.

"I bet you say that to all the girls." I'm digging deep for humor. Anything I've got to help me feel more like myself. More like I'm in control of what's going to happen.

The heat inside me builds, chasing away the coldness enveloping me.

I cannot hold the power for much longer, he says. *You must accept me.*

It sounds dirty the way he's saying it. It's coming across as an eager but patient boyfriend, questing for his girlfriend's virginity.

Let me in, he whispers, kissing my ear. *You are strong enough for this.*

"No!" A shrill scream slices the darkness in half. "No! Please!"

Maisie.

Heart wrenching sadness stabs through me. Anger. Fear.

Please hurry, a boy whispers. Not Gabriel. *I think she's in trouble.*

Maisie needs me. As afraid as I might be of what's going to happen to me, my fear for Maisie is greater. Giving myself a goal helps. I have some pressing task to complete and that urgency helps pull me out of the emotions engulfing me.

I let go. As soon as I do, a current pulls me in all directions, weighing me down as I swim hard for the surface.

My lungs swell to bursting, and the surface is still a million miles away. I thrash in darkness, unsure if I'm swimming toward salvation or my death.

Slowly, inch by inch, I begin to rise.

A sound vibrates the waters. It grows louder and louder, building in intensity until I can feel the rumble deep in my chest.

At first I imagine a boat with a giant propeller. It's too dark to see. A boat could roll right over my head, and spray my brains into the dark water. I wouldn't know what hit me. It's a horrifying prospect.

This isn't real.

There's no boat.

There's no dark water.

Yet the vibration in my chest is real. It has the sharp taste of reality. It isn't the cotton candy confectionary of dreams. And I'm about to find out what that vibration really is.

Ready? Gabriel asks.

Without waiting for an answer, Gabriel pulls me up.

I break the surface, gasping for air.

CHAPTER TWENTY-FIVE

MAISIE

om steps into Sam's bedroom, and at the sight of the scorched walls and clumps of black ash, she collapses to her knees.

She bends forward, putting her hands in it. With her skin coated black, she rubs her fingers together, as if trying to figure out what it is. But she knows. The tears and shaking shoulders say it all.

Her sobs grow louder, and Perry shifts uncomfortably behind me. He chose not to search with the others. I guess he wants to be near Mom in case Jesse shows up. But they're both treating me like I'm the enemy.

Her cries wind me.

Mom has been through so much. She was taken from her home and imprisoned in a torture camp. How hard Mom and Dad worked to be together, how hard he worked to free her from the camp, me sparking to life in Mom's belly when she was trapped in that place, and the morbid truth that they'd given her a break from torture for nine months, only because the scientists wanted me. A baby, brand new, and a clean slate for experimentation with a neurological disorder they knew little about—NRD. Necronitic Regenerative Disorder. It gives me, and all zombies like me, the ability to die but not stay dead. As long as the brain isn't damaged, we'll keep on kicking.

What would've happened to me if Dad hadn't taken me out of the camp and hidden me in the adoption system? What kind of life would I have had?

I shiver.

Mom turns on me with her red face and tear-stained cheeks. "Why didn't you protect him?"

Perry's hand squeezes my shoulder as if to warn me not to run.

My stomach clenches. I'm ready for more abuse—either from her or Perry. I brace for it the best I can. Knowing it's coming isn't enough to keep my heart from racing.

She pulls herself to standing, and grabs my forearms. She squeezes hard enough to leave bruises. I grit my teeth to keep from crying.

She doesn't let go. "You left him! How could you!"

A cocktail of emotions flood through me.

How can I be grateful to Dad for saving me, yet also relieved he's dead? I pity Mom. I can't imagine going through half of what she's been through, but I'm mad at her. I'm mad she won't work with Jesse, and that she won't listen to us. I'm mad she took Dad's side when she should have taken mine.

We're messed up. Our whole family is *so* messed up.

If I survive this, which I won't, I'm going to need therapy for years.

Her fingernails rake my skin. "Where is she?"

My heart's running like a rabbit at the sight of a dog. *Where is she?* It's a simple question. But it's as loaded as a gun in a game of Russian Roulette. My answer will determine how much I suffer and if Jesse and Sam will suffer with me.

Perry nudges me with the butt of his gun. His gun. My stomach rolls.

"The boy," Mom says. It's an accusation. Through her grief, she's replaying the last minutes of her life before she bled out.

"He left." I keep my voice and face flat. "He got scared and took off."

"No," she says. "He's here. Find him."

Anger makes my cheeks hot. I want to unleash on her. But I can't. Not only because there's a gun in my back, but because I can't forget my mom just lost the person she loves most in the world. It doesn't matter he was a wretched jerk who totally deserved to die. She loved him.

Still loves him.

"You killed his dad. I brought him back," I say. "I cleaned up *your* mess."

I watch her face for a reaction. I search her red eyes for any recognition of what I'm saying. I don't see any. Has she become totally callous to murdering people?

"It was his dad in the hotel," I say again. I want her to remember. Her expression doesn't change. "You lied to me. You said he let us use the house."

"Why does that matter?"

I blink back shock.

It isn't that she doesn't remember. She doesn't *care*.

"Your father is *dead*. You left your father to fend for himself. Even after I *begged* you to resurrect him and you went to go save another man?" Mom's nostrils flare. "You saved someone you didn't even know but your own father—"

My heart pounds harder. "Sam's dad is innocent!"

Innocent. Unlike Dad who's murdered hundreds of thousands of people. Dad who *chose* to fight and is—was—probably the entire cause of it all.

She shakes me. "You didn't know him! You didn't even know him!"

I don't know if she's talking about Dad or Sam's dad.

I don't respond. She's not yelling in my face because she wants an answer.

She's hurting. She's mourning. I understand. And she can be mad at me all she wants because Sam's alive and his dad is going to be okay and as soon as we're out of this town the better.

Mom's eyes flutter, blinking rapidly, as tears flow over her cheeks. She turns away with a sneer.

"Get her away from me."

Perry clamps down on my shoulder, and pulls me from the doorway. He marches me through the living room, out of the door and through the fence. He's leading me to the helicopter. He's going to make me wait in the scorching hot sun as punishment. And if I have any doubt how he views my behavior he says, "In some militaries, dishonor is punishable by death."

"I never joined the military." I wait for him to bring the butt of the gun down on the back of my skull and end my misery.

Instead, he shoves me into the white picket fence. He spins me around to face him.

I stare him down. There's nothing he can do to me that's worse than what my father did.

And he must know it by looking at me. His hatred softens to disgust. He smiles.

"You want to know a secret?" He's whispering, failing to

control the grin twitching at the corners of his mouth. "I'm not sorry you let him die. The bastard had it coming."

His face is close to mine and I can smell his awful breath. I'd bet anything he has a rotten tooth in there somewhere.

"If I must kiss someone's ass, I'd choose your mother's any day of the week."

His crude leer makes my stomach flop.

Then his smile is gone. "You need to know where your loyalties lie. If you're not with us, then we can't trust you. You know what we do to people we don't trust, right?"

Gun fire erupts at the back of the house.

Jesse!

Perry drags me toward the backyard. But when we enter the backyard, Jesse isn't there. No firebombs or purple shields.

There's a boy in the sand, on his back, coughing blood out of his mouth.

Did they find him? Did they find Jesse?

Or did he leave the safety of his hiding place for another reason.

It doesn't matter. The result will be the same.

"Sam!" I rush to shield him with my body, but Perry jerks me back. My shoulder aches.

No. *No.*

Why didn't you listen to me? Why didn't you stay hidden?

I blink back tears.

Another soldier puts a bullet in his chest. I watch the gun kick. I see Sam's body get knocked back.

"Sam!" I scream again as the bright red blood blooms through his Sun Devils jersey. The word *Devil* bleeds.

Hold on. I don't say it aloud, but I'm begging with all my being. The soft lips I kissed not long ago are caked in blood now. *Hold on. I'll bring you back. If you die, I'll bring you back. Don't be afraid.*

He knows I will. There's a clarity in his eyes, a fearlessness.

He believes in me. He has absolute faith my power.

Or he does until the moment Perry puts a bullet in his head.

CHAPTER TWENTY-SIX

JESSE

My eyes fly open.

I'm soaking wet. No. Not wet.

I'm cold. My skin and face are icy. And I'm shivering like I crawled out of a winter river. This is normal for someone who was dead and then decides not to be. But it isn't the low body temperature alone that has me quaking. I lift my stiff fingers, and *man*, they're stiff. My finger brushes cold and crumbly.

Dirt.

My heart blasts off like it's heading to the moon.

Dirt. Dirt. Oh god, I've been buried alive. *Again.* How do these things keep happening to me?

I stretch my arm overhead and don't feel the rough edge of a coffin or wooden box. No grainy splinters catch under my nails.

I pull myself to sitting position and nothing conks me on the head. Not buried. But definitely underground. I'll never forget the smell of packed earth. I exhale a sigh of relief, as much as my sore, achy chest will allow.

I'm sitting in some kind of cellar. A Coleman lantern resting on top of a stack of supply boxes illuminates the room. Dirt walls and floors. But there's the bench I'm on and another chair in the corner. Wait. Is this a bench or a cot? It's hard to see in the poor light.

But squinting in the dark, there's one thing I'm sure I don't see: a boy.

Please hurry. I think she's in trouble.

Who said that? Those words, like the vibration that woke me, had the sharp edge of reality.

Where's the boy?

And where's Maisie?

The vibration, whatever that was, is gone too.

But I remember the helicopter I saw in the distance before I killed Caldwell, before I murdered him and took his power.

His power.

Gabriel?

I reach up and pat my body. I pat my face and neck like I expect to find another nose or horns jutting out of my face.

"Gabriel?" I speak aloud when my mental desperation doesn't make him reappear.

I catch the scent of rain and a sudden heat washes through the cool darkness, but he doesn't materialize.

Go, he says.

That's it. A one-word command. No, "hey, how you doing? No, "hey, welcome back!" Or "I'm glad you're alive and not completely insane!"

Jesse!

Pop. Pop. *Poppoppop.* Pop.

My head jerks up at the sound of muffled gunfire.

Another gunshot followed by screaming. Maisie's screaming.

The muscles in my body go rock hard.

Without thinking, I open up. It's easy. I want to know if Maisie's okay one second. The next, I'm reaching across time and space to find her.

Only I'm not reaching with my arms or a stick. I'm reaching with my mind.

I find a soldier first and the thoughts and feelings pouring out of him—*god he's just a kid what a fucked up job this is I'm glad the bastard is dead I would resign this goddamn minute if I didn't think Perry would put a bullet in my fucking head the second*—

This mental vomit accompanies the image of a boy on the ground, writhing, coughing blood. A puddle oozes out from under his arm, turning the dirty sand red.

Is that happening now? Is some boy being murdered right above my head. The boy. Somehow, it's the boy who spoke to me when I was unconscious. *Hurry*. So, is he Maisie's friend? That's the only possibility that makes any sense.

Thinking about him makes me focus on him. I shift from the soldier to the boy. Pain hits me so hard I'm winded. I roll off the bench and hit the dirt on my knees. I'm sucking air and it's not coming in. My lung whistles, I'm drowning.

No. Not me. The boy's drowning. His lungs are filling up with his own blood, and every time his muscles contract against the pain, a flash of white hot agony tears through him and spots dance before his eyes.

Maisie skids to a stop in front me.

No, not me. The boy. I've got to keep reminding myself.

A man has Maisie by the arm, hurting her. I can see his fingers biting into her flesh. I want to kill him. Take his gun and shove it into his mouth.

Maisie's crying. *It's okay. It's not your fault. It's okay.*

Gratitude swells inside of me. For all Maisie's done for my dad.

My mind rears back. Fuck my dad. No, not *my* dad. The boy's dad. She did something for the boy's dad.

And she wants to save me too. I can tell, I can see it in her desperate face as she strains against the soldier holding her back. *And maybe she can save me, maybe—*

The man holding Maisie lifts his gun and points it at my head.

No.

I jump to the gunman's head. I reach inside him, and instead of finding the anger I expect, I find a cold emptiness. I try to seize his mind, seize his gun hand at the very least, and stop him from murdering the kid.

I'm either too slow or I don't have Caldwell's mastery of this power yet. He could be in several minds at once. The minds of a whole army. He could read them and control them as easily as his own body. I've seen him do it. But Caldwell had his powers for years.

I've had this ability for minutes.

I jump back to the boy the same instant the image of his mother standing at the back door smoking a cigarette flashes through my mind. *She's never coming back. She's never coming back, and if I die, Dad will be all—*

The gun goes off.

It's like someone yanks the plug out of the wall. Static, fuzz, and pictures and then pitch black dark.

I fall out of the boy's head and onto my forearms. I gulp air. The pain I've been struggling against leaves me all at once. I roll onto one side, desperate to breathe. Desperate to right the world again.

Jesse, Gabriel whispers. His hands press into my back. He's more solid than before. More solid with Maisie and Georgia above us. Is it the power? Is the power I absorbed his too?

Yes, he answers.

I don't know if he's saying this or me. I'm beginning to worry there isn't much of a difference anymore.

Move, Gabriel commands.

The tenor of male voices echo overhead.

They're coming.

"He came from in here," someone says.

I can't decide if I'm hearing the voice with my ears, my mind, or a combination of the two. My senses are blurring. Once, it was easy knowing the difference between seeing something and hearing it. Now I can't tell the difference between what I see and what someone else sees. What I feel and someone else feels.

Footsteps stomp on the ground above. Heavy boots come down on whatever separates this cellar from the world. Every time a heavy boot comes down, dirt tumbles from the ceiling. Little streams fall into my hair and hit my shoulders.

"Tear this place apart," someone says.

I'm pulling myself to a sitting position as objects are shifted and tossed aside. They bounce off the floor as they tumble down. It's only a moment before I'm discovered.

You must leave, Gabriel says again as if that's helpful.

Show me the freaking exit, I hiss inwardly.

I search the four walls and ceiling for a way out. Big mistake.

With my chin tilted up, a trickle of dirt hits me square in the face and I cough.

I swallow it. My eyes bulge with the strain of not releasing a cough tickling my throat. My eyes burn and water. As soon as I'm sure I can't hold it anymore, my mouth opens and I gulp air.

Only to sneeze.

The shuffling feet stop.

Go! Gabriel commands. He wants me to use Caldwell's power.

I don't know how! I fire back. *Yelling at me isn't going to make it happen!*

Caldwell's mind shit is disorienting enough. I'm not ready to open another power box and access all the fun shit inside.

I might not be ready, but I'm out of options, and time.

A scraping sound screeches overhead. I look up in time to see a square of light outline a panel. I dart into the darkest corner as fingers burrow into the ceiling and begin to lift the panel out of place.

A square of light hits the dirt floor and my cramped dark space isn't so dark anymore.

Gabriel!

Thrashing wings enfold me as more light pours inside.

CHAPTER TWENTY-SEVEN

MAISIE

S am.

Perry and two other men are in the shed, tearing it apart. Like a pack of wild dogs on a corpse, they're rough and thorough. A giant wrench and a stack of clay pots are thrown from the shed into the yard. The beautiful, sweet boy with his brains thrown across the sand lies there. No one is even looking at him.

I kneel beside Sam and take his hand. It's clammy. Cold but sweaty, with sand sticking to it. I turn it over and it rolls under its own weight, heavy as a lion's paw.

I touch his wrist bones, his elbow, and his upper arm. I don't go higher because I can't look at his face. I make it all the way to the collarbone, but the blood there makes me turn away.

I should look.

Someone should look. Because Sam deserves to be remembered. He deserves to have a witness to the horrible thing that happened to him.

He deserved much more, this boy in his Sun Devils T-shirt. Sam was brave enough to stay with me, to show me he could help me in repayment for saving his dad.

I wipe at my tears with the back of my hand, dragging the knuckles across my eyes.

"You should have gone to the hospital." My voice cracks. "You should have gone with your dad and you'd be alive. You'd be safe and sound in some waiting room now. Why didn't you go? Why didn't I *make* you go?"

"Did you hear that?" The commotion stops. "A sneeze."

"Look underneath," someone says. Perry? I can't tell. All the voices sound far away.

"Find the door. There's got to be a door."

They begin pulling up the floor.

A class ring on Sam's ring finger is nearly too hot to touch. I work it off the finger, wiggling it over the knuckle past the bone. The yellow gold ring rolls in my palm, sparkling in the sunlight. The gemstone is a deep red. The color of the blood oozing out of his chest. It's engraved on all sides. On one side, there's a basketball etched into the markings. In the other, the happy and sad face associated with drama.

I was right about the dramatics.

I cry again. Harder this time. I squeeze the ring until my hand aches.

Kill them all. Kill every one of them.

"Clear," someone shouts.

"Go down anyway. I want visual confirmation."

The stairs creak the way they had when Sam carried down my sister, something I could never have done myself. I wouldn't have known about the hiding place if not for Sam. They would have found her and killed her. There's so much I owe this boy for, and I'll never be able to repay him.

"Clear. There's nothing down here but supplies."

Big black boots skid to a stop in the sand beside me. Equally big hands grab onto my shoulders and lift me off the ground. I'm dragged away from Sam's body against my will.

I don't want to leave him alone and defenseless again.

Perry wraps his hand around my throat and lifts me into the air. My legs dangle. I grab his hand and forearm, trying to pull myself up and relieve the pressure crushing my throat.

"You'd save her, but not your own mother?" Perry shakes me and I'm certain my neck's going to break. Perry doesn't care. "She's going to destroy all of us. Is that what you want?"

And you thought he wouldn't? That Mom wouldn't?

He shakes me. He shakes me until my teeth rattle in my jaw.

"You've killed us," he says and drops me. Pain shoots up my legs and into my hips on impact. I draw in air, trying to breathe. My neck aches. It's already swelling.

What did Dad tell them? That he was the Messiah? He was the only one who could save the whole world? By serving him, they were protecting all of mankind, but especially their own butts?

What idiots.

I roll my eyes up to meet his. "Good! We should die. Every single one of us. We're not worth anything!"

I squeeze Sam's ring until my hand cramps, but I'm afraid if I don't, I'll lose it. I shouldn't take it. It should go to Sam's dad. I didn't know him. I can count on one hand the number of hours I spent with him. But holding it makes me brave.

Perry's face twists into a rage. I tense, expecting a giant boot to slam into my guts.

The intercom in Perry's ear buzzes to life. "They're here."

The earth shakes. I feel it rumbling under my palms. A huge black helicopter whizzes overhead. Perry and I both look up as it flies over the smoking town in the direction of the army base. Toward my defenseless friends.

Jesse! If she isn't in the underground bunker, then she's awake. She might be close, watching. If she's close enough to hear me, she needs to know about the danger. *The helicopter! It's headed right for them!*

I wait for any kind of recognition. I'm desperate for any sign Jesse heard my plea and is rushing off to save our friends. Nothing.

No telltale buzz in my head the way it felt when Dad snuck in and started poking around.

Only silence stretches in all directions, and the smell of smoke and blood from the town we've destroyed.

What if she isn't herself?

What if Jesse is as crazy as Dad was? It was a lot of power to absorb and now it's all inside her.

Azrael? I beg.

She is near, Azrael whispers, and with her words I feel the familiar breeze of her power blowing through me. *But she cannot help you now.*

I squeeze my new talisman in my fist. The blood-stained gold ring and Azrael's power blowing through me—

They're all I have left.

CHAPTER TWENTY-EIGHT

JESSE

Great black wings surround me, cocooning me in darkness. It's a tight space to squeeze through. Pressure builds in my head, and I have the distinct impression my ears need to pop.

When I'm certain my brains are oozing out of my ears, the dark opens like the expanding aperture on a camera, and I tumble out.

Literally.

My elbows scrape stiff carpet as I roll into the base of an armchair. Hard.

I groan, rubbing my elbow as electricity runs along the bone. Gee-*zus*. Freaking funny bone. Why in the world did someone name it the funny bone? There's nothing funny about it.

Before I can even pull myself from my knees to standing, minds press in on me again. It's stronger than before. Is that because I used the teleportation thingy?

The more I use the power, the more it will overtake me? That's *great*.

Now the dull roar of a cafeteria, a chorus of voices echoes in an enclosed space. Some dialogues are louder. Others barely a whisper. If I focus on one—

Oh god, Sam. What did I do? What did I do? I should have made you get in that ambulance. I should have made you get as far away from this place as—

I pull back, tears spilling over my cheeks. I blink rapidly but that doesn't seem to clear my eyes any faster.

Maisie.

I leap into her mind at once. Instantly, my throat is so sore I can barely swallow. Sweat pools in the small of my back as my damp shirt clings to me. My skin is covered in grit. I'm staring at the black boots that will kick my skull in at any moment.

Her fear rolls over me. She's crushed and in shock, and I feel all those feelings like they're my own.

How did Caldwell do it? How did he read minds without losing himself in the emotion? Or was he such a bastard no amount of emotion could chip at his cold heart?

You are stronger, Gabriel says. He's standing over me. He reaches out and pulls me up.

Again, I'm struck by how solid he is despite the nearness of Maisie and Georgia.

He could not go as deep as you can now.

I groan. "Lucky me."

A footstep falls, and still holding onto the overturned armchair, I turn to find a gun barrel taking aim at my head. The trigger is pulled and a bullet explodes from its black eye.

This is it.

I'm going to die.

I'll never survive a gunshot wound straight to the head.

Only the bullet doesn't blow out my brains. It pings right off me.

The bullet bounces off me and sails through the living room. It blows through a slab of drywall.

The shooter's jaw falls open. The scar running from the corner of his eye to the top of his cheek dimples as he does.

He pulls the trigger again and again, and sends those bullets zinging around the room after the first.

I lift my hands and gaze at the back of my knuckles in amazement. Then I turn my hands over, looking at the skin as if I don't know what it is. Bulletproof skin? No way!

Faint purple shimmers along my skin. My shield is up. It's so close to my body that I can barely see it. I erected it without even knowing it.

Ah, not bulletproof. Just permanently shielded.

The shooter raises his gun again, but I ignite him.

With barely a whisper of an idea, his body explodes in flames. Immolated on the spot.

The flames lick the ceiling, blackening the white popcorn surface. I screech.

I'm about to burn someone's house down. I've burned my own house down, and that was super depressing. Having someone else burn my house down would be even worse.

Water, I think. I need water.

I turn around the room once, trying to get an idea of where I might find a bucket or hose, but I freeze. Something rattles. A pressure is filling the room and I can feel it in my stomach, low, near the top of my thighs.

Are the walls *groaning*?

Water explodes out of the kitchen spigot. It sprays across the counters and floor like a fountain.

The walls vibrate as more pipes strain against the mounting pressure.

I pull at my face. "Oh my god, that's not what I meant!"

Cindy. The water thing was Cindy's power. I saw her explode a toilet once.

I glance around the room that is now not only burning, but incurring flood damage too.

At least the burning man has stopped screaming. Thanks to the growing puddle he's lying face down in.

And I'm not the only one who's tried to destroy this house today. All the furniture is overturned, some of it broken. The bedroom door is only half on its hinges.

I hope the owners have good insurance. But flood damage isn't covered in most policies. Maybe it would be best if the earth opened and swallowed it whole?

The earth starts to shake.

"Oh god, what now?"

Gabriel arches a brow. "You control the earth. The water. Fire and air."

The earth?

Dammit. *Liza.* In addition to knocking someone unconscious with the snap of her fingers, the partis could make the world shake because she'd killed her boyfriend Jake for that power. And who tore Liza apart for that power? Caldwell, of course.

"Stop!" I whine. I grab onto the overturned armchair. "I don't want the earth to shake."

But the pictures on the walls keep rattling. The silverware in the drawers keep jumping. The glasses in the cupboards clink together.

Jesse!

My name catches my attention despite the undercurrent of a dozen internal monologues.

The helicopter!

I focus on the voice and the world shifts.

Maisie. I'm in Maisie's head again, looking out through Maisie's eyes at the giant black helicopter barreling overhead toward the abandoned military base in the distance. Only the place isn't abandoned. Our friends are there. Ally, Gloria, and Gideon—and for some reason, Gideon's face is a little brighter, a little shinier in Maisie's mind. It has a gleam to it that the other faces don't.

Save them!

What about you? I ask.

Just go!

It surprises me that she can hear my thoughts and respond so naturally. Is that Caldwell's doing? Did she talk to him like that? Sadness blooms in my chest. So many questions I have for my sister and no time to ask them.

There may never be time.

I can't leave him. Maisie must know she's not safe with Georgia.

What if I jump out and grab Maisie now? Can I jump her away from danger? My first jump was sloppy. I can't imagine I've become magically better in the last few minutes.

And if I appear, I will only draw attention to myself. What if I get Maisie killed? Caldwell had tried to jump Georgia out of the military base for years after he first got his power, but he couldn't.

If I try to jump Maisie and fail, I'll be endangering her.

Come back for me, Maisie pleads. *Just go! Go to Ally!*

Ally.

The kid knows how to get my attention.

A knee-jerk fear consumes me. Some part of me casts itself across the desert, looking for her, wanting to know that she's safe.

Just like that, I'm gone.

The living room slips away and I'm in the tight void again.

The pressure squeezes my body, making it impossible to draw a breath. My lungs won't expand.

Gabriel, I can't breathe!

The aperture opens and I fall into the light again. My hands and knees hit scalding hot sand. Pain jars my palms, shooting up into my shoulders on impact.

"Ahh, crispy sticks. Shit." I roll over onto my back. "How do you land this thing?"

"How do you land yourself?" Gabriel asks. He stretches his wings wide as he touches down, the picture of grace. Freaking show off.

"You know what I mean! How do I keep from crash landing every time?"

"You must exit with intent."

I groan and roll up to sitting position. I shake the sand off my hands. "I have intent. I intend not to fall on my flippin' face. Gee-*zus*."

Intent, he whispers again.

The image of Caldwell flares to life in my mind. I see him stepping forward and disappearing. He takes a step backward and disappears. A dozen instances of Caldwell attacking or retreating, or even pulling me into his embrace and taking me with him. There's one thing every instance includes: a step.

I brush off my knees and take a breath. I close my eyes and picture Ally in my mind. Ally reaching out for me. Ally leaning forward with a grin on her face, puckering her lips to kiss me.

With my eyes closed, I step forward.

The compression seizes me, squishing my body. My head feels like it's in a vice.

The longer I'm squished, the more my panic rises.

Do not fold. Hold firm, Gabriel warns me.

My insides *are* folding. I'm caving under the pressure of

this place. I push back against the pressure and find enough room to breathe.

With intent, he reminds me as the world begins to open. The space blooms in my chest, somewhere in my heart space.

At the last moment, I step forward. The world tilts but I'm not tossed off the merry-go-round this time. My knees absorb the shock and I right myself.

Nikki stands from her chair, raising her gun.

My violet shield is in place, so I'm not worried about her blowing my brains out. Ally is stretched out on a cot beside the chair. A flat pillow rests under her head. Winston is sleeping in the crook of her knees. As soon as he sees me his cinnamon bun tail wags.

"Hey puddin' cup," I coo.

His tail wags harder and his little ears roll back with excitement.

Nikki's hard face softens. Her mouth falls open in surprise and her eyes round. "Shit, it's you. I thought you were Caldwell."

"She's dead?" I barely glance at Nikki. My heart is hammering is my chest.

"She's sleeping. She asked for you earlier." She removes her finger from the trigger.

I flip the pages of her mind, trying to understand her fear. "I'm not insane."

She doesn't lower the gun. "But you killed him. With all that power, you're a bomb."

We don't have time for this macho bullshit. A war helicopter with rockets and all kinds of other fun crap is coming here to murder everyone I care about. My anger spikes.

I shove myself into Nikki's mind.

I show her the helicopter and the men on their way.

She sucks in a sharp breath.

"Get over yourself," I warn her. "We don't have time for your ego."

She blinks back tears. I didn't make her sad. But I've had Caldwell push into my thoughts that way before. It's not much different than a fierce cold wind.

"How much time do we have?" she asks. The gun finally dips.

"Minutes. Where are the others?"

"Gloria's up and moving. She started drawing as soon as she opened her eyes. Her priorities are strange."

"That's more than you're doing. You're in here gawking." I don't know why I feel the need to defend Gloria. She's as badass as they come and can handle her own fights just fine. But there's always been something about Nikki that makes me murderous.

Oh, right. Could it be that I saw her holding Ally's hand? Fawning over her? Brushing her hair out of her face? The fact that she wants me dead and gone and Ally all to herself?

I don't know *why* that would bother me.

"What about Gideon?" I ask.

She relaxes at last. Is it comforting to see my normal level of bitchiness? Oh, I'm happy to provide that anytime.

"He's with Gloria."

Ally stirs and we both turn, looking at her expectantly. I go to the side of the cot and kneel beside her. I let my guard fall and the shield flickers to nothing. I don't care that Nikki is behind me with a gun. She could put it to my head and blow my brains out this instant.

I don't care because I want to touch Ally. I want to feel her breath and know she's okay. I run a hand along the side of her face. I wouldn't be able to feel her if the shield was between us, and this is much better.

Her cheek is soft and a little too warm under my palm. I

run my fingers along her jaw before tucking a stray hair behind her ear.

Her eyes flutter open and she sees me. As soon as her eyes open Winston takes this as his cue to lay on the love. He licks her face. I like to think he's saying *hey, wake up! Look who's here!* But I can't hear any pug thoughts to confirm this.

She tries to protect her mouth from the assault, and as she does, her eyes finally fall on me.

Her pupils constrict against the overhead light and recognition dawns on her face.

"Jess!" She's up and launching herself at me before I can react. I open my arms to catch her and she's all mine. Poor Winston is knocked aside without so much as a squeeze. I scratch his ears as he bounces around on the cot behind Ally.

"Hey, baby." I kiss her cheeks and breathe in the scent of her hair. The smell of shampoo is gone. It's replaced with gunpowder and smoke. My heart beats faster.

So close. How many times have I been this close to losing her?

Too damn many.

I hold her against me.

"You're okay," she says. "You're okay."

I snort. "That's debatable."

"Maisie?"

"Alive."

"Gloria and Gideon?"

"Alive, alive."

"Caldwell?"

And of course, my girl wants all the information and details straight away. Ally, my doer. My super planner. My action girl. But we don't have time for that. I might have bought some time by jumping ahead to the base, but that helicopter isn't going to stay in the air forever.

When I don't tell her I killed Caldwell, doubt flashes across her face.

The door opens and Gloria leans against the frame. Her hand remains on the handle. Her short hair is flat on one side and her eyes are red with exhaustion. Part of her face is swollen and a sizable bruise has bloomed on one side.

Gideon stands at her back. He lost his shirt, somewhere, and his stomach has a jagged line of stitches.

Rachel stabbed him. He'd risked his own life trying to bring her back to us.

I wonder what's hurting more: his stab wound or his feels?

He sees me staring and barely lifts one corner of his mouth. "It seems I'll live to see another day. Unfortunately."

I match his weak smile with my own. "You're in luck. There's a good chance you'll die before the sun goes down."

He brightens. "Really? Did you bring trouble back with you?"

"They're here." Gloria breaks into our banter with business. No *hello*. No *when did you get here*? Did she see me coming? Did she draw me in that notebook of hers?

"My team is twelve minutes away." Nikki adjusts her gun, probably thrilled by the idea she'll get to use it again so soon, the adrenaline junky.

Gloria doesn't even acknowledge her. Her eyes are fixed on mine. "Can you take us?"

I know what she means. Can I jump them? Can I slip each of them out of the military base before another battle ensues and more blood is shed in this god-awful place?

That's an excellent question.

Caldwell couldn't do it, but Gabriel keeps insisting I'm stronger.

But I'm no fool. Opening myself up to the power, using it at full capacity, that's where the real risk lies.

I turn to Ally again, and see the horror building in her face.

"You killed him," she whispers. Her voice is soft, and I wouldn't have heard it if she wasn't in my arms.

She searches my face, her lips pursed with unasked questions. I can practically see the cogs turning in her head as she puts all these pieces together, as she tries to figure out what this means for me.

For us.

I smile at her, hoping I don't look as scared as I feel. "Let's find out."

CHAPTER TWENTY-NINE

MAISIE

As they focus on their attack against Jesse and the base, I'm largely forgotten. So I cling to Sam. I apologize a thousand times. But no matter how many times I tell him I'm sorry, no matter how many times I wish he'd gotten into that ambulance with his dad and never looked back, this sick pit in my belly won't go away.

There's only part of his nose, but I try anyway. I blow into the caved nostrils several times, but that dormant stone in my belly won't spark.

I'm crying so hard it feels like a belt is around my chest, tightening. I can't draw a full breath. And I can't see because tears blur my world. But I see his sneaker and some black words scrawled on the bottom of the sole.

I wipe my eyes with the back of my hand and bend down to read what's scribbled there.

Happy birthday Sammy Boy—The fastest guard in the west.

There's a handful of signatures in different marker colors,

crowding in on the inscription, one even looping up around onto the side of the sneaker.

What had he said?

I'm not going to die here. I'll be playing ball at ASU in the fall.

The belt tightens again and I can't stop making these horrible sounds.

Someone grabs me under the arms and hauls me up. I dig my heels into the sand, screaming. "Leave me alone! Leave me with him."

A hand connects with my cheekbone and the world spins. I hang upside down in someone's grip. Whoever is holding me up isn't the same person who's slapped me.

I blink until the tears clear my eyes and I see Mom. She's standing in front of me, her hand hanging in the air. I search our connection, trying to get a read on her emotions.

Nothing.

I try harder and...*nothing*.

I can't feel her.

"Where is she?" Mom's wide blue eyes shake in their sockets. She looks more like an animal than a person now. Wild. Unreasonable. As if her heaving chest and trembling body weren't enough to clue me in. Her hand twitches and I brace myself for another strike.

"Who?" My voice cracks. Is it because of the screaming and crying? Dehydration and heat? Or because Mom hit me for the second time today?

All of it.

"Jesse! I know you can feel her. Is she at the base now? We need to know!"

I look away. I can't see the military base beyond the smoking buildings and smoggy air, but I don't need to. It isn't about seeing Jesse with my own eyes. I can feel her out there. I know she's made it to the military base, which means she can use Dad's powers to one degree or another.

I sag with relief.

Safe. She'll keep them all safe.

Mom searches my face. "She's there."

I neither confirm or deny. She turns to Perry.

"I want her," Mom says. She whirls away from me and then back again. Her movements are jerky. "I want to kill that bitch with my own hands."

Her hands tremble as she chokes an invisible neck.

"Do you want me to stop the chopper?" It's Perry's voice. His voice is the one in my ear. He's the one pinning me in place.

"No." She stops pacing. Sweat has pooled on her upper lip. "Don't tell them to take her alive. They need to fight their hardest."

"If they kill her—"

"They won't." Mom shakes her head. Her dirty hair flies.

"Do you want to go there? We can be there in ten minutes."

"No. That's pointless," she says. "She'll hear us coming and she can leave whenever she wants."

Is Jesse that powerful already? Could she read our thoughts as soon as we're in range?

Azrael?

A cool breeze blows on the back of my neck, but I can't tell if that's an actual breeze or Azrael. I want her to tell me if Jesse is okay. And I want to know why the connection with Mom is broken.

"When did you stop loving me?" My emotions flatline. My mind becomes a calm pool. "Was it before or after Dad died?"

How long has our connection been one-sided? Have I always been so stupid? Did I kid myself into thinking Mom was different? Maybe Mom was never the good one. Maybe she never loved me at all. Every kindness, every patient word or tender touch was a whim, empty of any real feeling.

Mom eyes me, but doesn't argue. She doesn't even try to assure me that she loves me. Her sliding glare is more hurtful than a direct insult.

My throat tightens.

"Was it before or after you killed Sam's dad? Before or after Sam was killed?"

The anger rises, warming my belly and throat, and exploding out of me.

"You could have stopped him. Perry will do anything you tell him and you didn't even try!"

Perry's grip tightens on my arms, and the pain shoots down my sides. I don't care. Hurt me. But I'm going to say what I need to say, before I'm silenced forever.

"You were always as heartless as he was, weren't you? I was too stupid to see the truth."

Perry snatches the back of my neck and squeezes. I scream.

"Yes!"

She might as well have kicked me in the face herself. Betrayal is a swift kick in the gut. She likes this? She *wants* to see me hurt?

"Hurt her again," Mom says. She stares down at me on my knees in the sand. Her gaze doesn't waver from mine.

Perry doesn't even hesitate. He twists my elbow, wrenching it until I howl.

"Our thoughts can't reach the base, but she'll feel her pain. It's pointless to chase her all over the desert. She'll come to us."

The red sparks dancing behind my eyes clear, but my arm burns.

I pant.

He wrenches it again and I feel the tendons snapping. I scream until I'm only wheezing.

"Why?" I say, feeling snot on my upper lip. "Why?"

"She'll come," Mom says. She's shuffling her feet. Her excitement makes me feel sick. I dry heave. My stomach contracts hard for a second and third time.

"She'll come. And I'll be ready for her."

Oh no. *No.* I'm not thinking clearly through the pain, but I finally get what Mom's doing. She's hurting me to draw Jesse out. She wants Jesse to come and fight.

No.

Our friends need her. She can't get distracted now. I won't let my weakness be the reason for *another* person's death.

I pinch my eyes shut against the pain.

Azrael, I beg. *Azrael, shield me. Don't let Jesse feel this. Don't let her know.*

Azrael's coolness rolls over me the second before Perry breaks the pinkie on my left hand. My connection to Jesse snaps with it.

CHAPTER THIRTY

JESSE

*A*lly won't let go of my hand. It would be super sweet if she wasn't also assailing me with her thoughts.

No pupil dilation. She's not sweating. Her gaze is focused. She can hold my gaze. No visible signs of distress. Maybe she can't utilize all her power yet? There's no pressure in my head. Maybe she can't read thoughts...

And beneath this intense mental chatter are rolling waves of concern. Love. Fear.

"Yes, I can." I stop dead in the hallway. I whirl Ally to face me, only she's got this pug cradled in her arms. Her brow remains scrunched as she searches my face, assessing my sanity.

"Yes, I can hear your thoughts. Yes, I can jump around. Yes, I can firebomb and heal and no, I don't know if I'm okay. I feel...overwhelmed and stressed, but not crazy. No, I don't know why."

"I can't feel you in my head like I felt Caldwell." Her brow softens. Her eyes light up. "This is good. Maybe you're..."

"Batshit crazy," I offer, running a thumb over her knuckles. It feels so good to touch her. To see her alive and *breathing*. She looks incredibly fragile, and I feel like this moment is going to be snatched away from me any second. I want to tip her back and do one of those Hollywood smooches. But that's a little over the top even for me.

"Functional," she counters. "He made unsound choices. And he was cruel, no doubt about that. But he was functional. He constructed plans and enacted them. If he was 100% insane, I don't think he would've accomplished nearly as much."

Her eyes are large and hopeful. And I can tell by the smile ready to erupt from her lips that she is also excited. But under that I catch *sane at least for a little while*.

"She will get worse," Gloria says.

We both turn to look at her.

"You read minds too, Jackson?" I ask, wondering if she'd plucked that thought out of Ally's head.

"I've seen it," Gloria says. Her face is blank. No regret or malice. She's giving me facts, nothing more. "Perhaps Georgia's death will tip the scale."

Georgia's death.

Oh yeah, you better believe I'm taking out that asshat. And when I do, will those two gifts be enough to send me over the edge?

Ally's face crumples at the same moment she adjusts Winston's pudgy butt in her arms.

"Hey—" I squeeze her hand back. Tears spring to her eyes. "Hey, look at me."

She does, but her soft brown eyes are shimmering.

"It'll be okay." When the hell did I become the reassuring one?

"There is no point worrying about what we cannot change." Gloria resumes walking with the quiet Gideon at her side. His uncharacteristic silence hasn't gone unnoticed. Did Rachel's death break his heart? I would know for sure if I jumped into his head to find out. But I don't.

I snort. "You're one to speak with your doodles and incessant interventions."

Nikki's watching Ally carefully, like she's a magician about to perform a trick, and if she blinks, she'll miss it.

I scowl at her. I would like to murder Sasquatch, but that might undo the argument I made for my sanity. Still, it's hard not to disembowel the person who's mooning over my girl.

"Blink, Sasquatch. Or you'll blow your cover," I grumble.

Her cheeks burn red. "What are you talking about?"

"Oh yeah," I grumble. "You're totally a robot from the past sent to kill us."

"Hear that?" Nikki asks, totally changing the subject, but her thoughts are loud and clear. Her emotions too. She wants Ally to be happy, even if that means being with me. But she totally wants Ally for herself too, convinced she can make her happier than I ever will with all my bullshit.

We agree on that.

But I'd rather drink acid than tell her so.

"It's the helicopter," Gideon says, breaking his silence.

I pull Ally against me and brush the hair off her face. "We can't worry about what's coming. We have enough to do right now."

Ally nods, folding into me. I kiss her head and smell blood. God help me, *blood*. I never want her to smell like blood. If it wasn't for Maisie, I would have lost her today. I can't forget that. I can't forget how much I owe that kid.

I don't ever want to let you go, Ally thinks. *You feel so good.*

You do too, I think back.

Her head lifts, mouth parted in surprise.

I give her a lopsided smile. "Sorry. I don't know how to turn it off."

"Can you move us before they arrive?" Gloria asks. Unlike Nikki who dreams of dumping my body in a shallow grave, Gloria isn't the least bit affected by Ally and me clinging to each other like a couple of sea otters. She's all business per usual.

I think about how poor my exiting skills are and how my elbow is sore from slamming into an overturned armchair. I decide not to embarrass myself. "I don't know. Full disclosure. I'm not great at jumping around yet."

Ally blinks at me. I can tell she's trying to decipher my noncommittal answer.

I flash a sheepish grin. "You *probably* won't die if I try."

Her eyes widen.

My face lights up. "I'll try it on Sasquatch first."

"Jess—" Ally begins.

The first blast strikes the military base. The whole building rocks with the explosion. The foundation erupts through the floor and ceiling tiles fall. I throw my shield wide.

The shield is brighter than ever.

Gabriel!

The shield thickens and widens. I've never seen it this shade of purple before. But it's large enough to enclose the five of us—six including the pug

Can I jump them?

You are not accepting your full power. Until you do, you will face limitations.

I'm about to berate Gabriel for his unhelpful response when Ally's gaping mouth stops me.

"What?" I ask, frowning. I've never seen her jaw quite so unhinged before.

"I can hear him," she says, her face in awe. "I heard his voice!"

What. The. Fuck.

You are projecting, Gabriel says. I see him materialize in the corner of my eye. *You are projecting your thoughts to her.*

Ally gasps and turns toward Gabriel. She knows where to look without a single clue from me.

"Oh my god!" Her hand covers her mouth. "Jesse! He's right there!"

"Is he?" I don't know what else to say. I'm trying not to vomit.

Her face pinches in confusion. "I don't understand. Is he there? Or if he is a projection of your mind, am I seeing him because you see him?"

I think of Caldwell's mind tricks. Once I saw him with pitch black eyes. Inhuman eyes. Did his eyes actually change? Or did he make my mind believe they did?

"I don't know."

But I do know I don't want Ally to see what I see. If my mind is all fucked up, I don't want Ally inside it. It's like sending her into a building that's about to explode. If Gloria is right and I do finally go supernova when I have all the powers, who's to say that power won't blast right through my mind and into hers?

That can never happen, I tell him.

Gabriel lifts his wings gently before they settle back into place.

Ally sucks in a sharp breath.

"Gee-*zus,*" I groan. "Because this really needed to happen right now."

A second explosion rocks the building. Observation glass from the rooms lining the hallway shatters, raining shards onto the cracked tiles. My shield shivers around us, taking the impact on our behalf.

"If you are going to jump, do it now," Gloria says. She's looking around, inspecting the shield as if expecting a hole to open.

"If I jump I'll take the shield with me." I can't knowingly sentence my friends to death.

A third explosion hits the building and the adjacent hallway collapses.

"The helicopter is shooting missiles at us. *Missiles,*" Gideon says with an eye roll. "No sense of finesse. Haven't they heard of the *art* of war?"

"Just do me," Ally says, pulling on my arm. She looks at Winston. "Us."

"Now?" I snort. "Tempting, but it's hardly the time. And I'm not cool with bestiality."

You care most for her safety. If you cannot move her, you cannot move the others.

"He's right," Ally says, agreeing with my hallucination. Wow. Weird.

Very true. Ally is the one I'm most desperate to get out of harm's way.

Tell me I won't explode her brains and I'll do it.

You will not harm her, Gabriel says. And I feel like he's probably lying to me so I'll move along.

Gideon is watching me with that heavy gaze again.

"You're shielding your thoughts," I tell him. Because I realize that he is. Was he able to do that against Caldwell during interrogation too?

I push harder and a small thought slips through.

Rachel.

Her face is bright in his mind the way Gideon was bright in Maisie's. Love, I realize. Love gives the memory of Rachel a brilliance it wouldn't have had otherwise.

I'm sorry I couldn't save her.

He blinks, surprised to hear my voice in his head. "How rude, Sullivan. At least buy me dinner first."

"If you're going to do something, do it. These walls were built to hold against an attack, but not forever," Nikki says. She presses the bud in her ear and it glows blue. "There's a second helicopter. ETA two minutes."

"Come on." Ally squeezes my hands encouragingly.

Gabriel?

With intent, he reminds me.

Ally's eyes widen at the silent exchange.

Somewhere safe, he suggests.

Where the hell is that? My house was burned down. Ally had an apartment, but she hasn't paid rent on it in months. No doubt they've moved someone else in there by now. Gideon is a wandering nomad. I'm not sure he has a place he calls home. I've only ever seen him inhabit posh hotel rooms. Even Nikki's place, a complex in Chicago, is far from ideal. I have no intention of running back to Jeremiah and his goons for any reason whatsoever.

Ally pulls her bottom lip into her mouth. "How about...?"

She searches for a place until her cheeks puff out in frustration. At least I'm not the only who can't think of somewhere safe.

"My house," Gloria says. "Go."

Ally closes her eyes. "I'm ready."

I snort. "I'm glad one of us is."

Gabriel?

I'm such a baby. I keep checking to see if he's there.

He stands behind Ally, unfurling his wings in an impressive sight. He looks ready to jump and that gives me confidence.

Ally looks ready to shit herself.

I take a breath.

I lift my leg, ready to take a step back. With intent.

Before I can put my foot down, a whistle slices through the air. A waterfall of crumbling walls starts to cascade at one end of the hallway.

The whole building is coming down.

I step back taking Ally and Winston with me into the crushing darkness, and at the same time, abandoning our friends, defenseless to their fate.

CHAPTER THIRTY-ONE

JESSE

The dark presses against us. Again, I feel like I'm being squished to death by giant plates of glass. The only difference is, this time I have Ally and Winston with me. I can feel their bodies crushed against mine. I'm about to scream, about to fly into a blind panic over the claustrophobia seizing me, when the breeze blows through. The pressure lessens as the aperture opens and we're pitched forward.

—oh god, I'm going to fall on her. Break something important, squish her little brains out of her ears if—

With intent, Gabriel says like the patient co-pilot surviving driver's ed.

Only it's hard to remember my intent when the world comes rushing back into place again. I tumble out of the in-between place into a jog. And I'm rushing forward, yanking them with me as I slide into Gloria's kitchen table and ricochet into her kitchen cabinets. My hip bumps off the side and a sharp pain runs from my knee to my armpit.

At least I'm Ally's cushion instead of crushing her. She bumps into my side too, giving me another sharp jab of pain as my hip bone connects with the counter's edge for the second time. But it could be much worse. We could have destroyed her table, gone through a window, or hell, down some stairs. Who knows how this thing works?

Ally is breathless, chest heaving as she pulls back. Winston leaps from her arms and scurries away from us as if he can't leave fast enough. He's not interested in another ride.

"What happened?" she demands.

"I think a missile hit the base the same moment we jumped."

"Jesus, Jesse. We have to go back!" She throws up her hands, her face red.

"*I* have to go back."

"With me," she says, her face twisting with fury.

"No," I say, preparing myself for an argument. Ally doesn't like not getting her way anymore than I do.

"You can't expect me to sit here and do nothing while you go back!"

"That's exactly what you'll do." I push myself off the counter, my voice rising to match hers. "How many times do I have to watch you die?"

She blinks like I've slapped her. And her cheeks are certainly red enough.

I'm lifting one foot, ready to bring it down in a military base in Arizona instead of a kitchen in Nashville.

Ally grabs my arm. "Jesse, wait."

Her eyes well up.

Oh god, don't cry. I hate it when she cries. I have absolutely no defense against her crying. Except my anger. But getting mad at a girl who is crying makes me feel like a bigger asshole.

"They need me," I tell her. "Al, I've got to go."

She's nodding, frantically, surrendering to my judgment, but the tears are streaming down her cheeks. She throws her arms around my neck and kisses me. It's a soft brush of lips at first. Her mouth is hot and sticky. Then she's kissing me harder and harder until I feel like she's sucking all the air out of my lungs. The entire front part of her body is pressed against me and the wetness of her cheeks moistens my own.

It feels like goodbye.

"I've got to go," I say again. I need to get back to the base before the others are killed. But I'm finding it so hard to leave her.

"Go." She shakes her head furiously. "Go but come back," she whispers. She pulls back and looks into my eyes. She blinks and fresh tears spill over. "Come back to me."

I'll try. That nagging doubt has me. I know my sanity is temporary. Caldwell. Rachel. Even Georgia. No one took on more powers and kept their minds for long.

I have no reason to believe I'm different.

Gabriel appears behind her, ready to help me with my jump, and I look up. Ally's expression ebbs toward wonder again.

"He's beautiful." All the stubbornness leaves her.

I snort. "Don't tell him that. He'll never get over himself."

"They are in danger." Gabriel's black wings twitch, those gorgeous emerald eyes watching Ally with a regard that I don't quite understand. "Go."

Measuring. That's it. He's measuring her.

Don't look at her that way, I warn him. *She isn't another pawn in your game.*

He flicks his eyes up to meet mine but doesn't deny my accusation.

When I step back from Ally, I'm moving toward Arizona. But even as the world opens and swallows me, the image of her lingers in my mind.

Ally standing in Gloria's outdated, mustard yellow kitchen. Every detail of her worried expression etched in my mind like an overexposed image burned onto the back of my eyes, as I tumble through the darkness,

I'm consumed by the vacuum, unable to draw air into my lungs as I squeeze through the distance between Nashville and Arizona, but maybe that's never going to happen.

Maybe this kind of darkness is never meant to be somewhere I get comfortable. I'm meant to get out as fast as I possibly can.

The pressure lessens and I know I'm sliding through again. I take a step, hoping that once I do, I'll put it down somewhere solid.

My heel connects and I'm pitched forward. My hands shoot out to catch myself and my shield blares to life around me, a flash of purple as the hamster ball encloses me, and then I'm rolling head over heels.

Once it stops spinning, I realize why my exit was so terrible.

The ground is uneven with crags and debris. Not only is the rubble—mostly concrete and dusty bits of broken glass— jutting skyward at weird angles, but the ground trembles too, making stability impossible.

"What the double mint chip?" I squint through the smoke trying to figure out what it is I'm staring at.

The smoke settles and I catch the glimpse of a white wall.

I'm in the base.

Correction. I'm standing on what's left of the base.

"They destroyed it." I turn to Gabriel. He's beside me, his hands in the front pockets of his suit. The air is thick with ash and fallout, but his black suit remains flawless, the white shirt underneath perfectly crisp. Is there a garment spray for that or something?

All that was left of Eric Sullivan is gone, Gabriel says.

I blink at the demolished building. Regret twists my insides.

Not everything. I say, "There's me. And Maisie."

"Jesse!"

I turn toward the sound of my name.

"Sullivan, over here!"

I slide off the chunk of concrete I'm balanced on and jump onto the adjacent slab. It isn't easy, but I clamber toward the voice. A flash of orange hair and a dust-covered shoulder emerges through the cloud.

"Sasquatch?"

She looks over her shoulder and her eyes fix on mine. A deep gash across her cheek is bleeding profusely, trailing down her jaw and neck. "Help me."

I follow her gaze to the rock she's trying to move. Beneath it is one slender black hand.

"Jackson," I whisper, freezing mid-stride.

"Move!" Nikki hisses and I launch myself forward. "We have to get this off her."

"I don't know if you're keeping score," I say as I collapse to my knees beside her. "But I didn't get the fancy moving power. Or super strength for that matter."

"Just get down here."

I slide down the rubble and place my hands on the side of the boulder. I push. *Surprise*! Nothing happens. *No, please. Not Gloria.*

I groan, giving up when my arms ache. "Where's some meth when you need it! This rock would be nothing for a meth head."

And I would totally do meth to save Gloria.

"Can you move her?" Nikki asks. Her own face is beet red,

either from wearing giant gear in the desert sun, or from trying to move the boulder.

"We'll never move this."

"No," Nikki says. She grabs my hand.

I pull back. "Eww. Sasquatch, no."

Nikki grabs it again and places it on Gloria's exposed forearm. "Go on. Try it."

Ah. I get what she's trying to say now. Thank *god*. Sasquatch is the last person I'd want to get sexy with.

A low whine builds and I look up in time to see a helicopter through the smoke. The tail end of a rocket ignites in a puff of fire and smoke.

"Fuck!" Nikki swears.

"Got it." I throw my shield up and enclose the three of us along with the offending boulder the second before the missile strikes. On impact the roar is awful. Aside from having my body totally blown apart, at the very least, my ear drums would have ruptured from the hideous roar.

The explosion rolls along the shield. Swirls of red, yellow, and orange curl around us. It's more fluid than fire, warm ink diluted in a dark pool.

Nikki can't take her eyes off it.

I grin. "Admit it. I'm cool."

Her gaze slides away from mine. "Her pulse is weak. We got to go."

If I go now, Sasquatch will get all melty.

Tempting.

I frown. "Isn't it dangerous to move someone who's been crushed by a boulder?"

"We don't have much choice. Don't move her and she dies. Move her and we have a slim chance."

I don't have a counterargument and the blast is starting to evaporate. The attackers are bound to know I'm here now. A rocket doesn't usually swirl in the air like this.

With my hand on Gloria's arm, I reach out and grab Nikki's shoulder. Her eyes widen to the size of tea saucers. "Let's hope I can do two for one. Even though you're the equivalent of ten pugs."

Her face explodes with outrage. "I'm not 250 pounds!"

I jump. This time it's easier, either because I'm getting better at it, or because I'm not as worried about what might happen to Nikki as I was about Ally. Poor Gloria has no say in the matter.

She and I never talked about a living will or a last will and testament, but I feel like "please save me from being crushed to death" is one of those things that goes without being said.

Or maybe that's just me.

The dark world squeezes us into pancakes, and then tosses us sun-side again.

Hot sand shifts under my hand. Brilliant sunlight says we're back in the rubble of the destroyed military base, except Gloria is stretched at our feet, sans boulder.

She looks like hell. Her face is covered in blood. Her leg is twisted in a direction I'm sure a leg isn't supposed to go. Seeing her like this gives me a nagging feeling I'm forgetting something.

"Gideon!" I say.

Nikki turns and I follow her gaze. Two helicopters.

A net sags from beneath one copter and inside it is Gideon. He's dangling in the mesh beneath the copter, his fingers latched onto the thick cord.

"They want him alive?" I ask, because it's the only reason they would bother to trap him.

"There's a bounty on his head," Nikki says. She's got her fingers pressed to Gloria's wrist. "Take us to a hospital. Now."

"But what about—"

"Come back for him!" Sasquatch barks. When I remain frozen on the spot she screams, "Or she dies!"

I give her my best hate face before turning back to Gideon. I make a motion which I hope he understands. *I'll be back, buddy. Don't get killed before I do.*

I hope that's a smile I see through the mesh enclosing him, but it's hard to tell from here.

I grab the women and I'm gone.

When I tumble through the other side, I know where I am instantly. The smell of chemical cleaners, bright fluorescent lights, and cold tile beneath me.

Nikki and I are crouching beside Gloria's unconscious body as we had in the desert. Our positions haven't changed one bit. I guess stepping with intent isn't required after all.

I didn't consciously choose a place when I jumped. I thought, *Help.* I wanted someone who could save Gloria.

And here I am on my hands and knees looking up into the startled face of Dr. York. He's standing in a doorway with the door propped open. Above the door is a giant *Exit* sign glowing red. In his right hand, he holds a cigarette billowing smoke into the night.

We sit in the hospital hallway not five feet from him.

The smoke he had intended to exhale the second before I popped into existence, pools in his mouth.

With a surprised cough, it puffs out. Out of his nose, mouth and ears—if that's even possible.

His face turns red as he struggles to draw breath into his lungs.

"She was crushed," I tell him, that way he knows what to do for her.

Choking, he tosses the butt outside, and lets the exit door swing closed. As soon as he's beside Jackson, touching her wrist, feeling for a pulse, I give him my last bit of instructions. "Update Ally as soon as you can." He looks up startled.

Nikki frowns. "Where are you going?"

"Where are *we* going." I grab her wrist and jump to

Gloria's house. When my feet find the shag carpet in front of a lumpy sofa, there's Ally and Winston. Winston jumps up barking and Ally rises from the loveseat.

"Stay with her until it's over. If anything happens, I'll kill you, Sasquatch."

I only have time to kiss Ally once, a light brush of the lips and then I'm gone.

$\mathcal{P}$erry drags the blade of his bowie knife across my upper arm. The white-hot steel opens my skin. I'm screaming again. But even as the heat spreads down my arm and blocks out all thought, it feels as if I'm seeing this from a great distance. Like I'm floating in the sky and down below is a different Maisie who's being cut and broken by people who were supposed to love her. Protect her.

This is what it was like when Dad hurt me too.

At first, all I could do was be in my body, feel every bite of pain. But after a while, something would shift.

I'd start to float away.

A professional would probably call this normal. It's a weird coping mechanism I've developed. Whatever it is, I'm grateful for it.

This is not a moment I want to be present for.

My jaw hurts from clenching.

"You should kill her," Perry says. He's looking at me, but he's talking to Mom. My heart skips several beats. Did he always feel this way about me or did my leaving Chicago with Jesse destroy what little friendship we had? "Her abilities will make you stronger, won't they?"

Mom eyes me. Her face is slick with sweat and grit. It looks like glitter on her skin. "Yes."

A shadow appears on the horizon, a vaporous waif of a body moving toward me. At first I think, *Sam*. It's Sam's ghost crossing the desert, made of water vapor and smoke. Here he comes to exact his revenge.

But this phantom is too short.

Jesse takes shape, emerging from the liquid horizon.

They can't see her. Mom and Perry are looking down on me. My body is on the sand between them, tears in the corners of my eyes.

"Yes," Mom says. "But her gift isn't an active power. It will only bolster what I already have."

But despite the blurred image, I know what I see.

Perry twists my knee. The tendon stretches, grows hot, and turns into a burn. I suck in a breath, preparing for the intense pain. Air whistles through my clenched teeth as a wave of anger hits me like a backhand.

Jesse disappears from the horizon and the anger disappears with her.

Then she's beside Perry. She yanks him back and his grip on my leg slips. They disappear.

Just like that, the wall of Perry that's been looming over me disappears and sunlight hits my face full force. Mom comes to attention beside me. Her hands open at her side, as if she's a gunslinger, ready to grab ahold of her weapon.

Perry reappears several feet away.

On his hands and knees, he screams. Flames lick the black

Kevlar clinging to his body. The fabric warps, melting to his skin. He collapses to his elbows, burning alive.

Mom throws her hands up and a wall of sand rises. It crashes down on Perry, extinguishing the flames. But it's too late. Perry isn't moving.

Another man screams. Shots are fired.

Jesse's killing all of them. One by one. And they can't do anything to stop her.

Mom turns in each direction, drawn by gunfire or a howl. But she doesn't have a target. Jesse's moving too fast.

I can't look away from Perry. My eyes are glued to the heap of black fabric smoldering several feet away, blackened like a log of wood. Am I sad? Do I regret his murder?

I don't know. And no one gives me time to process how I feel about it.

Someone twists my hair and pulls me to my feet.

The back door slams open and Jesse steps out. Her ponytail is loose. Stray hair falls around her face. The purple shield shimmers around her as she slides off the two concrete steps into the backyard.

"Wow," she says, her gaze sliding from me to Georgia. "This is an all-new low for you."

She pulls out the ponytail holder before gathering up her hair and retying it. Her eyes flick to mine.

Are you okay? Jesse's voice is loud and clear in my mind despite the distance between us.

Yes.

Liar, liar.

Dad. For a second, the sound of her voice, and the way she speaks to me—mind to mind—reminds me of Dad. It's something he would do.

A memory overtakes me. Dad slices open my palm with the edge of his pocketknife, the silver blade cutting into my life line *so you won't forget. A wound on the hand is like a wound in the mouth. You'll reopen it again and again, unable to help yourself. Each time the pain will be fresh.*

Jesse's face hardens with anger again.

I can feel her pull back from my memory. The warmth that radiates from her cools, and for the first time, I register Mom's slick sweaty palm on the back of my neck.

Mom keeps holding me in front of her like a shield. She doesn't think Jesse will kill me to get to her. And it's working.

Don't, I tell her. *She's a monster. Sam—what she did to Sam— I...I...so wrong.*

I'm a coward and I know it.

If it stops her—

Jesse's hard and angry expression falters. Her eyes soften and she stops circling Mom.

"None of this is your fault," she says. She uses her words. "Don't let her brainwash you with all that bullshit."

Sadness threatens to seal my throat shut. *I'm not worth it. Save them.*

Gideon. Gloria. Ally. Winnie Pug. Hell, even the whole world. Even one of them means more than me.

"You're wrong," Jesse says, tears in the corners of her eyes.

A breeze blows through me. Azrael's coolness slides down my spine. *Be brave little one. I am here.*

My heart beats faster. The last time Azrael told me to be brave, Dad hurt me. Bad.

This won't be different.

Mom's nails bite into the back of my neck until the skin breaks. Burning fire grows there.

The ground disappears. I gasp and look down. I'm floating. As if I've sucked in too much helium and instead of a funny mouse voice, I'm a balloon floating away. Five feet, then ten until Sam's body is a smear of red on the desert floor.

I can still feel Jesse. Feel her fear and anger like a second skin writhing on top of my own.

"Shield her or shield yourself," Mom says. She doesn't even glance at me. What's to see really? The moment Mom takes her power off me I'm going to fall. My brains are going to be all over the sand, like Sam's.

Jesse takes her gaze off Mom long enough to look up at me suspended in the air. She steps forward, moving to align herself beneath me as if she's going to catch me. Mom moves forward too.

"I won't let you catch her," Mom hisses. "Shield her or yourself. That's your choice."

It's like being at the top of a roller coaster. I know the drop is coming, and I also know my safety harness won't hold.

My palms sweat. My heart pounds. All I can do is wonder if I'll look as busted and broken as Sam when I hit the ground.

Because Jesse can't possibly save me. If she shields me, Mom will strike her dead and then she probably won't even stop my fall. I'll die the same moment Jesse does.

And if Jesse dies the whole world is lost. Me, Winnie Pug, and all our friends. Because Mom will honor Dad's vision of the new world order. She'll destroy it, and rebuild it in her subservient image.

Don't fall for it, I tell her. *As soon as she drops me, use your fire to kill her.* I know she can hear me. I know this distance doesn't matter at all with the mind tricks she's inherited from Dad. I say a prayer to Azrael while I'm at it. *Forgive her. She doesn't have a choice.*

Because none of this is Jesse's fault, and I don't blame her for a second.

I would never forgive myself.

My heart aches, but not with her emotion. Somehow,

Jesse only feels courage. And anger and a fierce determination to do what is right no matter the odds or the cost.

Jesse, don't!

The roller coaster drops, and my stomach falls with it as the sand reaches up to meet me.

CHAPTER THIRTY-THREE

JESSE

Maisie drops. A squeal of surprise erupts from her lips, and her arms go up over her head as if she's reaching for a ledge to grab onto. Her hair whips wildly around her, hiding her eyes. There's nothing but maybe five yards of air between her and the ground.

Gabriel!

Burn the darkness.

As hard it is to take my eyes off Maisie, I tear my gaze away long enough to face Georgia. She isn't even looking at Maisie. Her eyes are fixed on me. Her nostrils flared as she shifts from one foot to the other impatiently. She's waiting for me to drop my shield, her cue and chance to bring me down.

The black ribbons of death hang serpentine in the air around her. They're reared back, ready to strike with the first opportunity.

Burn the darkness, Gabriel says again. He's at my back,

lending me his strength. I feel one cool hand between my shoulder blades.

Without looking up, I reach out and test the connection with Maisie. Her fear and panic rushes through me. Instead of trying to sever the connection, and protect myself from the intensity of her emotions, I open myself wide. I note her edges, the outer border of her body, and I throw my shield around it.

My first instinct is to jump away. To take myself out of Georgia's striking path. But as soon as I try, I find that my feet are stuck to the spot, rooted. She's using Rachel's telekinesis to pin me down the way Rachel pinned Caldwell.

Burn! Gabriel screams as the black smoke strikes.

At the same moment, Georgia's death tendrils rush forward to engulf me, I throw my fire. An enormous stream of flame rushes out of me, colliding with the darkness. A spray of sand pelts us too, probably from Maisie's impact. But if she's inside the shield, her body should be unhurt. I won't know until this is over. I don't dare look, because Georgia is at my feet.

The power pouring through me is unlike anything I've ever felt before. A reckless euphoria rolls over me, making me weak in the knees. It's nearly orgasmic, but somehow my legs don't fold.

The flames continue to pour through me, driving the darkness back.

More, Gabriel urges. *More.*

I open myself wider. The channel inside me spreads and I can feel part of the universe coming through. I see myself for what I am. A conduit. A doorway into this world, a way for power and energy to govern here.

Reality slips. This cocoon of darkness and fire entrances me and in this in-between, I see the truth. Layers and layers of the universe lie on top of one another. The interconnectedness of them. The way one can bleed into another, the osmosis of this exchange, and how certain beings have taken it upon themselves to control the fate of other planes. They are the midwives of the world, committed to helping us birth a more beautiful future—no matter how difficult that birth will be.

Even as these truths pour through me, my mind rejects them. Mental barriers erect. Radical ideas are drowned in the pool of my disbelief.

The sand under my feet becomes real again. The heat of the desert and my fire becomes real again. Gabriel, an icy relief, fades.

Georgia collapses, her darkness falling limp beside her.

I could pull back. I could stop here and pardon the bitch of all her sins.

But part of my mind remains in that other place, sees this situation and life from a higher perspective. And that part of my mind says this is simple. One thing must be done and I can do it.

Easy peasy.

The fire blasts right through Georgia.

It latches onto her hair and body. Her clothes blacken.

I advance, intending to put my hands on her. After all, I can't absorb her powers and fulfill my divine power until I sink my fingers into her gray matter.

Georgia tries to push me back. Her telekinesis hits my chest like a wall, winding me. The fire falters, but thankfully, because her smoke is already retreating, I'm able to renew my attack without getting struck by her death ribbons.

She uses her smoke the way I use my shield. She's protecting herself from immolation. Until her resistance evaporates like water in the desert.

A shimmer of purple in the corner of my eye catches my attention. I turn and see Maisie standing halfway between her mother and me. Tears stream down her face and great sobs make her chest convulse.

Besides relief that my shield held and she landed safely, other emotions rage inside her. The desperate impulse to protect her mother, to give her own life for Georgia's, and the understanding she shouldn't because the woman doesn't deserve it.

Maisie shouldn't have to see this.

Gabriel flutters nearby, more solid than ever, but not at full strength with three partis so near to one another.

She does not have to, he whispers. *She does not have to see.*

A bright image of Liza comes to mind. A face I haven't seen in a long time.

Liza in a hotel room in Ohio, raising her fingers and snapping them before my whole world was engulfed in darkness.

Caldwell took that power from her, and now I've taken everything from him.

You're right. Maisie doesn't have to see this.

I raise my left hand, the only hand I can snap with, and I press my middle finger and thumb together.

Maisie never even looks my way. I know she can feel me as clearly as I can feel her. But she isn't paying attention to me now. She can't tear herself away from Georgia.

I feel the power uncurl inside me and when it grows too hot to contain, I snap my fingers.

Maisie collapses on the spot. She crumples like a robot whose power cord has been ripped out of the wall.

She lays on the sand, unmoving except for the gentle rise and fall of her chest. The purple shield is alive, vibrating a couple inches above her skin.

I refocus on Georgia.

She looks up at me through her lashes, her face a mask of fear and hate.

I give her my best wolfish grin. "Now you can have all of my attention."

Spittle foams at the corners of her mouth. "You fucking bitch. If you think I'm going to roll over and—"

"No, no," I say, cutting her off. "I know you'll fight to the end. Bitterly. And lose."

She pulls herself up, trying to ready herself for another attack. But her knees knock together, the left side of her body is charred black from her hip to her neck. She must have turned into the fire, protecting her dominant side. Smart.

I know from Caldwell's memories of Georgia, that I could have learned a million things about pain from this woman. About living with disappointment and uncertainty. She was nothing if not a survivor. I respect that about her. Even if she is a worse mother than my own.

"Last words?" I ask her.

Because I'm not going to draw this out. I care too much about Maisie. Also, because I don't have the luxury of time. I murdered all her henchmen and destroyed one of the two choppers that carried them, but it's only a matter of time before someone else comes.

Georgia growls at me, her eyes feral.

"Nothing at all? No apology for hurting your daughter? No regrets?" I want this to end knowing I tried.

"What about you?" she hisses, her fingers curling into claws. "For killing the man I loved. For killing the only good thing in this world."

Her voice cracks and her lower lip quivers.

"If that's your definition of good, then we definitely don't want you establishing the new world order."

She screams. "Fuck you!"

Georgia launches herself at me, unrepentant to the end.

"Not today," I say, and throw my biggest firebomb yet.

CHAPTER THIRTY-FOUR

MAISIE

 open my eyes slowly. I blink, and water leaks from the corners of my eyes down across my temples. A great blue sky stretches in all directions with puffy white clouds rolling by. Wisps of black smoke dilute the blue.

I sit up. Sand rolls off my chest and legs, granules tumbling off the fabric of my clothes. The pressure between my ears is horrible, like the time I got a sinus infection during a winter. I open and close my jaw until I hear a soft *pop*.

I come onto my knees, turning, trying to see what is on fire.

It's the shed.

The white paint is black with thick plumes of smoke billowing into the sky. Sparks of crackling wood and cinders caught on the breeze float up into the sky. The door, weakened as the fire eats through its frame, cracks and falls to the sand.

Sam burns.

I run to him.

I want to throw myself on his body and protect him from the flames.

I rip off my shirt and start slapping him with it. My shirt catches. The cheap fabric incinerates.

I run into the house. The back door slaps the house viciously as I grab a blanket off a sofa and run back outside. I beat Sam with it.

I'm crying so hard my lungs threaten to give out long before my arms do.

When the blanket begins to look like another failed attempt, I drop to my knees beside him and start scooping sand onto his body.

I manage to extinguish the flames licking his legs. But not before they've done damage. The melted fabric breaks off in ashen pieces, carried into the air. The skin beneath is raw.

At least he didn't feel the fire.

That small condolence isn't enough to keep me from sobbing into my hands. Granules of sand get into my eyes, scraping my skin and eyelids as I wipe at my tears.

My mind begins to register my surroundings for the first time. It dawns on me how many bodies were in the house. The bodies I clambered over in my blind panic to grab the singed afghan.

A body in the yard lies on a heap of ash.

I stand on shaking legs and stumble toward it.

I recognize the nest of chestnut hair even before I roll her over.

Jesse. Dead.

This is twice today I've found her in a pile of ash. The soot coats her face and neck.

Her fingers are soaked black with it.

She killed Mom.

I roll Jesse onto her back and rock onto my heels.

A void opens inside me. A big vapid space swallows up all my feelings.

The heat leaves my body and leaves a cold, cramping pit inside me. The raging fire at my back doesn't stop me from shivering. I might as well be in the arctic rather than in the Arizona desert.

I have no idea how long I sit like this. No thoughts. No feelings. I know I'm beside Jesse's body. One hand on hers, the burning shed and Sam's body behind me. I can register on some level that the house is full of bodies and that was Jesse's doing. I can even register that my face and neck are sunburned. Or maybe even burned by actual fire. The skin is tight and stings. Once the sun goes down the pain will *set* in.

If I'm alive to feel it. It's all I can do just to keep breathing.

I sit there, my body aching, until a small sound catches my attention. I begin to pull out of the void.

Whump. Whump. Whump. Whump.

The sound grows.

An enormous bird passes overhead, blotting out the sun. The whole yard is cast in its shadow.

I look up and see it's not a bird at all. It's one of Dad's helicopters.

One of *Dad's* helicopters. What are they going to do when they realize that both Mom and Dad are dead?

The world snaps into focus and I throw myself over Jesse's body at the same moment the helicopter lands.

Men with guns lying across their chest hop down onto the sand, running toward me.

They shout questions at me, demanding to know where my parents are.

They don't like my answer.

As I knew they would, guns whirl on Jesse.

"No!" I scream. I throw myself over her. I try to protect

her head above all, but also her vital organs. I should have blown into her nose while I had the chance.

"Move!" the gunman shouts. With the sun behind his head, he's only an angry black blob growling.

"She's already dead!" I shout.

"The fuck she is!" His voice is muffled by a faceguard. The end of his gun in my face is perfectly clear.

"Please," I beg. "She's no threat to you."

My voice wavers even though I'm telling the truth. Jesse got her revenge against Dad. She took out the only other evil person who was a threat to the world. They have no reason to fear her.

But if I'm being honest, it's more than that.

I love her. Not only because she's my sister, but because she's all I have.

She's the only person I have left in this big empty world.

"Move or I'll put a fucking bullet in your head," the soldier screams. It seems that even without Mom, Dad, or Perry, his orders are clear. Kill Jesse Sullivan at all costs.

I'm prepared to be that cost.

I take a breath and I close my eyes.

I imagine the bullet going in. I imagine it blowing through my skull the way the bullets blew through Sam.

Maybe the world will be okay.

Our partis powers—mine and Jesse's—will be blown to the four corners of the earth. Twelve new people will be chosen to save the world or destroy it. Maybe they'll do a better job. Maybe they won't screw up and kill each other like we did.

One could hope.

I breathe in the darkness.

I settle into the thick shadow of my fate and wait.

A gun goes off.

I expect white hot pain. Or more realistically, nothing at all. It's a big gun and bullets travel fast.

But I feel nothing.

Another gun goes off and someone shouts. Then the shadow moves and my shade disappears. Sunlight hits my face and burning neck.

More screams, and I open my eyes. A man with wild black hair brings the butt of a gun down on a skull. I flinch the second it crunches and the soldier's knees buckle. Before I can even process what I've seen, the wild man flips the gun, twirls it in his hand like a baton and takes aim at my soldier, the one who is going to take my life.

The gun in his hand blats.

Kevlar-clad knees hit the dirt. More blood paints the desert floor.

Then warm, sweaty hands are touching my cheeks, slapping me lightly.

"Love," my savior purrs. I know that British accent anywhere. "Darling. Open your eyes."

I see Gideon. His hairline is soaking wet, and a trail of sweat runs down the side of his face. But his eyes are bright and clear with relief.

"Thank god," he says. He drops the gun and drags me across Jesse's body.

Before I know it, he's got me in a bear hug, twirling me and laughing.

"We did it!" he laughs. "We bloody did it. Bad guys dead. Good guys alive. Oh hell, I need a drink!"

My throat closes. "Not the bad guys."

"What?" he sets me on my feet. "What's that, love?"

"Not just the bad guys. Good guys died too."

Gideon looks down at Jesse. "Oh, don't worry about her. She'll be alive and raising hell in no time."

My throat tightens even harder and I don't think I can squeeze out the words. "There was a boy."

Tears spring to my eyes.

"There was a kid, like me. He lived here. This is his house. And that—" I point at the collapsed shed and the burned corpse half-buried beneath it. "That's his—that was him."

Gideon's humor vanishes like an oasis. He grabs me and pulls me into his arms. "I'm sorry. So *so* sorry." He kisses the top of my head.

My chest caves under the weight of his apology. I can't draw air into my lungs.

"And my mom—"

"I know." Gideon strokes my hair. "I know. You were terribly brave. I'm proud of you. We all are."

I pull myself away from him. "I'm not. If I was brave, I would have protected him. I would have done more. I would have killed Dad myself or stood up to Mom or not let Perry hurt me or—" My sobs cut my voice short. "His dad is going to come home and find his house ruined and his kid dead and it's my fault. It's all *my* fault."

Gideon's face hardens. "That's not true."

"It is."

"No," he says and pulls me into his arms again.

"It is!" I slam a balled fist against his chest. "It is! All of it. I'm stupid and weak and—"

I keep punching his chest until he hugs me against him. He holds me there in his arms and won't let me go. It's like being crushed by a boa constrictor. I try to wrench away, but he's stronger than me. And the more he coos apologies in my ears, the weaker I feel.

I want to believe him that Sam isn't my fault. That Sam's dad wasn't my fault. That all the thousand things I could have done differently, weren't my fault.

But they are.

They always will be.

Azrael pointed at the hotel. We stopped there because I said something.

"Nothing I do is right," I sob into his shirt.

"I am sure if you think about it, you won't be able to count on one hand all the brave things you've done today.'

"You're wrong," I say, my breath hitching.

"You saved the pug's life. And Gloria's and Ally's. There's three."

I say nothing. There's no point.

"You stood up to your mother. You protected Jesse. I saw you. That's five acts of bravery I can think of without trying. I bet if I tried, I can come up with 24. One for every hour."

I pull back and look into his eyes. Tears stand in the corners of his long dark lashes.

"Not to mention you saved my life." He plants another kiss on my temple. I feel the plump, wet lips on my skin long after he pulls back. "Thank you for that."

"I could have done more," I say.

He grins. "At least I know where you get your stubbornness from." His eyes fall to Jesse. "Shall we get her out of the sun? You too. You're quite red and it's not your color, love."

He takes a step back, his eyes on Jesse.

"Freeze!"

I whirl and see the police.

Of course, they came. With the helicopters, with the guns and fires and chaos, why wouldn't they respond?

"It's the girl!" A female cop with blond hair like mine recognizes me. My face was all over the news. But she only spares me a glance. "And she's wounded!"

She won't take her eyes off Gideon.

"Drop your weapon!"

"Now wait a minute," Gideon says, showing an empty palm. He doesn't drop the gun.

I know what she's going to do the moment before she does it. I can see it in her eyes. I've seen that look a thousand times on my parents' faces when they decided to kill someone.

"No!" I step between Gideon and the cop a heartbeat before her gun goes off.

The bullet punches a hole through my chest.

And the ground rushes up to meet me.

CHAPTER THIRTY-FIVE

JESSE

I'm on the beach of my dreams. Gray-white sand stretches left, only ending when the mouth of a forest swallows it. It extends right until it disappears behind a large lighthouse. The top of the lighthouse is barely visible in the ghostly fog.

Behind me, the beach slopes up to a house. An A-frame, its front propped up on stilts. Enormous windows of black glass reflect the water and the clouds rolling through its dark frame.

I bend and dig a rock out of the damp, compacted sand.

It's a rose-colored stone, smooth and wet like a tortoise shell between my fingers.

"It's real," I say. I crane my neck from where I crouch and smile at the angel beside me.

His black wings are out, stretched behind him. The breeze ruffles the soft downy tips near his ears. The longer, sleeker feathers near the tips trail in the sand. The tide is out.

"So is that it?" I ask. "I'm dead, right?"

I look at the dark horizon in the distance. Thick storm clouds are forming. A flash of lightning glows inside the smoke-gray bodies.

Gabriel doesn't say anything. His hands rest in his pockets with only the white cuffs showing at the edge of the black sleeves. His hair whips around his head in the ocean breeze. Maisie says she sees Chicago and Lake Michigan in her special place.

But this is the ocean. The salty brine stings my nose as I pick at the white granules in the sand.

"I have all the powers except for Maisie's, and here I am at the beach house again." I frown at him. As peaceful as this place is, uneasiness cramps my guts. My lower abdomen squirms and his silence is only making it worse.

"I'm not going to kill her," I tell him. "You know that, right? You say Caldwell murdering Chaplain started all this and we should see it through, but I'm not going to murder her. She's a kid. A *good* kid."

"That is not a problem," he says.

"She can be saved?" I practically squeal with delight. "Tell me how." He finally looks at me. Like a thousand times before, goosebumps rise on my arms the moment those bright green eyes meet mine.

They're so bright. I've never seen a person with eyes that bright. And there's something feline about the shape. But it's the sense I'm looking at an illusion that scares me.

I'm being *tricked*.

Deep down, I know he's something else, only pretending to be insubstantial. In a way, I can detect his gaze moving, his body softening and reforming as I look at him.

The wind pulls tears from my eyes and I'm forced to look away.

He turns back to the horizon, concerned about the storm

building in the distance. "Your choice must be conscious and informed."

I frown. "I'll get the rape whistle ready then. One wrong move and you better believe—"

He cuts me off. *So like a dude. Look. They're coming.*

With his voice in my head for the first time, I realize I can't read his mind the way I was listening to the others. No aimless prattle. I can only hear what he wants me to hear. Not sure how I feel about that.

I turn back to the storm as another brilliant flash of lightning cracks open the sky.

It's begun to rain. I watch droplets fall from fat clouds to the water. From this distance, it looks like static between the cloud and the surface below.

Look closer.

I squint.

It's not rain.

A thousand wings flap. A swarm converging above the blue-gray waters.

My gaze sweeps across the horizon. Angels. Or creatures that look like angels. Part human. Part bird.

And they're headed this way, with a torrential storm at their backs.

"What the fuck?" I ask.

This is the last gate. Once they reach it, if it is not closed, they shall pass.

"Then let's close the freaking gate!"

You must make an informed decision.

I gesture at the approaching swarm. "Then hurry up and inform me!"

Give me permission, Gabriel says. He pulls me up from the sand and laces his fingers with mine. Rough granules scrape my palm, trapped between my hand and his.

He pulls me against him. He pins me against his body

with one arm pushing into the middle of my back, forcing me to arch against him. It's a very possessive gesture.

Give me permission, he says again and I realize he's repeating himself because I'm just standing here doe-eyed and drooling.

"Permission to do what?" I ask, aware that his thighs are pressing against mine.

To inform you.

"Is this a sex metaphor?" I try to pull back but I don't even manage an inch.

You must know the consequences. He slips one hand under my hair, clasping it against the back of my neck. I've never been so trapped in my life. Okay, well, I was buried alive that one time. And locked in a gas chamber before that. But this is a new kind of trapped. And I don't have time to figure out how I feel about it either. Not with the angel swarm halfway here.

I look up into big green eyes. "Okay. Show me. Let me know the consequences of saving the world."

His wings extend around me, pulling me even tighter against his body. He takes flight, my stomach dropping as the scenery shifts.

When he unfolds his wings, we stand in the middle of a meadow. Tall grasses stretch as far as the eye can see.

Your species views time as linear. I will show you time as such for clarity.

"You have no faith in my brain, do you?"

His gaze narrows.

"Is now a bad time for sarcasm?" I pout. In my opinion, every time is a good time.

Let's begin at the beginning.

"Good place to start," I say, despite the unfriendly gaze.

The meadow is replaced by dust. A thick cloud whips in all directions like a dervish. It doesn't last, this massive dust storm. It settles into hard rock and a sky, which becomes water, then softer earth, and then a meadow full of tall grass. It fast forwards like this, animals coming and going at a speed I'm unable to process. At best, I catch a scaly whip-like tail here and downy white feathers there.

I point at the fleeting wisp. "Aww, was that you? Was that baby Gabriel? Rewind that."

We disagree.

"I didn't say it was you. I was just asking."

My...people.

He stumbles on the word *people*. Is it because they aren't people? I mean, obviously. Look at him.

We are your creation. We exist because you exist. You dreamed us into this existence. Mankind believes God existed first. That creation begins at point A and flows until point Z and all that occurs between is the act of creation. But this is not true. Time is not linear. God is your descendent and all things were dreamed into life from a consciousness that evolved naturally, true. But we affect the continuum. We reinforce its existence by stretching our hands back down the line. Once the consciousness is fully formed, we go back. We alter the present reality. You are the dreamer as much as the dream.

If I could put all the sense that made into one hand, I wouldn't even be able to buy a bus ticket across town. I blink at the meadow, which isn't much of a meadow anymore because it has become a small village and then a bigger town, a bigger city.

"There must come a time when the creator no longer controls the creation, but becomes as much a myth as the object itself. A symbiotic relationship that must continue in tandem with one another. Our existence depends upon yours. But we disagree on what form of our creator should take, as you disagree on what form your creation should take. Some believe your kind can be recreated. *Improved.* They believe our imperfections are the result of your imperfections. If we perfect you, we perfect ourselves."

I snort. "Don't tell the humans. They have a pretty high opinion of themselves already."

Others believe that you must be allowed to evolve imperfectly. You must wrong if you are to right.

I want to reach out and touch the tall grass around me, smell its grassy scent, feel the breeze. But there is something purely visual about this landscape. My body isn't experiencing this place as much as my mind is.

I frown at Gabriel. "You're the second group. You don't believe we'll become better if we just destroy everything and start over."

"No," Gabriel says, his lips pursed. It isn't until now that I realize he's switched to speech. "Growth is life. Life is growth. All you need is time."

Time.

"So you chose me because you thought I would shield the Earth, that I would protect it from being destroyed. Because what we need is time."

He turns away, watches a bridge spring up across a river in the distance.

"But you said before that you chose the partis because at some point in their life they *wanted* to die. If you want to find someone who'll shield Earth, it seems stupid to choose from a bunch of suicidal people!"

Gabriel smiles. *You wanted to die, but you also wanted to live. Both desires must be present.*

I sense the turn in the conversation.

"What's the bad news?" I ask him. "I have a feeling that *informing* me is another way of telling me the bad news. What did you tell the other three partis before me, the people who chose to blow up and become stars—what did you tell them that was so horrible they decided not to protect Earth?

"Darkness lies ahead." He steps toward me and I don't know why but I step back. I step back like he's a boiling pot of water and I don't want to put my hand in it. He grabs onto me anyway.

Everything in me says, *No. Don't look. Turn away while you can.*

"Growth is not without pain," Gabriel says. He's pressing himself against me again, thigh to thigh, hand in the middle of the back. "Growth is not without setbacks."

Black wings engulf me.

In the blackness, it's like a cinema. Images assail me. First, at a pace slow enough that I can process what I'm seeing.

The earth begins to die. Life is unsustainable under the strain of overpopulation and depleting resources. Wars begin over scarcity. Millions flee. Bodies float in the ocean, bodies of those who didn't reach the other shore. Borders close out of fear.

Children are bought and sold. Slavery swells.

Even the wealthy nations struggle to sustain their populations. The poor starve. They revolt against the rich. War spreads into the wealthier nations as they fight over what is left.

Diseases spring up in the changing climates and populations are confronted with viral strains they have no immunity for. More death. Our health weakens as our ecosystem weakens.

Destruction of beautiful cities. More disappear underwater, masterpieces lost forever in a toxic sea.

Cruelty on every level imaginable.

And the truth is I could prevent it. I could take us back to the beginning. I could make it so that we start again, in a simpler time. I could erase all the horrible things we've done to each other in the past. All the genocide. All the rape. All the fear and anger and heartbreak. I can undo it. I can make sure the worst never comes.

Because the worst *is* coming.

In one blast, I can blow this universe apart. Erase all our fuckups past and future. Somehow, my body would become the entry point for an enormous influx of power. It's already started. Somehow that angel storm I saw on the horizon blows through me and another—*Bam!* Big bang again.

A fresh start.

And a chance to be better than we were.

Hope.

Choose, Gabriel whispers to me through the dark. Heat washes over me. I feel the air in my chest a moment before I break the surface.

I'm alive.

Gabriel lifts me out of the darkness.

Choose wisely. Choose for us all.

CHAPTER THIRTY-SIX

JESSE

Maisie is on her knees in front of me, blood pouring out of her chest.

"Thank god," Gideon says as soon as my eyes open. He's got her by the shoulders, propping her up. Two officers lay dead on the ground several feet away. I'm able to piece from his memories—because my telepathy is back in full swing—that Maisie protected Gideon from the gunshot before he was forced to shoot the cop himself.

Regret wafts off him.

"Save her." His voice is too high. "Come on. What are you bloody waiting for?"

I take Maisie into my arms, cradle her like a baby.

She coughs blood and I wipe it away with my thumb, smearing it across her cheek like some slutty rouge. She coughs again, and I realize she's trying to speak.

Don't, I tell her. *You'll only make it worse.*

I tried. I tried to be brave like you.

You're way braver than me, kid.

You can have it. I never wanted this power anyway.

She's shot in the right lung. That whistling sound is air trying to get through a hole filling with blood.

Kiss Winnie Pug for me. Tell Gideon—

But whatever she wanted me to tell Gideon dies with her.

Hold on, kid.

I reach deep down inside myself and call on a power that I haven't used in a long time. It's always been mine. I used it before I knew what it was and calling on it now is no great feat.

My vision changes, and with it the knowledge that despite everything that's happened, I'm what I've always been.

A death replacement agent.

And death is the transformation of energy. When someone is about to die, a tiny black hole is created inside them. Like a black hole in space, it looks like an empty swirling vortex. This vortex sucks all the warm, living colors out of a person, leaving nothing behind that can survive.

I see Maisie's little flame flicker, threatening to go out at any second. And here I am, a bright brilliant blue flame beside her. A sparkly blue. Electric blue so harsh it hurts to look at it.

A familiar hot-cold chill settles into the muscles in my back and coils around my navel like an invisible snake.

"I'm sorry," I tell the dying girl in my arms. "There's no other way. We have to finish what we started."

Gideon screams. "No, you can't."

But he's beating only air. I've erected the shield around me and Maisie. He can thrash and wail and scream all he wants, but I'm not stopping now.

I saw our future and our horrible past. There's only one way to fix all that.

Maisie's heart stops.

In the darkness, Gabriel showed me a trick. A death replacement agent can't replace someone with NRD. But if I use her breath—her power to rekindle life in the same way I perform a replacement, that might work. If Maisie willingly gave up her power, her body wouldn't incinerate.

And I have to try.

Not yet, I tell her. I take all her blue fire into my body and kindle it against my own. Then I bend down and blow air into her nose. My throat burns. My nose burns, but I do it again. And again.

Three times and Maisie's heart kick starts. All the flame that was hers is mine now, but she's breathing.

She's alive.

I lay her down and look at Gideon. He's stopped pounding on my shield long enough to wipe his tears.

"Take care of her," I say, before collapsing into the darkness one more time.

I DON'T HAVE A BODY.

I'm floating through time and space, unbound.

A tirade of sins flicker against the black screen of my unconsciousness. Babies dead in their mothers' arms. Soldiers murdering a woman's children, and then raping her as their bodies grow cold on the floor. More souls in the bottoms of boats, drowning when they capsize, and the terror that overtakes them as their lips slip beneath the water.

In a field, a boy, gay, and surrounded is beaten to death by his friends from school. Blood dries on a baseball bat.

A police officer luring a little girl into a car.

The final moments of a 14-year-old who never comes home.

A cripple in the street, kicked by a passerby, because he dares beg for his next meal.

The people living in squalid camps on foreign shores. The natives who burn these makeshift homes to the ground.

I'm not imagining this. These evils are not the product of my imagination. They're happening across the globe in this very moment.

And it isn't only human consciousness I'm riding—because that's what I'm doing somehow. In this bodiless state between life and death, I'm jumping from mind to mind. For that moment, I'm in their mind, I can taste their fear, raw and burning, in the back of my throat. I feel the tremors in their bodies. I'm rolled by the crushing wave of loss, fear, uncertainty, and betrayal.

It isn't the countless cruelties I witness from the perspectives of the victims. It's the hate and fear in the minds of the perpetrators. The relief a man feels when the back of his hand connects with his wife's face. The utter ecstasy that rolls along his spine when another pulls the trigger. The excitement tightening a man's guts as he threatens a young girl, sees her fear, knows he has power over her.

I can't let this go on.

My heart beats in my chest. I draw my first breath and the tether connecting my spirit and body warms. My omniscient gaze narrows. The world dims to a specific place and time.

"Restraining her is pointless. What could that possibly do?"

"We can't leave her like this. She's breathing. We have no idea what she'll do once she's awake."

"Whatever she does I'm sure it will be more rational than what she'll do if she wakes up restrained," a voice quips. Annoyance grates against my skin. Gideon is fighting for my freedom. "Even with all the powers, she didn't kill Maisie. She could have, but she saved her. That is an excellent sign."

"I've seen what she will do," the other man says. There's something familiar about this voice. It's uptight and clipped.

"I've seen the visions. I've followed her progression since the beginning. Every vision has come to pass. I have no reason to believe that my next won't also come to pass. If she ascends in her current state, that's it for everyone. The end of us all. We have to reason with her."

"If that's true," Gideon says. "I advise you against the restraints. I speak from personal experience. Reason is quite difficult when I'm tied up."

"You have no idea what she's capable of."

I open my eyes and Jeremiah takes a step back.

Of course, he does.

I take in the room. It's a bedroom in a small house. Someone darts past a doorway, carrying out a body. So, Jeremiah caught up to us and is cleaning up our mess. My mess. Lucky me.

Gideon is braver. He holds his ground. "Hello, beautiful. How are you feeling?"

"Maisie?" My voice cracks and I dry cough. I sit up in the bed.

"Alive, thanks to you. We've stitched her up, and she'll be fine. Her NRD will heal the bullet wound. She should be as good as new in a few hours."

I turn on Jeremiah. A quick flip through his mind tells me all I need to know. "Prophet."

His back stiffens.

"So you saw me destroy the world?" I'm not even surprised. I saw what he saw. The memory is one of the most vivid in that dense skull of his.

I'm standing in the dead of winter, a frozen landscape stretching in all directions until a purple light blows me apart. I go quasar.

It will be mercy.

The explosion will be so enormous and so quick no one

will feel a thing. Isn't this preferable to another 1000 years of pain?

"You don't understand," I tell him. "You've seen a lot, but not everything."

I give him a taste of it. I shove all the painful images I collected from Gabriel's confession and my short time without a body into his mind.

I let him see the dead children washing onto the shore like trash from the open sea.

A cry escapes him.

"I can't let that happen."

"What about Alice?" Gideon asks. His heart is hammering in his chest a mile a minute. I feel it in my own head like a second pulse. "You would kill her?"

"To save her from a lifetime of suffering? If Brinkley was being tortured and you couldn't stop it, wouldn't you shoot him in the head? Wouldn't you see that as a mercy?"

"You can stop it. You'll find a way to stop it. I don't believe that you saved Maisie only to take her life away, did you?"

I can't explain it to them. I can't possibly make them understand. I can scare the shit out of them, as I've clearly done with Jeremiah. He's on his knees on the floor, weeping like a baby.

"I can remake the world. I can make it into anything I want. I'll make it better, Gideon. I'll make you and Maisie and Ally, and hell, maybe even me. I'll make us all over but without all the bullshit. Without all the fucked-up parts. I'll make it right."

Gideon's jaw sets. "That's not what Brinkley taught us. He taught us to keep moving forward. To keep trying no matter how fucked up a situation is. He taught you better than that."

His words sting.

"You don't understand," Jeremiah cries, still on his knees.

"It is not an imagining. It's what you are. If you remake the world, you will only make it what you are."

He opens his mouth to explain, but I can't listen to him anymore.

I know what I've got to do.

I'm going to take this enormous power and use it for good. I'm going to take away all the pain. I'll erase all the cruelty. I'll dream up a better world for all of us.

"No, wait!" Gideon reaches out to grab me, but his feet clip Jeremiah hunched on the floor.

I slip through the darkness before he has a chance to stop me.

The in-between world squeezes me, but this time, I don't find it nearly as claustrophobic as I did on my earlier trips.

When I pop out the other side and find Ally, I'm not even breathless this time.

She stands the second she sees me. She's holding Gloria's hand. The woman's unconscious but breathing beneath the snug bedsheets of a hospital bed. Her red coat is thrown over the back of a chair.

"Jesse!" Ally sighs. Her relief washes over me like a cool cloth to a feverish brow. "Thank god, you're all right."

My resolve melts instantly. Half a second ago, I was ready to say goodbye. I had absolute conviction that remaking the world was the right thing to do. Gabriel said himself it's going to get worse before it gets better.

But considering these big brown eyes, my prepared speech leaves me.

Ally's brow furrows. "What's wrong?"

"I have to." Of all the super lame things I could have said, the best I manage is *I have to?* Really? Good job, Sullivan.

"You have to what?" Ally lets go of Gloria's hand and advances on me.

Oh no, no, no. Don't touch me. Don't make this harder.

Ally stops mid-stride as if she's run into a brick wall. Her mouth falls open in surprise. "Jess!"

It's accusatory. And I realize it's because I've stopped her using Rachel's gift.

Rachel's gift is inside me because Georgia killed her for it. And I killed Georgia and even that small part of the journey is proof enough of what horrible, wretched people we are.

"Don't come any closer," I say.

"Why?" she asks. Her sadness socks me in the gut. Sadness and betrayal.

"I—" I try to breathe around her mixed emotions. "I have to tell you something and if you get all touchy, feely I don't think I can do it. So please, stay there."

"Jesse—"

"Promise you'll stay there and I'll stop holding you back."

Anger warms her chest, fueled by her fear. "I promise. Now tell me what's going on."

"When I rebooted, I saw all kinds of things. Horrible things. I could show you but I don't want to. Just imagine the most malicious crap ever and then multiply it by a bazillion."

"How did you see this stuff?"

"Gabriel showed me. He showed me what we've done—"

"We?"

"People. It's going to get worse, Al. More wars. More death. It's unbelievable. But it doesn't have to be that way."

"It doesn't have to be that way." She repeats it but not in agreement. She repeats it as if she doesn't understand the words coming out of my mouth.

"I can choose a do-over. I can take us back to the beginning and we'll try again. We can make better choices this time."

"That sounds—"

"—perfect! Think about it. Undo all the suffering. All the

murder. Rape. Crime. I can take it all back and make us better than we are now."

"Life isn't perfect. It never will be. I don't think even Gabriel can create a do-over like that. Are you sure you understand what—"

"I have to! Okay? I didn't go through all this so you'd have a long and miserable life. No. *No.* I refuse."

I'm crying. Somewhere in the middle of my tirade my voice breaks and the tears stream down my face.

Ally cries the second she sees me cry. I don't take it personally. She cries whenever anybody cries. Even television people.

"I can make it better. I can make it all donuts, all the time. No heartburn," I say. "It'll be amazing."

"This isn't a joke," she says. Leave it to Al to refuse my humor at such a crucial time. "Be serious."

I short jump in front of her and take her hands in mine.

"Be serious? I love you, seriously. That's the only thing worth being serious about." I kiss her. I kiss her before she can yell at me or slap me or maybe even pull my hair. Her lips are warm and sticky on mine. Her wet cheeks slide against my own. I squeeze her so hard I'm sure she can't breathe.

Don't be afraid, I whisper into her mind. *I'd give you anything. Creating a world worthy of you will be enough. Because the world I imagine* will *have you in it. How could it not? You're the only good I've ever known.*

Her fear spikes. "What about what I want?"

"What do you want?" I'm prepared to give her anything.

"You!" she grabs on to me. "This can't be right, Jess. You're missing something. Let's talk about this."

Her doubt flares. My own conviction wavers.

"I will take you when you are ready," Gabriel says into my ear. Ally's eyes widen. I'm still broadcasting, damn it.

"I've loved you forever and always will. I don't need to

love the whole world to save it. Loving you is enough of a reason."

I kiss her cheek.

"Jess, no. Listen."

Before my doubt can overtake me, I let go.

I let go of Ally. I let go of my hold on the world and I slip through the darkness one last time.

When I open my eyes I'm on a cliff. The air is stupidly cold. The tears on my cheek freeze instantly. Wind whips my hair around my face and I grab onto it, trying to hold it out of my face. Gabriel is beside me, watching me with those feral green eyes.

"Let's get this over with," I tell him. Because I don't think I can hold onto my nerve for much longer. Ally's tear-stained face burns in my heart and mind.

"Ascension is complex. The timing must be perfect," he says.

I shiver. "Just show me what to do."

He takes me into his arms. He's warm like the sun on my cold skin. He pushes one of his hands through my hair as the other stays locked around my waist.

"Do you know what you want?" he asks me. His tie fades from green to a deep midnight blue. His eyes do the same. They become star-filled waters at midnight, the reflection of a million stars shimmering on the liquid surface. I haven't seen that in a while—the tie mood ring thing.

Do you know what you want? he asks again.

I thought I knew what I wanted about two minutes ago. Now I'm not sure.

You must know what you want, he says. *You must see the world you wish to create.*

I picture Ally. Ally smiling. Ally wrapping her arms around me. Ally leaning in to press her lips to mine. Because if I'm being honest with myself, I'm doing this for her. Sure,

I'll save the world, but I'm doing it for the person I love most. I wonder if the three partis before me were as selfish. Did they choose to become stars over shields because they wanted to save everyone?

Or some*one*?

I know my answer. My one wish.

Ally untouched by sadness, pain, or heartbreak.

Ally happy.

Ally safe.

Gabriel's hold on me tightens.

I'm ready, I say, and fall into midnight waters.

IF YOU ENJOYED THIS NOVEL, JESSE'S STORY CONTINUES in *Dying Day, Dying for a Living, Book 7.*

GET YOUR THREE FREE STORIES

Thank you so much for reading *Dying Breath*. I hope you're enjoying Jesse's story. If you'd like more, I have a free, exclusive Jesse Sullivan story for you. See Ally survive her first death replacement gig, during her first week as Jesse's assistant. You'll also discover how the lovable Winston came to be Jesse's loyal companion.

You can only read this story for free by signing up for my newsletter. If you would like this story, you can get your copy by going to my website and joining my free fiction newsletter at:

www.korymshrum.com/free-starter-library

As to the newsletter itself, I send out 2-3 a month and host a monthly giveaway exclusive to my subscribers. The prize is usually a signed book. I also share information about my current projects, and personal anecdotes (like pictures of my dog).

So if you want these free stories and access to the giveaways, please sign up.

If this is not your cup of tea, you can follow me on social media to learn about new releases.

ACKNOWLEDGMENTS

Always so many people to thank—and what a great problem to have!

Thanks to the fans first and foremost. If it wasn't for your enthusiasm for this series, I would've definitely given up by now. Every gushing compliment on social media or via email has given me just enough steam to power on—and I can never thank you enough for that.

Watch me try:

Thank you for reading the book, liking the book, telling me that you like the book, telling your friends you like the book, and showing your enthusiasm for the next one. All of this is more important to me than you know.

A round of applause to my critique group, The Horsemen of the Bookocalypse: Angela Roquet, Monica La Porta, and Katie Pendleton. They're always the first to approve—or veto. Thank heavens.

Thanks to my ever-eager proofers. For this book we have: Joe Thomas, Misty Neal, Lisa Morris, Rachel Menzies, Charles Colp, Colleen McGuire, Kerri Krauter, Rebecca Shannon, Andrea Cook, Ashley Ferguson, Nick Graham, Michelle Harrison, Claudette Bouchard, and Wendy Nelson.

Eternal gratitude to John K. Addis for my author photo and the original cover for this book. Thank you to Christian Bentulan for the second edition cover. Not only am I grateful for their immense talent, but also for their patience and generosity.

As always, thanks to my wife, Kim. Thank you for reading

my drivel. Thank you for liking it. And most of all, thank you for wiping my tears when I don't feel good enough. Someday I'll learn how to have faith in my talent and I'll stop being so needy.

Probably.

Maybe.

Until then I'll just be really, *really* grateful I have you.

ALSO BY KORY M. SHRUM

Dying for a Living series

Dying for a Living

Dying by the Hour

Dying for Her: A Companion Novel

Dying Light

Worth Dying For

Dying Breath

Dying Day

Shadows in the Water series

Shadows in the Water

Under the Bones

Danse Macabre

Carnival

Devil's Luck

What Comes Around

Overkill

Silver Bullet

Hell House

One Foot in the Grave

Blood Rain

First Light

Castle Cove series

Welcome to Castle Cove

Night Tide

The City 2603 series

The City Below

The City Within

The City Outside

The Borderland series

Blade Born: A Borderlands Novel

Standalone novels

Jack and the Fire Eater

Short Fiction

Thirst: new and collected stories

Final Cut: stories

Nonfiction

Who Killed My Mother? a memoir

A Well Cared for Human: self-love strategies for transforming pain into power

Poetry

Birds & Other Dreamers

Questions for the Dead

You Can't Keep It

Learn more about Kory's work at www.korymshrum.com

ABOUT THE AUTHOR

USA TODAY bestselling author Kory M. Shrum has published more than thirty books including the bestselling *Shadows in the Water* and *Dying for a Living* series.

She is the host of two podcasts: *Who Killed My Mother?* a true crime podcast about her mother's tragic death, and a second show, *A Well Cared For Human*, which focuses on debunking self-care myths, while offering concrete strategies for improving one's mental health and personal power.

She also publishes poetry under the name K.B. Marie.

When not writing, podcasting, or planning her next adventure, she can usually be found under thick blankets with snacks.

She lives in Michigan with her equally bookish wife, Kim, and their very spoiled rescue dog, Max. Learn more about Kory and all the mischief she gets up to at www.korymshrum.com